Paperback Writer

Also by Stephen Bly in Large Print:

The Outlaw's Twin Sister
Fool's Gold
The General's Notorious Widow
Hidden Treasure
Last Swan in Sacramento
Picture Rock
Proud Quail of the San Joaquin
Red Dove of Monterey
The Senator's Other Daughter
The Marquesa
Miss Fontenot
Sweet Carolina

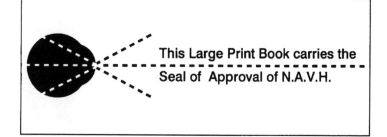

This Large Print Book carries the
Seal of Approval of N.A.V.H.

Paperback Writer

Stephen Bly

Walker Large Print • Waterville, Maine

Published in 2005 by arrangement with Broadman & Holman Publishers.

The text of this Large Print edition is unabridged. Other aspects of the book may vary from the original edition.

Set in 16 pt. Plantin by Liana M. Walker.

Printed in the United States on permanent paper.

The Library of Congress has cataloged the Thorndike Press® edition as follows:

Bly, Stephen A., 1944–
    Paperback writer : a novel / Stephen Bly.
      p. cm.
    ISBN 0-7862-6880-8 (lg. print : hc : alk. paper)
    ISBN 1-59415-050-8 (lg. print : sc : alk. paper)
    1. Detective and mystery stories — Authorship —
Fiction. 2. Fiction — Authorship — Fiction.
3. Imagination — Fiction. 4. Novelists — Fiction.
5. Large type books. I. Title.
PS3552.L93P37 2004
  813′.54—dc22   2004052239

With thanks to
William Saroyan,
who taught me
at an early age
how a man can live
within
the words
that he writes.

As the Founder/CEO of NAVH, the only national health agency solely devoted to those who, although not totally blind, have an eye disease which could lead to serious visual impairment, I am pleased to recognize Thorndike Press★ as one of the leading publishers in the large print field.

Founded in 1954 in San Francisco to prepare large print textbooks for partially seeing children, NAVH became the pioneer and standard setting agency in the preparation of large type.

Today, those publishers who meet our standards carry the prestigious "Seal of Approval" indicating high quality large print. We are delighted that Thorndike Press is one of the publishers whose titles meet these standards. We are also pleased to recognize the significant contribution Thorndike Press is making in this important and growing field.

Lorraine H. Marchi, L.H.D.
Founder/CEO
NAVH

★ Thorndike Press encompasses the following imprints: Thorndike, Wheeler, Walker and Large Print Press.

"In every man's writings,
the character of the writer
must lie recorded."

Thomas Carlyle, *Goethe*

"The most solid advice, though,
for a writer is this, I think:
Try to learn to breathe deeply,
really to taste food when you eat,
and when you sleep, really to sleep.
Try as much as possible to be wholly alive,
with all your might."

William Saroyan
Preface to the First Edition
*The Daring Young Man
on the Flying Trapeze and Other Stories*

ATLANTIC-HAMPTON PUBLISHING
COMPANY
books by
PAUL JAMES WATSON

The Distracted Detective Series

Arctic Ice Murders
Atrocity in Athens
Autumn Ambush in Alberta
Avery's Arms
Backstreet Baltimore Blackmail
Black Box, Black Door
Blood Red Pacific
Blue Days, Red Nights
Boston Blackmail
Cairo Customs Charade
Casablanca Suspect Slaying
Countdown to the Reluctant Countess
Deception in Geneva
Denmark at Daybreak
Diamond Dandy Disaster
Distracted in Dublin
Double or Nothing
False Truth in Frisco
Flames over Havana
Georgia Never Minds
Hawaii Reins

High Tea, Low Life
Hong Kong Poison Princess
Lady's Other Tiger
Last Digit to Go
Last Time in Tulsa
Long Night in Laguna
Manhattan Moon
Maui Mother's Mayhem
Mexicali Melee
Mile-High Murder
My Time to Fly
North Shore Nanny
Offshore and Dangerous
Over Easy in Omaha
Pirates of Battery Park
Renegade Rembrandt
Rocky Mountain Misery
Saigon Siren
Salamander's Last Skin
Samoa Sunset Suicide
San Pedro Profiles
South Padre Pardon
Steel-Eyed Susan
Sunken Pleasures
Texas City Tornado
The Princess Who Kidnapped Herself
Too Wild to Be Free
Tragedy in Toledo
Tunnel to Heaven
Twenty-Three Minutes to Midnight

When All the Bridges Burned
Why Not Now?
Widow's Wig
Wrong Ticket to the Right Town
Yellow Sea

prologue

the life of
a paperback writer

Paul James Watson never impressed his world . . . or himself.

But that is not to say he was a total failure.

Society sets a man's value by what he accomplishes in the midst of others. A man measures himself by what he achieves when alone. It is possible to be a success at one and not the other. And, of course, one can be a failure at both.

A man who finds success in public and knows, in private, that he is a failure will never be understood by the general public. He will be called a moody workaholic who continues to drive himself.

The man who finds success in his private world but not in public is considered an underachiever, a man who lacks drive, one who never lived up to his potential.

When Paul James Watson's youngest son, Peter, came home from college for the summer, he declared, "Dad, you will always be just a minor celebrity. Real celebrities need no introduction. But no one knows you until you are introduced."

If the people in Bridgeport, Montana, thought about Paul James Watson at all, they concurred. After all, he did write books. They were published all over the world and read by thousands, perhaps millions. They knew there was some fame connected to that.

But Watson's books weren't read by the people in Bridgeport.

It's not that they ignored their resident author. It's just that life was crammed with hunting, fishing, endless garage sales, bowling leagues, pine needles to rake, and a garden to put in, if it ever stopped snowing.

They all had an autographed copy of a Paul James Watson novel around the house . . . somewhere. And every week or so a pilgrim would wander into town from some distant land asking the location of the home of the almost-famous novelist. Folks pointed to the big log house on Tomahawk Drive on the north side of a dead-end gravel street.

His editors in New York thought of Paul James Watson as a self-exiled iconoclast. If they thought of him at all.

Of course, he thought about himself.

Not as often as his wife, Sheila, thought he did. Still, there were times when his eclectic mind turned inward. He thought about himself in those few glorious days after one book was finished and before the next one began.

Five times a year.

Some would not think that obsessive, but they don't know how intensely he thought about himself.

And, right at the moment, Paul James Watson was between books.

chapter one

"Are you having a bad day, darlin'?" Paul James Watson drawled.

The onions on the three-egg Spanish omelette would give him heartburn all night. That's why he ordered it with no onions. But the message somehow got lost in the scribble of the red-eyed waitress and white gravy from the thumb of the cook with a hair net over his bleached-white ponytail.

But Watson didn't complain.

It wasn't his style.

When the waitress resloshed his thick, chipped porcelain coffee cup, he glanced at her tightly drawn, narrow lips. She brushed the dangling strand of wispy pale almost-blonde hair out of her eyes as she wiped up the coffee spill with a once white damp rag. "Why did you ask me that?"

"There was something in the way you said, 'Oh, crap! I don't need this!' after

16

dropping my Tabasco sauce on the floor."

She tossed the rag into the soapy water, then folded her arms across a weak chest. "Mister, I am having a bad day, a bad night, a bad week, a bad month, and a bad year. With any luck I will have a bad life as well. Any more questions?"

The coffee burned more than the tip of his tongue. "No, ma'am."

She leaned her red, water-shrunk fingers on the counter and gazed out the window into the dark, east Montana night. "And if I am really lucky, you will leave me a bad tip. And frankly, mister, I just don't give a . . ."

"I believe I heard Clark Gable say that same line," Watson interrupted.

Two girls bounced into the café and giggled their way to a back table. The waitress bused two tables and took their order. Then she leaned into the sink with one hand pressing the small of her back. She didn't turn to face him.

"It's a good movie," she finally murmured.

Watson stopped dissecting the lump in the slate-colored gravy to glance at the back of her pink-and-white-striped uniform. An oval sweat stain marked the cotton cloth just above her apron knot.

17

"You like *Gone with the Wind?*"

"Yeah, I liked it. It's been years. I ought to see it again."

He studied the back of her head and noticed that her hair was not the same color at the roots as at the tips. "It's not necessarily a happy movie," he added.

"But it makes you forget yourself and think about something else. For that I am always grateful."

"Who are you trying to forget?" he asked.

She tossed the plates in the sudsy water and splashed soap foam on her cheek. "Crap," she mumbled. "I didn't need that."

He sprinkled pepper on the gravy-like substance. "Sorry, I'm through prying."

She glanced back over a narrow shoulder and shook her head. "No, that wasn't it. I mean, I don't need this soap in my face, or the Tabasco on the floor, or lousy pay, or some trucker groping at my backside, or this stinking job."

He scraped dried green food substance off his fork with his thumbnail. "Have you been putting in long hours?"

"All the extra time I can get. I've worked twelve straight today."

"I presume you need the money."

18

She wiped a thick, off-white ceramic plate over and over. "Yeah, are you going to give me a million dollars so I can retire?"

He grinned. "No, but I have been thinking about giving you a five-dollar tip."

"Whatever." Her shoulders rose, then sank. "I don't deserve it tonight."

"Think of it as a partial repayment for all the times you did deserve it and got stiffed."

For a moment she stood straight, and her body filled out. "Ain't that the truth?"

Her hair hung down her back in a ponytail like a teenager, but the lines that framed her eyes said she would never see forty again. Paul James Watson considered her a pleasant-looking lady. Nice features. Pretty face. She wouldn't stand out in a crowd of beautiful people, nor would she look out of place.

She flipped around and slammed another stack of dishes into the sudsy water. "I'm working long hours because I'm trying to forget the person that ruined my life."

"How long have you been trying to forget?" Watson scraped the gravy off the toast with a knife and plucked out onion bits with a tine of the slightly bent fork.

"Twenty-three years."

"That's a long time to be so angry at someone."

"I didn't say I was angry."

"Why else does someone not forgive?" Her voice softened. "Because they are hurt?"

"That's true." He scooted his plate over to the light. "Do you have any idea what this purple substance is in my omelette?"

"Eggplant."

"In my Spanish omelette?"

"Don't you like eggplant?"

"No."

"Then it's not eggplant, it's onion."

"I don't like onion either."

"Mister, you are a pain to get along with. What do you like to eat that's purple?"

Watson rubbed his square, clean-shaven jaw. "Boiled cabbage?"

"That's what it is. It's boiled cabbage."

"Thank you."

"You're welcome. Do I still get the five-dollar tip?"

When he laughed, he felt his steel-gray eyes relax. "I was considering lowering it to $3.50."

"Yeah, that figures."

He sliced the limp, soggy toast with his fork. "Tell me about the person who ruined your life twenty-three years ago."

"A selfish, dumb, naive kid that had absolutely no thought of others or the future . . . bad habits, disastrous relationships, and mind-numbing debt that could never be repaid. It's a tragic tale of stupidity and grief."

"Not totally unlike *Gone with the Wind*."

"Yeah, but there was no Clark Gable, that's for certain."

The toast caught in his throat. He raised his napkin to cough. "What is her name?"

Her smooth cheeks flushed when she spun around. "Whose name?"

"The one who caused you all that grief."

"Who said it was a her?"

"You are talking about yourself, aren't you?" he pressed.

She rubbed her arms as she crossed her chest. "Are you a detective, or what?"

"No," he laughed. "But I do write detective novels."

She wiped her hands on her wrinkled cotton apron. "No fooling? I've never met an author before." She strolled over to the counter. "What's your name? Have I ever heard of you?"

He grimaced, then shoved another bite past his thin, chapped lips. "Probably not."

"Aren't you going to tell me your name?"

"Not until I know the name of the eighteen-year-old who ruined your life."

When she rolled her eyes to the ceiling, Watson surveyed her smooth complexion and pouting lips. "Barbara Joy DuPree," she announced.

"And what is that same woman's name now?"

"It's Barbara Joy DuPree. But in between it has been Barb Cripane and Barbie Collins. Now that you know my name, what's yours?"

"Paul James Watson."

She glanced at the gold ring on his left hand. "That sounds formal. What does your wife call you?"

He grinned. "In the daylight . . . or at night?"

"Hah!" For a moment her tired eyes flashed. "How about in daylight?"

"Paul."

"Paul, do you have a pen name you write under?"

"Nope. I'm afraid that's it."

"You're right, I never heard of you." She avoided his eyes. "You really got some books published?"

Her straight, white teeth caught his

gaze. "Ninety-eight."

"You have ninety-eight books published, and I've never heard of you?" The faint outline of girlish dimples framed her tan face.

"Yes." He drug his fork across his plate. "Do you have any idea what this stringy thing is in my hash browns?"

"Paul James Watson, do you ever eat your food? Or do you just play with it?"

"I guess I'm not very hungry, Barbara Joy DuPree."

"Then why come into the diner at ten o'clock at night and order breakfast?"

He leaned back on the red vinyl stool repaired with gray duct tape. "Just to visit, I suppose."

She laughed and leaned over the counter until she was only a foot from his face. "With me?" She winked. "You came in to visit with me?"

She was in his space, but he didn't pull back. "To visit with anyone, darlin'. I've been locked in my motel room way too long."

Barbara Jo Dupree stood up. "That's where you write?"

Watson trailed his fork through the omelette. "Yep."

She reached for the top white button on

23

her dress as if to make sure it was fastened. "Where's that wife you mentioned?"

He spun the gold band on his left ring finger, then smiled. "She's at home in Bridgeport."

"Bridgeport?" She brushed her hair back with her fingers. "That's seven hours from here."

"I wrapped up the final chapter of my latest book tonight. I'm going home tomorrow."

"What's it called?"

"*Diamond Dandy Disaster.*"

She locked her hands on narrow, shapeless hips. "So, you are celebrating tonight?"

"You might say that." The coffee was cold but strong. He took two sips before he set the cup down.

"By ordering an omelette you don't like and talking to an over-the-hill waitress who is ticked off?"

"Yeah, I really know how to live it up, don't I? If it's any consolation, you don't look over-the-hill."

Her eyes softened, and she stroked dangling, Indian-bead earrings that he hadn't noticed until that moment. "Thank you, Paul James Watson. But you are as pathetic as I am."

"No, Barbara Joy DuPree, I am more pathetic." He combed his graying dark brown hair back over his ear with his fingers.

"How do you figure that?"

"You haven't been pathetic as long as I have. I'm a good ten years older than you."

She studied him from waist to hair. "You don't look it."

"Thank you. The tip just went back up to five dollars."

She carried an order of nachos and a plate of curly fries to the two teenage girls in a booth at the east end of the café. Then she returned and filled his coffee cup.

She packed an aroma somewhere between French fries and vanilla musk perfume. "If I was celebrating, it surely wouldn't be at this café," she murmured.

Watson pushed his plate back. "Where would you go to celebrate?"

"The Pinto Club," she announced.

"Why there?" he asked.

"They've got live music tonight."

"Who's playing there?"

"Trampis and the Desperadoes." She tilted her head. The weak brown eyes now sparkled. "You ever hear of them?"

Paul Watson studied her face. "No."

"Gary's a local guy who works for Allied Chemical. He used to be married to Nancy

Mason. He sounds just like George Strait."

"So you'd like to hear a little 'Amarillo by Mornin'?"

"I was thinking more like, 'Lead On.' " She started toward the kitchen, then turned back. "Paul, I get off at eleven. If you want to go to The Pinto, I'll ride over there with you. What do you say?"

Paul Watson looked at her brown eyes. They looked like a former homecoming queen's that dreaded another rejection.

Then her face blurred like poor television reception.

When Watson's mind cleared, she looked different.

A lot different.

Her eyes looked impatient.

"Well?" she demanded. "What do you say?"

Paul James Watson glanced back at the sticky, plastic-covered menu on the empty gray counter in front of him. "I can't decide."

"Mister, you come in here and stare at the menu for ten minutes and can't decide what to eat? There aren't twenty items on the dinner menu. It can't be that tough," she snapped.

He stared down at her chipped red fingernail polish. "I can't decide whether I'm hungry or not."

"Don't order the meatloaf."

He glanced at the gap between her upper front teeth. "Bad, huh?"

"No, it's good, but it's gone."

"Maybe I'll just have breakfast."

She brushed a long, loose strand of sandy blonde hair over her ear. "At ten o'clock at night?"

"It says, 'Breakfast all day.' "

"Do you believe everything you read?"

Watson laughed and shook his head. "No. I spend most of my time with fiction."

"Me too. I like romance novels, the trashier the better. Are you going to order or not?" she pressed. "My back hurts, and I've got dishes to wash."

"I'll take your Spanish omelette, no onions, with wheat toast."

"Out of wheat. And no sourdough either."

He scraped dried egg off the menu with his thumbnail. "What do you have?"

"I got white bread."

"That's fine."

She pushed her way back into the kitchen. Watson glanced at his watch. *Why do I do that, Lord? I script out the entire scene before it happens. But reality is never as good. I get lost in fiction all right. Sometimes it's like I never get totally out of it. I should probably call Sheila. But it's late. She said to call when I finished the book, but she'd be worried to get a call after ten. If Ruth Ann is home, she'll have the line tied up with the Internet. I can leave early tomorrow. I can get home by two; that's soon enough.*

He pulled a small calendar from the back pocket of his jeans and studied it.

I've got an Old Bridgeport Days meeting at 7:00 if we have a quorum. That wasn't the night of the coaches meeting, too, was it? I'll call Brett. He doesn't need me. If I get home in time, I'll change the oil in the truck. That pile of gravel needs to be spread in the alley. I doubt if Pete got to it, what with the new job. I could put the blade on the four-wheeler, but the starter needs to be replaced. Just as easy to use the wheelbarrow, unless that tire went flat again. Everything waits. Like street gangs in a dark alley, real life waits in ambush. If I glance up more than two minutes from my writing, real life imprisons me.

He pulled a pen from just below the top

button on his beige long-sleeved shirt and wrote on the paper napkin. He had filled one side with a scene about a waitress at an all-night diner when the front door of the café banged open. A wide-shouldered man, with square jaw and suntanned face, swaggered up to the counter. The blonde-haired waitress scooted out of the kitchen holding a plate with a chicken-fried steak lapping over the edges.

The man, with strong spice aftershave, thick dark-brown mustache, and black golf shirt labeled "The Old Course at St. Andrews," plunked down two stools away. His wide grin revealed straight white teeth. He flashed the waitress two deep dimples. "This is your lucky night, babe!"

She brought him an empty, unchipped coffee cup. She glanced over at Watson, then back at the man. "It hasn't exactly been lucky so far," she mumbled.

He laced his hands behind his head and leaned back on the stool. His biceps bulged in the short sleeves of the black golf shirt. "Tell her who I am, P.J."

She turned to Watson. "You know this guy?"

Paul James Watson shoved his half-empty coffee cup toward her. "Yes," he replied. He studied the anticipation in her tired eyes. "This is none other than Tobias Patrick McKenna. Most of the ladies call him Toby."

She filled McKenna's cup with coffee, then paused. "Yeah, right, and I'm Scarlet O'Hara."

McKenna puckered his lips, then took a sip of coffee. His arms were as tan as his face. "You see that, P.J.? The cute babes never believe who I am. Remember that supermodel in *Manhattan Moon*? It took me until chapter 6 to convince her who I was."

A deep red flooded her face. "Oh, my word. . . . Is he really Toby McKenna? The famous detective?"

Watson studied the blush in her otherwise plain, pale face. "That's him," Watson nodded. He pointed to his coffee cup. "None other than the distracted detective himself."

She shoved the coffeepot toward him, then handed McKenna a bowl of sugar cubes. She leaned on the counter, her chin resting on the palm of her unringed hand. "You want a menu, Toby?"

He reached over and squeezed her fingers. "I can already see what I want, darlin'," McKenna drawled.

Her eyes widened. She looked twenty years younger.

He pointed to a plastic case behind her. "Give me a big slice of that apple pie."

"You like it warm?"

"The hotter the better, babe, with a melting kiss of vanilla ice cream, if you don't mind. Now, tell me" — his eyes glanced to her name tag — "Barbara Jo, darlin', where are we goin' when you get off work?" McKenna insisted. "Do you feel like dancin', cute thing? I feel like dancin'."

"The Pinto Club is nice," she murmured as she carried the pie back into the kitchen.

Paul James Watson sipped his coffee, then glanced over at McKenna, who waved at the two teenage girls in the back booth. "Hi, Little Darlin'," he called out. "You growed up as purdy as your mama!"

The girls giggled.

"Toby, you don't know either of those girls, and you don't know their mamas."

McKenna balanced his knife straight up on the counter. "I don't?"

"No, you don't."

He peered back at the girls. "Shoot, partner, I just brightened up their day anyway. There's nothin' wrong with that, is there?"

"But it's all fiction," Watson protested.

"Of course it is. But the blonde girl does look like Corina from *Georgia Never Minds*, doesn't she?"

"Corina was African-American," Watson insisted.

"Other than that, they look similar."

"Toby, what are you doing in this café, anyway?"

"Just like you, P.J., I'm celebratin'."

"But we said good-bye an hour ago. I told you I didn't want to see you for a month."

"I didn't know you were in here," McKenna explained.

"A world-class detective, and you don't know where I am? We both know that's a lie."

"Look, I knew you'd be havin' trouble talkin' with the waitress, so I figured I'd stroll in and pump you up a bit."

"I don't need help talking to a waitress."

"Why don't you ask Barbie girl if you need help?"

"I'm not the one who needs to hit on every waitress in North America."

Toby laughed. "North America? How about that Arab beauty in *Casablanca Suspect Slaying*? She was a waitress." He rubbed his chin. "Or was she a belly dancer?"

"McKenna, I don't want to talk about your women."

"You're in a sour mood for a man who just finished a book. I'm goin' out and celebrate how I finally cracked the *Diamond Dandy Disaster* case."

"You cracked it?" Watson exploded. "You were stuck in that dead-end alley with the Palestinian kid and the rocket launcher before I found you a loose brick. You were dead meat until I figured how to get you out of there."

McKenna sipped his coffee and stacked sugar cubes on the counter. "I didn't know anyone still used cubed sugar." He leaned back and stretched his arms. "One loose brick? That was your help?"

"It worked, didn't it?"

"Only because of my years as a minor league pitcher for the Sea Cats. I would have found my way out on my own."

"Toby, you would have been blown to kingdom come."

"No chance of that," McKenna boasted.

"Oh?"

"L. George Gossman told you that you can't kill me off until sales are consistently under thirty thousand. We ain't there yet, partner."

The waitress returned with two big

scoops of vanilla ice cream melting down over the double portion of apple pie. She wiped a fork clean on her apron, then set them down. "I can't believe Toby McKenna is at my counter. I read about you in the *New York Times*."

"Sort of makes your heart jump, doesn't it, darlin'?" McKenna blustered. "But I never did like New York City. You probably heard about how I solved the mystery of the missin' cab drivers in the book *Yellow Sea*." McKenna chomped down on a big bite of pie, then wiped his mouth on the white paper napkin and leaned forward. "Say, total cuteness, are you related to Faith Hill? You look just like her, only shorter and thinner in places, if you catch my drift."

She grabbed the coffeepot from in front of Watson. "Is he really THAT Toby McKenna? The one in *Twenty-Three Minutes to Midnight*?"

"And in *Long Night in Laguna*, *Tunnel to Heaven*, *North Shore Nanny*, and about fifty more. That's him, in all his glorious ego," Watson replied.

"Of course," McKenna blurted out, "you can't always believe P. J. Watson. He might be stringin' you along. I might be a truck driver from Des Moines. He's a known liar and a thief."

Her hand went to her mouth, and she stared right at Paul James Watson. "You mean, he's a crook?"

"It's much worse than that." Toby McKenna shook his head and bellowed, "He's a paperback writer!"

chapter two

Daylight slammed against the pale blue sky and reflected across the steam that rose from the blacktop of the Western Way Motel. Paul James Watson shoved the box of books behind the seat in the extended cab of his gold Silverado pickup and trudged toward the double glass doors marked "Lobby." Eastbound clouds had leaked enough during the night to suppress dust — at least for awhile.

Two women in army camouflage fatigues huddled around a tiny table and two blueberry muffins as they watched the early morning news on a television set that had a wavy vertical black line down the middle of the picture. Watson grabbed a Styrofoam cup and deliberated on the dispensers.

"The decaf's on the right," the olive-skinned soldier called out.

Watson couldn't decide if she had a slight scar on her cheekbone near her eye or if her mascara had been ill applied, but

36

he chose not to stare. "Thanks." He reached for the spigot on the left. *I wonder why she assumed I wanted decaf?* He stood straighter and sucked in his thirty-six-inch stomach. Then he sighed and relaxed.

He parked himself next to the "Do Not Remove from Lobby" newspaper on the counter and banged the small silver bell. A middle-aged lady with short blonde hair and a beautiful upturned nose seldom seen in gals over twelve ambled out of the back room. "Hi, Paul. Are you leaving us this morning?"

He sat down the coffee and smiled. It wasn't a "do you like me" smile but rather an "it's so nice to be among friends" smile, and it felt good on his face that for two weeks had experienced few real smiles. "Carrie, I got that sucker finished last night, and now I have to scoot home."

Tiny emerald studs blossomed in her earlobes, pulling color and class from the starched green collar of her satinlike blouse. She studied the computer screen below the counter. "Now, Paul . . . I thought you were home!"

"Sometimes it feels that way. I've spent more time in Room 220 than most any other place away from Bridgeport."

"You had a phone message while you

were loading your truck." She handed him a small note. "Some man named L. George Gossman with Atlantic-Hampton Publishing Company. Is he your editor?"

"Yeah."

"And he called you at 7:00 a.m.?"

Watson folded the note and tucked it in the pocket of his dark blue, long-sleeved cotton shirt. "He's in New York. He doesn't believe in time zones."

Carrie punched the keys on the computer. "I suppose he wanted to know if you were done with the book."

"Kind of like vultures, aren't they?" Watson said. "Hovering over the carcass, waiting for an opportunity to devour."

She handed him an invoice. "Just initial the rates and sign at the bottom. You know the routine."

Under a sketch of a fedora hat, he scrawled, "Paul James Watson."

Carrie stacked the papers and stapled them together. "You know, you never did take me up on that home-cooked supper."

He studied the petite woman's narrow, flawless chin. "I never seem to have time. I don't reach my quota of pages until late in the evening, and I'm always too tired to do anything but crash. Sorry about that. Maybe next time."

"Next time? I feel like the short-armed kid grabbing for a ring at the merry-go-round. It's always next time. You can't survive on vending machine food and bottled water." She brushed her short blonde bangs off her forehead.

"You are right about that." He glanced across the lobby at the counter of muffins and sweet rolls. "I did go out to eat last night at the Miles City Café."

Carrie locked the cash drawer, then dropped the key into the pocket of her black denim skirt. "Is that place still open? I heard it was closed down."

Watson swallowed and could taste onions. "It was open last night."

"Now, I am insulted, Paul." She strolled around the counter and stood next to him. "You chose the Miles City Café over coming to my place for chicken alfredo with homemade noodles."

He grinned and shook his head. It wasn't a we-have-a-secret grin but more like a we-could-have-had-a-secret grin. "Yes, but I don't have to explain to my wife why I ate at the Miles City Café."

"How is Sheila?" she asked.

"Incredibly busy as always. Too busy. She's been lecturing at the University in Missoula, has a show in Great Falls next weekend, and is still trying to finish that twelve-by-twenty-foot mural for the Department of Lands. Then there's her pride and joy, the huge running horse sculpture for the state museum in Helena. It's at the foundry. At least, I think it is."

"You two seem to live in different worlds."

"Yes, but we still do manage to collide every once in awhile," he replied.

"Paul James Watson, do the sparks still fly when you collide?" Carrie giggled.

He studied her face. *There is something innocent and healthy about the way a woman never forgets how to giggle.* "Carrie, darlin', there are times when Sheila and I light up like the Fourth of July over Flathead Lake."

She shook her head and smiled. "Shelia's a lucky lady, Paul."

"Well, thank you. I'll tell her you said that."

Carrie rocked back and forth on her black high heels. "Don't you dare, or she'll never let you come back here again."

"How could I ever write a book without you and the fine staff at the Western Way Motel?"

A telephone rang in the back room. She

strolled away with a quick wave. "Just ring if you need me."

Paul James Watson burned his lip on the coffee in the Styrofoam cup as he banged his hand down on the silver bell. He glanced back across the narrow motel lobby and rubbed the bridge of his nose. An unshaved trucker in a plaid flannel shirt stared at the rerun of a celebrity camel race and scratched his armpit.

Watson turned back and rang the bell again.

A gravelly voice shouted from the back room. "I'll be there in a minute. I'm washin' towels. What do you want?"

Watson cleared his throat and tried to peer around the divider. "I need to check out."

She wore red leather clogs, black stirrup pants, and a black untucked T-shirt that was a size too small for her 250-pound frame. The T-shirt read "I'm with stupid" and pointed to the window, which at the moment acted as a mirror reflecting the image back at herself.

"Yeah, what room were you in?" she asked.

"Room 220." Watson handed her the plastic card.

She scratched her nose on the back of her hand and studied the computer screen. "Twelve days? You were in that room for twelve days?"

He rubbed the stiffness in the left part of his neck. "That's right."

She leaned over the counter and screwed up her fleshy face. "No one stays in this motel for twelve days except drug dealers from Seattle. You aren't a drug dealer, are you?"

He folded his arms across his chest and immediately sucked in his stomach as she continued to study him. "Not hardly."

"Where are you from?" She continued filling out the form using a purple ball-point pen with a long purple feather attached to it.

"Bridgeport," he replied.

She tickled her nose with the feather. "Is that in Montana?"

"It's between Bozeman and Butte."

She laid the pen down and scratched at the black roots of her auburn hair. "Never heard of it."

"Where are you from?" he asked.

"California." She shoved papers across the counter and slapped the purple pen down next to them. "You got a message here."

42

He reached into his shirt pocket, but there was no note. "I suppose it's from L. George Gossman at Atlantic-Hampton Publishing Company?"

"Yeah." She reached under the collar of her T-shirt and tugged on her bra strap. "How did you know that? Are you psychic?"

He tugged off the tiny yellow sticky note. "No, but it's way too difficult to explain to you," Watson mumbled.

She plucked up her purple pen. "Is that so? Do you think I'm stupid?"

He stared at her T-shirt. "Eh, no, I don't think you are stupid."

"So how did you know who phoned?" she pressed.

"I write novels."

"What does that have to do with anything? My aunt wrote a novel once. She was doin' eighteen months in the county jail and didn't have anything else to do, what with the TV broke. Do you mean you actually have somethin' published?"

"A number of books. But sometimes my imagination runs away with me, and I live a scene out before it happens. While I was standing here waiting, I sort of lived out this scene. That's how I knew about the phone call."

"That's really weird. Does it always turn out the way you imagine it?"

He stared at the large lady and thought about a fictional lady named Carrie. "It seldom, if ever, turns out the way I imagine it," he replied.

She tugged on the sagging lobe of her triple-pierced ear. "Are you sure you aren't a drug dealer?"

When Paul James Watson returned to his truck, a familiar face greeted him from the passenger side. "McKenna, what are you doing here?"

The man in the Dockers and deck shoes reeled the seat belt around him. "I need a ride, P.J."

Watson pulled on gold wire-framed sunglasses and shoved the key in the steering wheel column. "What happened to your Corvette?"

McKenna scooted the electric seat back as far as it would go. "It's a long story. It's in the body shop."

Watson turned west on Interstate 94 and merged between a Wal-Mart eighteen-wheeler and a turquoise motor home with Florida license plates. When the traffic settled down, he turned to Toby McKenna. "Are you going to tell me what happened to the classic Corvette?"

"She kicked off the emergency brake," McKenna explained. "That's all there is to say."

"Who did?"

"Barbara Joy, the waitress from the Miles City Café."

"I don't think I want to hear about this."

"Not much to say. We'd barely got started, and she wiggled around and hit the emergency release, and we rolled down toward the river." McKenna shrugged. It wasn't a startled look, but more like a man who hits the same sand trap every time he plays that hole.

"You dunked your Corvette in the Yellowstone River?"

"We would have, if we hadn't hit the boulder."

"What did you do then?" Watson punched on cruise control.

"I thought you didn't want to know."

"You mean, after all of that you . . . you . . . you . . ."

Toby McKenna laughed as if someone had taken his tone control and set it on bass. "P.J., virtue looks good on you. But on me it's like baggy pants and a cheap cigar. Do you know what I mean? It just doesn't fit my image."

Watson rubbed his clean-shaven chin. "Image or not, you have to act responsibly, Tobias Patrick McKenna."

McKenna dropped open the glove compartment and dug around. "Why?"

"Because we are accountable to a higher person," Watson lectured. "What are you looking for?"

"A fingernail clipper. There it is." He clipped at a hangnail. "P.J., are you gonna lay that religion stuff on me again?"

"Toby, God is real. You've got to deal with that."

"No, I don't. You have to deal with it. I'm fiction, remember? You created me. I'm responsible to no one except your imagination. Which, I might add, is wearin' thin lately."

"Don't get too cocky. Even fictional characters can die off," Watson insisted.

"Not legendary heroes like Toby McKenna. There's no way you can do that. Besides, popular fictional characters never die."

"You can go out of print."

"Yes, but I will live forever in small town libraries, old ladies' bookshelves, and in the Library of Congress," he bragged.

"Toby, you have to live in a responsible manner because you are real in the minds of readers all over the country."

"And the world. Did you see the German translation of *Offshore and Dangerous?*" McKenna bragged.

"That's my point. You are known all over. You are forty-two years old. You have to act in such a way as to have a more positive influence on the readers."

"We were both forty-two when we met, remember?"

Watson glanced in the rearview mirror at the deep creases around his own eyes. "Yeah, I remember."

"You were crankin' out prairie stories and nearly starvin' before I swaggered into your life," McKenna said.

Paul Watson felt his neck stiffen. "I was writing historical fiction. I was doing OK."

"Well, you are doin' better now, P.J."

"Yeah, maybe. But still, I think you need some changes in lifestyle. Maybe I'll create a fictional heaven and hell," Watson suggested.

"You can't do that; it would ruin my image." McKenna leaned back and popped his fingers. "Besides, you know in your mind you like me the way I am."

Watson flipped off the cruise control as they approached the back of a slow-moving cattle truck. "How do you know what's in my mind?" As they slowed, a black car zoomed past them.

"Are you kiddin'? I've spent my whole life in your mind. Whoa, did you see that blonde in the Camaro? Speed up and catch her."

Watson pulled in front of the cattle truck. "I'll set it on cruise control at 75. That's the speed limit, and I have no intention of going faster."

"That's the trouble with you, P.J. Your life's always on cruise control. Someone — some *thing* — controls all your life."

Watson studied the rhythmic motion of the quarter-section sprinklers that watered the hayfield next to the freeway. "There's nothing wrong with that."

McKenna sat up and unfastened the top button of his golf shirt. "But you never get to dance."

With both hands on top of the steering wheel, Watson stared straight ahead. "I don't like dancing."

"That's not what I mean. You hadn't said ten words to anyone in over two weeks, so how come you didn't visit with that waitress last night? She would have visited with you. I'll tell you why. Because your life is on cruise control."

"I didn't feel like visiting," Watson mumbled.

"You visited with her in your mind, didn't you?"

"What's that have to do with anything? I write fiction. I'm always writing scenes in my mind. I'm plagued with scenes. They flood in like water rushing through a busted dam. There's no way to hold them back."

McKenna waved a strong, suntanned finger at him. "But you never live them. You write out of your mind but not out of your life."

"If I only wrote out of my life, Toby McKenna would never have a murder to solve. I've never been around a real murder."

"Point taken. But the fact remains, your life is on cruise control, and you like it that way."

"Plenty of surprising things happen to me," Watson challenged. "How about last week when I pulled the old man from the burning building?"

McKenna rolled down his window, stuck his head out, took a deep breath, then pulled it back. "You didn't save him. I yanked him out."

Watson glanced at the oil gauge, the amp

meter, the radiator temperature, and the fuel gauge. "You saved him?" he mumbled. "It seems like I was there."

McKenna rolled up his window and combed his thick dark brown hair with his fingers. "I risked my life, saved the old man, then you up and deleted the whole scene."

"It didn't work."

"Didn't work?" Toby grumbled. "The old man in the burnin' building thought it worked."

"He's just fictional."

"Maybe so, but he won't end up in the Library of Congress. Man, he'll be tossed in some unmarked grave in the back of your brain."

"We saved a little boy from a burning riverboat casino in *Steel-Eyed Susan*. It seemed redundant to have another fire scene so similar," Watson insisted.

"We? Why do you keep saying 'we'? I saved the boy."

"Wrapping him in the wet felt off the craps table was my idea," P. J. Watson said.

McKenna waved both hands as he talked. "Yes, but your eyebrows didn't get singed off when the propane tank under the high-stakes Baccarat room exploded."

"Are you complaining, Toby?" Paul challenged. "If it weren't for that accident, you would have never met that redheaded emergency room nurse."

A wide smile broke across McKenna's face. "Whatever happened to Synthia Ann? I keep expectin' her to show up in another book."

Paul Watson tapped his fingers on the top of the black steering wheel. "She married a writer and is raising a family in California."

Toby McKenna sat straight up. "Oh, no! You got to be kiddin'. Synthia Ann with a writer? A paperback writer?"

Watson pushed his sunglasses high on his nose. "What's wrong with that?"

"Synthia Ann with a writer? She could have done better than that. I bet he has her livin' in a double-wide in Fresno. She probably has to keep workin' in the emergency room just to support them. Yet she did look nice with a stethoscope."

"She had cute ears," Paul Watson mumbled.

"Synthia Ann?"

"Yeah, remember, she had tiny, delicate earlobes with those teardrop jade earrings," he said.

"I'm proud of you, P.J., you remembered. You usually forget the women."

"That's ridiculous. I remember every one of them. I created them. I made each one of them what they are. Without me they are nothing," Watson declared.

"But you never remember the details. I was right. You are just on cruise control. You remember where the road starts and where it ends, but you never remember all the details along the way."

"Of course, I remember the particulars."

"In *Mile-High Murder*, which of the twins had the little mole next to her right eye?"

"Candy," Watson said.

"Nope. It was Lacy," McKenna insisted. "When you looked at Candy, the mole was to your right, but that is her left eye. Lacy had one on the other side."

"I wasn't locked in the tool shed with them for a long weekend like you, McKenna."

"OK, P.J., here's another. Which gal has a field of freckles the size of a silver dollar on her lower left hip?"

Watson passed a four-horse trailer pulled by a dark green Dodge pickup.

"There's a couple of barrel-racin' angels," McKenna blurted out as he stared at the truck. "Maybe I should stay in Montana a little while." He turned back to Watson. "You didn't answer. Which gal has the little field of freckles?"

"Laramee?" Paul guessed.

"Not hardly. She ended up in the full body cast."

Watson tapped on the steering wheel. "That Templeton woman, what was her name?"

"Sonya?"

"Yes, her."

"P.J., you are losin' it, man. You gave Sonya the birthmark in the shape of a horse's head under her right ear."

"OK. I don't remember who had the freckles on her hip."

"Her lower hip."

"Good triumphs over evil. That's what my books are all about. The ladies are not the most important part of a Distracted Detective book," Watson declared.

"Well, they are to me." McKenna studied the far side of the interstate. "Whoa, was that a Ferrari convertible? Why don't you ever give me a convertible? Thomas Magnum always drove one."

"Jim Rockford never did," Watson added. "Now, which one of my gals had the freckles?"

As they passed a dark green minivan, McKenna waved at a little boy whose nose was pressed against the window. "It's

Sheila. She has the freckles."

Watson gazed at the highway in front of the gold pickup. "Sheila? I don't remember a lady named Sheila."

"Aha!" Toby McKenna sat up and shouted. "Exactly my point, P.J.! It's your wife, Sheila, who has the freckles, and you don't even remember."

"Oh, sure, of course," Watson mumbled. "I assumed you meant one of the characters I created."

McKenna pulled a dark blue golf tee from the pocket of his alpaca sweater and chewed on it. "As far as I know, you did make her up. You never let me stop by to meet Sheila. I've always wondered why that was. Are you a little unsure of yourself?"

Watson stepped on the brake just hard enough to kick off the cruise control. "Wait a minute, McKenna. How did you know Sheila has freckles on her hip?"

"Her lower hip." McKenna flexed his arms across his chest. "Eh, you can let me out at the Billings airport. I'll fly back to Florida. I can pick up the Corvette in the next book."

Paul James Watson felt his neck and shoulders stiffen. "McKenna, you didn't answer me. How did you know about Sheila's freckles?"

"You talk in your sleep."

"That's absurd."

"Hmmm, I wonder why you are afraid for me to be around Sheila? Could it be that you are just too boring? Could it be she will like Toby McKenna more than Mr. Routine? Let me see that picture of your wife that you carry in your wallet."

Watson resumed his speed and reset the cruise control. "I've got to call L. George Gossman."

"You're changin' the subject. Let me see that pic you keep in your boot wallet with that folded hundred-dollar bill. You know, the one where she's wearin' that cute little white . . ."

"McKenna, I can write you out of this rig right now. I could have you run over by a cattle truck and dragged all the way to Butte."

"Hmmm, a little touchy, I see. Relax, P.J., I'm just teasin' you. You've been away too long. All right, no more talk about your poor wife. Even that writer guy that runs around in your mind would be more fun for her to be with than you."

"I will not discuss my private life with you."

"How do you know which is your private life? What if Toby McKenna is real, and he writes stories about P. J. Watson, a paperback writer? Whoa, doesn't that blow your mind away? I think I'll write a book someday." McKenna pushed the electric controls until his bucket seat jammed against the box of books behind him.

Paul shoved his sunglasses up on his forehead, rubbed his left eye, then tugged them back down. "I just thought of something, Mr. Macho McKenna. In the next book in the Distracted Detective Series, I'm going to have you marry Nancy Morratt!"

McKenna sat straight up. "What!" he shouted. "She doesn't have a brain in her head."

"And your point is?" Watson laughed. "You seem to be fond of the rest of her."

"What about that illness? I can't even pronounce it," McKenna declared. "She's bedridden half the time."

"You need to spend some time taking care of an ill wife. It will give you depth of character."

"I don't want depth of character. I like bein' shallow and superficial. It fits me," McKenna insisted.

"I think a tender, caring, sensitive Toby McKenna would be a welcome change. Especially for the women readers."

"Hmmmm. You wouldn't dare."

"Mention my wife and her freckles again, and you'll find out."

"On the other hand, a tender, caring, sensitive Toby McKenna sits by his poor, dying wife's side until . . ."

"I didn't say she was dying."

McKenna grinned. "Of course she's dyin'. Look at her all peaked and pale. There will be a big funeral, and then women all over the world will want to show love and support to the grievin' widower."

"That's crass, McKenna. Invent a wife just so she can die and you can get sympathy from the ladies."

"Relax, P.J., it's not like this is a real woman. It's all fiction, remember?"

"Sometimes I forget," P.J. murmured.

For several minutes the only sound was the whine of all-season tires on the pavement and the rhythmic thump-thump of the seams in the concrete of Interstate 94.

McKenna dug through the stack of CDs. "Where's your Jimmy Buffett?"

"Don't put one on yet. I need to phone Gossman."

They had just crested Blue Elk Hill and the "Ranch Exit, No Access" sign when Watson punched the numbers into his dash-mounted cell phone and flipped on the speaker.

The voice that answered sounded like a teenager. Or more like a woman who has been a teenager for twenty-five years. "Atlantic-Hampton Publishing. How may I direct your call? Or did you just call to visit with me?" she giggled.

"Hi, Spunky, darlin'! What are you doing answering the phone? I thought you retired from that years ago?" Watson said.

"Whoa!" McKenna hollered. "The boss's wife is back at the reception desk? Hi, Spunky, this is your Toby. I hitched a ride with P.J."

"Toby," she giggled, "how is my teddy bear?"

Watson feigned a gag.

McKenna laughed and shook his head. "I still haven't forgotten Scottsdale."

"Spunky, is George in the office?" Watson asked.

McKenna scooted down in the seat and lay his head on the back of the bucket seat, then tugged his fedora over his eyes. "Ah, Scottsdale."

"Sure, Paul, but he's in a grumpy mood. I'll get him on the line. Bye, Toby," she purred.

"Bye, sweetie," McKenna said.

"L. George Gossman, editorial vice president of Atlantic-Hampton Publishing, speaking."

"Hi, George, this is Paul."

"My word, where are you? I've been trying to reach you all morning."

"I'm on the road in eastern Montana."

"Are you near a fax machine?"

"Not in my truck."

"We have some cover changes you've got to approve by 3:00 p.m. eastern."

"On which book?" Watson asked.

"*The Salamander's Last Skin.*"

"What's wrong with the cover? I told you I like it."

"We put a different dress on the blonde," Gossman reported.

"What kind of a dress?"

"A black, slinky one, slit up to the thigh, and a little more revealing neckline."

"What?" Watson gasped. "She's an elementary schoolteacher on a field trip. She doesn't wear something like that."

"It's a dynamite cover. You'll love it. The marketing boys said it will sell."

"George, that's not my style at all. You know my readers. They trust me to keep it clean."

"We aren't changing the text. Besides, the dress is not all that radical. It's the kind of thing Spunky wears to work. Can you get to a fax? I'll shoot you a sample sketch."

"No, I can't, George. I want the cover left just like it was. The turtleneck and wool skirt looked good. Leave it as it is," Watson insisted.

"But you have to take a look at it."

"No, I don't. We all agreed on that cover three weeks ago. I didn't change my mind. Enjoy your day, George. Tell Carolyn hi for me. I'll check in with you in a day or two."

"Watson, you're getting as miserable to deal with as John Grisham."

"Thank you. Bye, George."

Watson glanced over at the reclining Toby McKenna.

"Well?" McKenna said.

"Well, what?" Paul James Watson asked.

"Are you gonna call the toupeed, elevator-shoe-wearin' L. George Gossman, or can I put on a Buffett CD?"

"Yeah, I'm going to call him," Watson replied. "I've just been mulling over what I want to say."

"You mean you lived the whole scene out in your head?"

"Yeah, sort of like that."

"Well, how did that guy in your head do? Did he take care of L. George Gossman?"

"He was confident, aggressive, and decisive."

"Good, now let's see if you can really do it," McKenna challenged. "Because thinkin' about it and doin' it are two different things."

chapter three

Paul James Watson pulled off the interstate at exit 93. Clumps of clouds bumped across the sky like white tumbleweeds on a light blue prairie. "I can't believe I'm doing this," he muttered. "How did I let Gossman talk me into looking at this new book cover? I know I'm not going to like it." *Lord, why do I feel a need to do everything everyone tells me to do? I'm not sure I want to know the answer to that.*

McKenna twirled his fedora with his right hand. "I can't believe you didn't tell L. George to shove it. I'd have told him to put the cover the way I wanted or my attorney would be at the door with a violation of contract suit."

"He's a friend, Toby. I don't treat friends that way."

"They use you, P.J., and you never do anything about it. Do you think they do that to Tom Clancy?"

"No, but Tom Clancy needs no intro-duction. George wants my opinion on the cover by his three o'clock committee meeting. At least, this way, I can tell him specifics on why I don't like it. But where in the world am I going to find a fax ma-chine in Forslip, Montana?" Watson pon-dered the scattered old buildings along the gravel street. "Am I supposed to go door-to-door and ask for a fax machine? In Gossman's mind, Montana is merely a re-tired football player." He turned right on the deserted street and crept along, in-specting each structure.

"Remember that time in *Countdown to the Reluctant Countess* when I needed the combination to the marquis's wall safe and I ran into a Victoria's Secret just to use their fax machine?"

"I hardly remember anything in *Count-down*. At least, I don't remember too many quality scenes."

"That's where I met Lady Ashleigh."

"In Victoria's Secret?"

"No, in *Countdown*. How come you never let me catch her?"

"It wouldn't have worked. She's much too classy for you, McKenna. The readers would have protested and said, 'What does she see in him?' "

"Hah, so that's it. I'm not good enough for her?"

"That's it, Toby, you're stuck with your kind."

McKenna scratched his thick mustache. "I can change," he murmured.

"Do you want to change?"

"No, but Lady Ashleigh was quite a gal. Don't think I've ever met a babe who could fly a Blackhawk helicopter through enemy fire, then win the grand prize at the county fair for her baking powder biscuits."

"Yes, she is quite a gal."

"Why don't you bring her back in a story? You know, a chance meeting at a little café along the dock at Key West at sunset?"

"Key West at sunset? You mean just you, her, and ten thousand loonies?"

"I like Key West," McKenna replied. "I can always blend into the crowd."

"It's not Lady Ashleigh's kind of place. But don't worry, Toby, you two will always have Omaha."

"That's not funny, P.J. Did you ever notice how shallow and superficial all my relationships are?"

"Isn't that the way you want them?"

"I like Lady Ashleigh."

"You said that before." Watson pulled over next to an abandoned wooden grain store. "There aren't any open stores in this town."

"How about over there?"

P.J. studied the building. "Odetta's Café?"

"Give it a try," McKenna insisted.

"Any place that has a faded tin sign for Orange Nehi in a bottle can't have a fax machine."

"That might be . . ." Toby pointed, "but it also says, 'Check our weekly specials on www.odettasgoodeatin.com.' "

Paul James Watson parked the truck in front and glared at the handwritten sign on the door. "Does everyone on earth have to have a Web site?"

"Now, don't start on that, P.J., just because the Toby McKenna Web site gets five times more hits than the Paul James Watson one."

"I am not jealous about that," Watson replied.

"Hey, I did let you link up to it."

"Yes, you are such a generous fellow."

"That's just the way I am," McKenna blustered. "You aren't expectin' me to go in there with you, are you?"

"You wait here. I'll be right back."

The wooden handle on the screen door was polished smooth and concave from decades of wear. Watson's boot heels struck the old gray linoleum like a heavy stick on a tired snare drum. The counter held six empty green vinyl stools. The kitchenette table in the corner was surrounded by five chrome and yellow plastic chairs and a wooden bar stool. The front of the tiny café was racked with potato chips and other snacks. Behind the counter the wall displayed dozens of small, hand-carved wooden signs sporting wise sayings.

Watson waited for someone to appear and read, "You Cain't Never Tell Which Way a Pickle Will Squirt." Finally, he hollered out, "Excuse me. Is anyone here?"

"You are too late!" a gruff voice shouted from the back room.

"Too late for what?" Watson challenged.

"Too late for breakfast and too early for lunch. Go away. I'm busy."

"Do you have a fax machine?"

"I said, 'I'm busy.' "

"I need to receive a fax from my publisher. Does anyone in Forslip have a fax?"

"Are you a writer?" the voice shouted.

"Yes."

"What's your name?"

"Paul James Watson."

From behind a curtain of beads that served as a door, a short man with a long gray ponytail charged out. "Paul James Watson who wrote *Wrong Ticket to the Right Town?*"

Watson grinned. "That's me."

"I must have read that book six times." Dark circles sagged under his droopy eyes like wet towels tossed on the bathroom floor.

"Thank you. That's very encouraging."

"That Toby McKenna is quite a guy," the man said. "How he knew that perfume was also an antidote for slyzene poison is beyond me."

"Yes, Toby is quite amazing."

The man reached out his suntanned hand. "I'm Crawford Newross."

"Crawford, is there any chance you have a fax machine? I really need to receive something from my publisher." Watson towered above the man.

"Sure, come on into the back room. You know, I wrote a book one time," Crawford declared.

"Oh?"

"*Charles Manson and the World Bank Conspiracy*," Newross explained.

"That's an intriguing combination. Manson had something to do with banking?"

"He still does."

"I thought I read he was in maximum security in Corcoran, California."

"No, that's his double. Manson's been out for years and lives in Cyprus," Newross declared.

"Working for the World Bank?"

"Yeah, it's all in my book. Do you want a copy? I've got fourteen hundred of 'em in the garage."

Watson squinted his eyes and rubbed the back of his neck. "Can I order it on-line? I'm on the road and can't read it now. But I would like to buy some snacks on the way out."

"Sure. Mention you stopped by, and I won't charge you for the autograph. That's a five-dollar savings."

As soon as Watson pushed his way through the translucent, multicolored beads, he was confronted with six computer monitors and a row of keyboards. A black leather executive chair was parked in front of them. "Crawford, this is quite a setup. What have you got going back here?"

"I do a little buying and selling on eBay,"

Newross admitted. "My handle is MontanaMothers. I sell those little wooden signs with wise sayings. I buy them from a dealer in Hong Kong for $1.26 each and sell them for $12.60. My daddy always said I should be happy with 10 percent. Not bad, eh?"

"How are sales going?"

"The sign business is always good, but you have to know which ones to inventory. I've got a company in Denver that does my warehousing and shipping. This month the big seller is 'Custer Had Pierced Ears and Other Body Parts.' "

Watson gaped at the man.

"I'm joking. Just some local humor. Now, I'll shut this machine down, and they can fax you here." He scribbled a number on a small, square, yellow sticky note. "This is the number. Say, if I dig up your books, will you autograph them?"

"Sure."

"I have a couple dozen of them."

"Bring them on."

"How much do you charge?"

"Autographs are free."

"Really?" Newross pondered. "That's quite generous of you."

The short man disappeared into another room as Watson stared at the phone number on the sticky note.

There's no area code. Yellowstone 5-1951? That can't still be the phone number. They haven't used prefixes like this since the 1950s. This isn't a fax number.

"You gonna stand on that porch all day? Try the door," McKenna hollered from the pickup.

Watson turned around. "The door's locked. I told you this place was closed."

"That gas station down the road isn't closed. I saw two rigs pull in there while you were readin' all those signs," Toby said.

Paul James Watson climbed back into the truck. "Some of those signs I haven't seen since I was a kid."

"I figured you fell asleep."

"I was working on a scene."

"P.J., doesn't your mind ever rest?"

Watson locked his eyes on McKenna's. Took a deep breath and let it out slow. "No." He eased up to the gravel road and waited as a car roared past.

"Whoa," McKenna hollered, "that gal in the green '62 Impala is in a hurry. Probably on her way to see her boyfriend."

Paul James Watson pulled out and followed in the dust of the green car. "At this time of the morning, in the wilds of Montana? That's a dumb assumption, Toby. You'd never make a novelist."

"And where do you say she's goin'?"

"To her mother's to leave the baby, so she can go to work as a bookkeeper at a mine in Colstrip. Her husband has been laid off work since April, and she's working two jobs to make ends meet."

"Nice try, Watson, but that's pathetically boring too. Let that writer guy in your mind take a crack at it."

P. J. Watson gazed at the distant horizon. "OK, she's headed to an abandoned Strategic Air Command silo forty miles north of here, where, unknown to the United States government, radical Laotian terrorists are reassembling a short-range missile that will be aimed at Fort Peck Dam. Similar counterparts are planning simultaneous attacks on Hoover, Grand Coulee, and Bonneville dams. While the western states reel in death and destruction, a crack team of Laotian operatives huddle in the desert outside Hawthorne, Nevada, waiting to break in and confiscate two tons of heavy plutonium, which they will sell to an unnamed Middle Eastern nation so they might have enough money to hire

Britney Spears to make a series of 'See Laos First' commercials."

"You see, Watson, P.J. is the real writer. I love that story. But you didn't say what this lady in the green Impala has to do with that story."

"She has just found out that the Office of Homeland Security has confiscated the tanker car of rocket fuel they counted on hijacking, and she's rushing to warn them to abandon the silo."

"You're a master, P.J.," McKenna mused.

"It's a ludicrous story."

"Write it. I'll play the part of the guy that saves the world and catches Britney Spears as she dives off the train speeding through the Laotian jungle."

"She's too young for you, McKenna."

"Too young for what?"

The speeding green car slammed on its brakes and parked in the middle of the gravel road. A dark-haired lady who looked about thirty and wore a green sweatshirt and jeans jumped out of her car and waved her hands and arms at them.

Watson pulled up next to her and rolled down his passenger-side window. "Do you need some help, ma'am?"

"Do you know who won the bull-riding

at the rodeo?" she cried.

"What?"

"Who won the bull-riding?"

"I have no idea in the world. Is that why you are crying?"

"I need you to help me," she begged.

"With what?"

"Please! Just follow me," she sobbed.

"Do you need me to phone 911? I have a cell phone, and I could . . ."

"No!" she shouted through her tears. "Just follow me! For heaven's sake, just follow me!"

"But, where are you . . . ?"

"Please," she begged. "You have to follow me."

"Does this have to do with bull-riding?"

"No, it's a matter of life or death."

"You want me to phone the sheriff?"

"No! Just follow me!" she hollered, then jumped back into her car and fogged dust as she spun her tires in the loose gravel road.

"Follow her?" Watson mumbled. "I have to find a fax machine. I have to look at a book cover. I have to go home."

"Hurry, P.J., she's pullin' away," McKenna insisted.

Watson stepped on the accelerator, and the pickup's tires spun in the gravel. "I don't even know where she's going."

"Of course you don't; that's the mystery. That's the joy. That's the adventure!" McKenna shouted. "Yes! You finally get to live it out instead of just dreamin' it up."

Watson sped after the old green Chevrolet. Buildings disappeared, and the road was otherwise deserted. Sagebrush and brown grass stretched across the low, rolling hills.

Lord, this is insane. I have no idea why I'm driving down a gravel road after this near hysterical woman. I wonder if I should phone the sheriff, just in case. I think I'm still in Rosebud County.

When they reached the blacktop, she turned west on Highway 12, then burned rubber racing away.

"She's got someone with her," Watson mumbled.

"Looks like a little boy standin' in the seat beside her," McKenna added. "This is excitin', P.J. I'm sorry about sayin' how borin' your life is. I didn't know things like this happened to you."

"Things like this never happen to me. This is crazy. I've got to call the sheriff's office."

"No, she said not to call. Maybe her

other children are kidnapped, and if you call the police, they will slit little Julia's neck and toss her in a desert cave," McKenna cautioned.

"That's . . . that's preposterous," P.J. replied. "No one who drives an old '62 Impala has their children captured for ransom."

McKenna pulled a pack of Beeman's out of his pocket and shoved two sticks of gum in his mouth. "A '62 Impala is a classic."

"Not that one. The muffler is dragging, and it's burning oil." When P.J. rubbed his cheek, he could feel places he missed with the razor.

"OK, what is your explanation?" McKenna challenged.

"I think she's afraid of running out of gas and wants us to follow her home."

"What?" McKenna gasped. "There's a station right back there in Forslip."

"But she didn't have any money, and she's too embarrassed to ask for money," Watson suggested.

"But she flagged you down to follow her and wouldn't tell you why?"

"She knew if she told me, I wouldn't follow. That's why she said it was life or death, just to sucker me along." Watson surveyed the highway leading up into the hills. "How far is she going, anyway?"

"What's down this road?" McKenna asked.

"Nothing until we get to Roundup."

"Then she's goin' to Roundup."

"That's a hundred miles away."

"With no gas in the tank?" McKenna shook his head. "I think you had the wrong story. What does P.J., the writer, say now?"

Paul Watson rapped his fingers on the steering wheel. "What if a band of Eastern European gypsies are prowling the region?"

"Therefore the old car?" McKenna said.

"Precisely. But they try to avoid the locals who might turn them in."

"How would she know that?"

"The question about the rodeo. Local people would know the answer."

"And you didn't."

"So what if the scam is for her to do her little act, then lead us up some gravel road to a box canyon where her brothers and cousins are waiting to steal my truck, rob us, and leave us with a bullet in the skull behind some boulder."

"Us?" McKenna added. "I'm fictional. Remember?"

"So, when I need some help, you'll cut out?"

"You don't need my help. But I'll be with you in spirit." McKenna grinned wide enough to reveal dimples. "If you go down, I'll go down with you. Of course, I won't be buried in a pine box."

"Yeah, I know, you'll live forever in the Smithsonian."

"The Library of Congress."

"Whatever." Watson eyed the green car ahead of them. "She's not turning north, so I guess we are headed to Roundup."

"Gypsies carry knives, P.J. Have you ever been knifed?"

"Other than almost slicing my thumb off when I was trying to whittle a moose as a kid, no, I haven't."

"Well, I have," McKenna reported. "Remember that scene in *Steel-Eyed Susan*? TriLisha yanked that straight razor out of her . . ."

"Her boot," P.J. insisted.

"Yeah, that was what I was gonna say. Anyway, she sliced through my arm before I could punch her out. I had to hike out of the swamp next to the river with two hundred pounds of dangerous plastic explosive under one arm and an unconscious, 106-pound, redheaded man-hater over my shoulder. All the time I was gushin' blood. If not for that Girl Scout troop, I would have been in real trouble."

"Do you have a point to this, McKenna?"

"Don't get ambushed by knife-wielding gypsies."

"I don't intend to, but she keeps driving faster and faster. I'm not going to drive that fast."

"Why not? Are you afraid a deputy will pull you over for speedin'? Then you could tell him about this crazy lady."

"I don't think she's crazy," P.J. murmured as he sped up.

"There's always a possibility that's she's a looney and seein' things. You know, paranoid about aliens tryin' to abduct her."

"I can't believe this conversation."

"P.J., for a man of faith, there sure are a lot of things you can't believe. You can't believe this conversation, or this lady, or this chase. I should think a paperback writer like yourself wouldn't have such doubts. What if this is one of your divine appointments?"

"You mean, the Lord leading me to this woman?"

"Yep."

"This is not the way he does things. This is not the way anyone does things. I'm calling Sheila."

"What is she supposed to do?" McKenna challenged.

"I just want someone to know where we are."

"So they will know where to look for your body?"

"I didn't mean that."

Watson reached over and pushed the first speed-dial button. He grabbed the phone out of the holder.

"So you don't trust your ol' pal Toby to talk to the wife, eh? Speaking of paranoia."

"How fast is she going?"

"We're doin' 85 and losin' her," McKenna reported.

Watson waited for the phone to ring.

Is Toby right? Did you lead me out here? Or is this a demonic sidetrack? Why isn't it easier to tell the difference between the two? I just want to go home, that's all. I don't like bein' on the road two weeks, especially locked in a motel room. I start talking to myself.

"Watsons."

"Hi, babe."

"Oh . . . Paulie, I'm glad you called. I needed to talk to you."

"What's up, darlin'?"

"Your signal isn't very good. Where are you?"

"You wouldn't believe it."

"Nor would you. Paul, the foundry in Kalispell called. They have my piece *Rough Day at Canyon Rim* ready for me to examine. Isn't that incredible? I thought this day would never come. You know how hyped I am about that piece. It will be my most famous, I'm sure. Anyway, I'm going up to see it."

"Now?"

"Yes. I'll spend the night with Marty."

"But . . . but . . ."

"Honey, you've been gone two weeks. One more day will be all right, won't it?"

"I guess."

"The kids are fine. Pete's staying over at Jared and Marcia's, so little brother can fix big brother's computer. Rudi will be home about three unless they give her some overtime hours. There's leftover roast in the fridge. Don't forget you have a Bridgeport Association Meeting tonight and a dentist appointment at ten in the morning. I'll be home about the time you get back from the dentist. Mom called and said Dad was depressed again, so I promised we would spend Thanksgiving with them in Colorado Springs. You have a couple of calls. George Gossman phoned, said it was an emergency, so I gave him your truck cell number."

"Yeah, I talked to him."

"And the other call was from Theodore Revelage," Sheila said.

"What did Theo want?"

"Did you know that he and Terri aren't together anymore?"

"Eh, no. Listen, darlin', I need to tell you . . ."

"Anyway, Theo is working on a new conspiracy project. He seems to think you can help him out."

"I'll call him when I get home. Sheila, listen, we took Highway 12 . . ."

"We? Who's with you?"

"I meant, I took . . . I've been having a running dialogue with Toby McKenna."

"I certainly hope you aren't taking advice from him," she giggled. "Paul, I think it is so marvelous the way you dialogue with your characters."

"Here's the point. A lady flagged us, . . . eh, flagged me down and wanted me to follow her home. She was in some sort of distress but wouldn't tell me what. So I'm on Highway 12, driving 85 miles an hour . . ."

"Ninety," McKenna blurted out.

"And I still haven't figured out what is going on."

"Paul, you are so creative," Sheila said.

"But this is true."

Her voice was soft, gentle, like snow dripping off pine trees on a sunny spring day. "I don't know how you do it. You are a natural novelist. Your mind fills up with such incredible ideas. You are an inspiration, honey. Don't ever change. I love it when you are in one of your zones."

"But, darlin', this is real. I'm really . . ."

"I know, baby. I know. Just let it flow, sweet Paul. You know you are my favorite author of all time."

"Shelia, listen to me."

"I'm losing your signal, Paul. Drive carefully. I'm heading out right now. I'll see you in the morning, honey."

"Sheila?"

"You lost her," McKenna reported.

"I most certainly did not," Watson snapped. "I merely lost the cell connection."

"That's what I meant," McKenna retorted.

"Oh. Yes, well, anyway, she knows I'm on Highway 12."

"Not for long. The woman in the green Impala is turnin' off," McKenna reported.

"Where does that road go?"

"The sign said Big Porcupine Creek

Road," McKenna said.

"I can't see the rig anymore. Can you see it?"

"No, just follow that dust cloud," McKenna reported.

"How far do we do this?"

"Until we spot the band of murderin' gypsies, or the gas gauge is halfway down," McKenna suggested. "I don't ever think I've been this remote. Not countin' bein' lost at sea for fourteen days in *Flames over Havana.*"

"I'm about ready to stop and turn around," Watson insisted.

"You better check that out with the boss."

"There's no cell phone reception out here. I lost connection with Sheila."

"Not that boss," McKenna insisted. "If this is a divine appointment, you'd better get the man upstairs to approve you abandonin' her."

"Are you getting religious on me, Toby McKenna?"

"Isn't that what you are always houndin' me about?"

"You're saying that God is leading us here?"

"Leadin' you, P.J. I'm nothin' more than a parable," McKenna added.

The ring of the cell phone caused them both to jump back as they bounced down the gravel road toward barren, brown hills.

"I'd say you got reception now," McKenna mumbled.

Watson punched the speaker phone and kept both hands on the black leather steering wheel. "Hello?"

"Hi, Paul, this is . . ."

"Hi, Spunky, tell George I haven't found a fax machine yet."

"Are you close to one?"

"I doubt it."

"What are you doing?"

"He's chasin' a lady across some back road of Montana," McKenna blurted out.

"Oh, Paul, you naughty boy! Now you are chasing women! You've been hanging with my teddy bear too long."

"Not that kind of lady," Watson insisted.

"Just what kind of lady are you chasing?" her high-pitched voice teased.

"I don't even know who she is."

"Do you know that's how I met my first husband?"

"I'm not chasing a lady. I'm following her because she asked me."

"Good for her. Montana women are more assertive than I imagined. You be careful, Paul, and give us that fax number within a half hour, or Mr. L. George Gossman will start pulling out what little real hair he has left. Bye, teddy bear."

"Bye, babe," McKenna called out.

"I'm not going to find a fax in a half hour," Paul complained.

"It's no big thing, right?"

"It's the cover of the next Toby McKenna book."

"Did you tell them about my idea for embossed letters with gold foil?"

"I told them. They said it was cost prohibitive."

"Whoa, did you see that? She turned off and busted through that chained drive."

Watson turned right on the dirt road and followed her. "What's that sign say?"

"No trespassing, U.S. government," McKenna reported.

"Are we on BLM land?"

"How do I know?" McKenna shrugged. "You never set me in Montana before."

"She's stopping by that little shed."

"It's an outhouse," McKenna mumbled.

"It's not an outhouse.

Watson pulled in behind her and pulled himself out of the truck when she ran over and shoved a five-year-old, blonde-headed boy in his arms. "Do you have a gun?" she shouted.

"Not with me," Watson murmured.

"You'll have to stop him if he shows up."

"Who?"

"You'll know when you see him. He's armed and dangerous. You have to stop him at all costs," she insisted.

"What is this all about?"

She turned toward the tiny shack. "You don't want to know."

"Where are you going?"

"To get my things, of course."

"In there?" Watson pointed to the broom-closet-size building.

"It's much bigger than it looks," she called out as she scampered to the little wooden shed. "Hold him. Don't let him wander around."

The young boy smelled of campfire smoke. He peered at Watson with wide blue eyes.

"All right, young man, what is your name?"

The boy stuck a knuckle in his mouth and sucked on it.

"My name is Paul. What's yours?"

"Hey, P.J.," McKenna called out from the other side of the pickup. "Look at this old rusty sign."

"What does it say?" Watson asked.

"NO TRESPASSING: Strategic Air

Command." McKenna called out as he hiked closer. "Maybe your fiction story was close to the truth."

P. J. Watson felt his throat grow tighter. "It really is a missile bunker."

"What's the boy's name?" McKenna asked.

The blonde-haired boy wiggled to get free.

"He doesn't talk," Watson reported.

The boy kicked P.J. in the shins. "I'm Frederick the Great, and my daddy's going to kill you!"

chapter four

"You surely got a way with kids, P.J.," McKenna chided. "I wonder where the buildings used to be around here? There aren't even any concrete foundations left." He scratched the back of his thick, dark hair as he paced the grounds.

Frederick the Great stopped kicking. "Put me down!" he demanded.

"I was told to hold on to you."

"Do you always do what you're told?" the boy whined. He punched with his fists, and Watson grabbed his hands.

Toby laughed. "Son, P.J. is the poster boy of obedience. He obeys people he doesn't even know."

Watson tried to study the rusted equipment that littered the facility. "Your mama will be right back, son. Then you two can go home."

The boy rubbed his flat, round nose. "This is our home," he sniffed.

Watson stared at the tiny shack. "Where?"

Frederick the Great pointed down. "In the dirt."

"You live underground?" Watson asked.

The boy nodded his head.

Toby McKenna strolled back with a short, rusted iron pipe in his hand. "There really is a facility under here?" He stomped on the dirt.

"Perhaps that little shed leads to a shaft inside some underground bunker," Watson said.

McKenna glanced at the wide, deep blue, cloud-littered Montana sky. "Right out here in the middle of nowhere?"

Watson shifted the boy to the other arm. "What's under the dirt, son?"

The boy's chin was on his chest. "My mama."

"Maybe P.J. the writer was right. Perhaps this is an international conspiracy," McKenna mused. "What do you think of the title *Big Sky Spy*?"

"It stinks," Watson replied. "No, I think it's much more threatening than international intrigue. I think it's a domestic quarrel. Those are the most dangerous and violent."

McKenna plucked up a discarded padlock from a sagebrush. "This has been hacksawed. You sayin' the old man will show up ridin' a mule and totin' a shotgun?"

"Or maybe show up on a dirt bike with an AK47," Watson said.

The shed door opened up without the woman being visible, and a large cardboard box was shoved outside in the dirt. "Put this in the trunk of my car!" a voice shouted. "I'll go get the rest."

P.J. glanced at Toby McKenna.

McKenna shrugged. "She wasn't talkin' to me. I don't think she even knows I exist."

Watson lowered the boy, then drew a circle in the dirt around him. "Frederick, don't step out of that circle. You could blow yourself to bits. There are land mines all over here."

The boy nodded. "I know," he mumbled. "I know." He stood motionless as if at attention.

Paul James Watson hiked over to the box in the open doorway of the ten-foot-square shed.

He knows? Good grief, are there actually land mines here? Why?

He paused and glanced back at the boy. He still hadn't moved.

Lord, this is scary. Not just because it is strange, but because I can't tell if it's true. I don't know if I'm living one of my stories or not. That frightens me. I've always lived in my stories, but I could come back anytime I need to. But what if I can't get back? What if instead of being "highly creative," I'm merely delusional?

Watson struggled to lift the huge box.

What is she moving, the woodstove?

He staggered toward the green Impala.

"Watch out for the land mines," Frederick cautioned him.

McKenna waited for him. "You really think there are land mines?"

"It's getting really difficult to be certain of anything," Watson murmured as he shoved the box in the back of the car.

"What's in the box?" McKenna asked.

"I didn't look."

Toby flipped open the lid. Watson peered in.

"A laptop? Satellite phone? A paper shredder? She's taking the paper shredder?" Watson gasped.

"It's modern times, P.J. They don't fight over the toaster anymore. What's that?" McKenna fingered a gray metallic box.

"It's an old reel-to-reel tape recorder."

"What does she want with that?"

"I don't know, but here she comes with another load." Watson hiked toward the woman.

"You got Toole standing still." She nodded a round chin at the boy. "How did you do that?"

Paul James Watson took the box from her hands. "I warned him that there were land mines. His name is Toole?"

"Yeah, you're right about the land mines. I don't think his father even remembers where he buried them. What did Toole say his name was, Joseph Stalin?"

"He said he was Frederick the Great. Your husband actually buried land mines around here?"

"I didn't say that," she snapped. "I didn't say anything."

She grabbed another box out of the shed, and they shoved them in the backseat of the Impala. Paul James Watson stepped back from the car and slipped his hands into his back pockets. "What is this all about?"

She tugged up the waist of her jeans. "Go get Toole for me."

"Look, are you in trouble with the authorities?" he pressed.

"Hah!" she blurted out. "If they knew what I know!"

"About what?"

She slid in behind the steering wheel of the Impala. "About who, you mean."

Watson hiked over to where the little blonde boy stood in the circle in the dirt. "Come on, Toole."

The boy folded his arms. "My name's not Toole."

Watson reached down. "OK, Frederick the Great, Mama wants you in the car."

"I'm not Frederick the Great."

P.J. shook his head and sighed. "All right, just who are you?"

"I'm Generalisimo Francisco Franco!"

"It's so good to see you again, General. I trust Spain is surviving your autocratic rule. How is your pal Mussolini?" Watson plucked up the boy and ambled toward the car.

"They hung Mussolini in the plaza with his mistress," the boy explained.

Watson stared at the woman as he shoved the boy into the Chevy.

"He's a bright boy," she offered. Then she stepped on the accelerator and left Watson in a fog of pale yellow dust.

McKenna smirked in the truck. "OK, P.J., are you gonna let her drive away like that?"

"The further the better. This can't be happening to me. I think I'm having a breakdown. Too much stress. I'll wake up in a padded room somewhere." He glanced at the floorboard in front of Toby McKenna. "What's that?"

"I found it out in the sage. 'NO TRESPASSING! Strategic Air Command.' It's a cool sign."

"Toss it out."

"I'll take it with me to Florida. I'll nail it on the palm tree next to my hammock."

"No, you won't," Watson barked. "You'll leave it here. It's just my luck to get pulled over and have to admit I was back here. Toss it, Toby."

"You're paranoid, P.J."

"I said toss it."

McKenna rolled down his window. "OK, slow down. I wonder if I can sail it over that rise? Remember that time in *Samoa Sunset Suicide* when I tossed the Studebaker hubcap across the Burger King parkin' lot and hit that drug dealer in the back the head?"

P.J. shook his head. "You missed the drug dealer and hit the used-car salesman."

"It's hard to tell 'em apart from the other side of a Burger King. Anyway, I'll

94

bet you five bucks I can toss this over that mound of dirt."

"You don't have any money to bet."

"And yet I'm never broke. Have you noticed that? Never, ever, in any book you wrote did I not have money. One time in *Atrocity in Athens*, I was down to my last one hundred bucks, but then that rich Bulgarian lady helped me out."

"She was Hungarian."

"Whatever. Watch this!" McKenna sailed the one-foot-square sign high in the air like a Frisbee. "Yes! Toby McKenna, you are still the . . ."

The sign dropped out of sight; then the dirt exploded. Debris jetted into the air and drifted toward them.

"Land mines?" Watson stepped on the gas and shot down the dirt drive. "We're going to get arrested."

"Not me, buckaroo. I'll just crawl up on some library shelf and park it until you write your next novel from jail," Toby grinned.

Watson pushed his sunglasses up on top of his gray-streaked, dark brown hair and squinted into the dust. "I should never have driven back here."

"Look at how tedious your day would have been again," McKenna said. "You don't want to spend your entire life bored spitless."

Watson pushed the electronic button and rolled up the passenger side window. "My life is not boring. It's peaceful. I like it that way."

McKenna turned on the CD player. "Peaceful is just another way of sayin' you are in a rut and can't get out."

Watson studied his rearview mirror. "Jesus came to bring us a peaceful life."

"Now, P.J., explain somethin' to me. I've heard lots of stories about Jesus. . . ."

"Are you going to tell me you read the Gideon Bible in your motel room?"

"Eh, no," McKenna replied, "but remember that short little Baptist flight attendant in *Black Box, Black Door*? When I struggled to get the 737 out of a nosedive, she started readin' the Bible over the loudspeaker. Now, the Jesus she read about lived a mighty excitin' life. How come you want your life to be dull?"

Watson gripped the top of the black leather steering wheel. "I can't believe you would try to compare my life to Jesus'."

McKenna sunk down in the seat. "P.J., maybe you are right. It could be that you are just losin' it, havin' some sort of breakdown. It used to be, when I brought up

Jesus, I'd get a whole sermon about how I need to change my life."

The cell phone rang as they bounced through the dust toward the blacktop highway.

"Yeah?" Watson called out on the speaker phone.

"My word, Paul, we have to have your approval in less than a half hour."

"Look, George, I'm a little busy. I'm in the middle of Montana at an abandoned Strategic Air Command silo where a mysterious woman just stole a laptop full of secret information that the government is desperately trying to get. On my way out to the highway, a land mine went off, and I'm about to choke to death on dirt spewed from the crazy woman's Impala. I can't get to a fax machine right now, and please stop calling me about it!"

McKenna flashed him two thumbs up.

For a moment there was no response.

"Maybe you lost the signal on the bald, bombastic Brooklyner," McKenna mumbled.

"I'm from Queens. Who is that with you?" Gossman demanded.

Watson leaned forward toward the microphone mounted above the windshield. "That was Toby McKenna."

"Where have I heard that name? Anyway, I like your new story. Send us that blurb for the spring catalog. I don't know how you get those ideas. Of course, if I knew that, I'd be a rich and famous author instead of an obscure editor."

"Some people are destined for obscurity," McKenna blurted out.

"Paul?"

"I'm here."

"There seems to be some interference. Where are you really? Are you still in Montana?" Gossman asked.

"About seventy-five miles from Roundup, Montana, approaching Highway 12," Watson reported.

"Splendid. Just a minute. I have some instructions for you. Can you hear me?"

"I can hear you, George."

"OK, now turn down Willow Creek cutoff and go south thirteen miles until . . ."

"Do you know this country, George?" Watson asked.

"The wife and I were going to stop by to see Lynda and Brady Stoner's twins last summer. She used to be an editor here before she ran off and married the cowboy. She still does freelance for us when she isn't busy having babies. She edits all of

Joaquin Estaban's books, that is, whenever he decides to send them to us. Anyway, we didn't make the trip in August because Carolyn got rice stuck in her nose at Joseph's wedding and had to have surgery to remove it. But I have the instructions to their house right here. She has a fax machine you can use."

"Look," McKenna called out, "that gal is waitin' for you at the highway."

"What did you say?" Gossman challenged.

Watson watched the woman get out of the car and lean against the door. "What does she want now?"

"What does who want now? Paul, what is going on out there?"

"George, I'll call you tonight. I've got a situation here. Bye."

"Wait. Wait. Wait. Tonight will be too late."

"Then stick with the original cover. It's the only one I approved. Good-bye, George."

"But, Paul, Mr. Hampton needs to know what you think about that cover today."

"Tell him the new cover stinks and I want the old one."

"You haven't seen the new cover."

"Good-bye, George. Of course, if you

want to wait until tomorrow, then I'll give you my opinion after I see it. Fax it to the house."

"Hmmm, well, I suppose we could wait until tomorrow."

"You see?" Toby triumphed. "You've just got to stand up to him."

"What was that?" Gossman demanded.

"Nothing, George. I'm just mumbling to myself. I'll fax you back tomorrow."

"Bye, Georgie," McKenna piped in. "Hug your toupee for us."

"What?"

Watson turned off the phone and pulled up next to the Impala. The woman marched to his door as he rolled down the window.

"Was that a land mine, or did he throw a hand grenade at you?" she asked.

"He has hand grenades too?" Watson gasped. "I think it was a land mine."

"Look," she said, "thanks for going in there with me. If he had been home, it would have been a violent mess. He's become a total psycho. I shouldn't have led you back there, but I was desperate. If you read in the paper anything about me getting killed, I need you to phone someone for me." Her round face creased with stress and torment.

Watson gazed into her light-green eyes. "How will I know if you get killed? I don't even know your name."

She studied the traffic on the highway. "You'll know. It will be spectacular." She strolled back to her car. "Hand me that pen, Timmy." Then she stepped back to the pickup.

Watson looked over at the little boy who sat in the backseat. "Timmy? I thought you said his name was Toole?"

"Did I? Imagine that." She reached into the front pocket of her Levis and pulled out a wad of papers. Something dropped to the dirt. "Let me write a phone number for you."

"You dropped a fifty-dollar bill."

"Oh . . . yeah." She scooped it up, then continued writing. "Here's the deal. If you read that I was murdered, call this phone number. He will have a question for you. You are to answer: Hank F. Calf."

"You're kidding me," Watson mumbled.

"Just do it." She handed him the card, jumped back in the car, then roared west on Highway 12.

Watson turned to McKenna. "This is bizarre. Did you hear that?"

McKenna rubbed his strong, square chin. "Hank F. Calf? You ever hear of him?

101

I never heard of him, and I hear a lot of strange names."

"Are you kidding?" Watson pulled onto the highway after a cattle truck rattled by. "That's got to be an acronym for something."

"I don't know," McKenna said. "Remember, that gal in *Arctic Ice Murders* was called Calves . . . or was it Thighs?"

"That was Ankles."

"Whatever. And then there was a lowlife called Joe Kidney."

"Joe Kidd."

"Was that his name? No wonder he kept tryin' to punch my lights out. I thought his name was Kidney. 'Hank F. Calf.' Let me see that card, P.J." McKenna jerked his head around. "Look at what's comin' at us. A shiny black Hummer. Is that like the one I drove over the cliff in *Too Wild to Be Free*?"

"Maybe. Look back there," Watson said. "Did he just drive off the road into the sagebrush?"

"Whoa, he's headed to the silo, I bet. Maybe that's her old man! Talk about good timin'. We got out of there just in time. Paul James Watson, you are livin' right today."

"We don't know he's going back there."

"Where else would he be going? Turn around, P.J. Let's follow him. Have you got a carbine behind that seat?"

"No. And I'm going home."

"You'll regret it," McKenna said.

"What do you mean, I'll regret it?"

Toby McKenna continued to watch the dust from the Hummer in the side-view mirror. "Someday when you are sittin' in your wheelchair at the nursin' home, watchin' *I Love Lucy* on the television, you'll put down your Tupperware bowl of tapioca puddin' and have one lucid mental moment and say to yourself, 'I should have followed that Hummer.' "

"You're quoting me in *Boston Blackmail*. That's all fiction, and you know it," Watson protested.

"Of course it's fiction!" McKenna bellowed. "Everythin' I say is fiction."

"I'm tired, Toby. I'm going home."

"You've got to take me to the airport in Billings first."

"I will be happy to leave you in Billings."

"I want an aisle seat next to a tall gal with champagne hair named Oliole who's read all my books," McKenna said.

"They are my books," Watson corrected. "Your life but my books."

"You must be tired. You're crankier than

a two-year-old after losin' a spirited game of Duck, Duck, Goose," McKenna declared. "Remember, seat me next to a lonely blonde."

Watson released a long slow sigh. "I could put you between a two-year-old boy named Adolf Hitler with weak bowels and a three-hundred-pound lady wearing a string of garlic around her neck."

Toby McKenna stared at the business card the woman had given Watson. "Hey, P.J., don't you know this guy?"

"What guy?"

"She wrote that phone number on the back of this business card."

"Whose card is it?"

"Some guy in Marina Del Rey named Theodore Revelage."

"What? Give me that!" Watson demanded.

Watson studied the card that read, "Theodore Revelage, Esq. Confidential Investigations, Old Coins Appraised, Special Assignments."

Watson shook his head. "That's the second time in an hour his name has been mentioned, and I haven't seen Theo since doing research for *San Pedro Profiles*."

McKenna rolled down his window and sailed his hand through the breeze. "Oh, don't remind me of that one! You promised never to bring that one up again."

"Toby, I explained to you why she had to die."

McKenna pulled his hand back inside and slammed it on the tan dash. "I could have saved her, P.J. I know I could. I can swim five miles; you know that."

"The water was too cold, Toby."

"Then I should have died tryin'. You always tell me there are things worse than dyin'."

"And what about all those other adventures you would have missed?"

"But what if I made it? What if I saved Traci Martin? And so what if I died? It's not like I have a grievin' family, P.J. You're always tellin' me that you need to do those things you would regret not doin'. Well, how about me? I regret not tryin' to save Traci's life. Besides, you could just wake me up at the beginnin' of the next book and tell everyone I was just dreamin'."

"I don't need dreams to get me out of a jam. Besides, you are wrong. There would have been grieving lady readers all over the globe mourning your death."

"Yeah, I never thought of that. Still, that was not a happy plot."

"I'm not going to discuss old plots."

Watson pulled over to the side of the highway. "Besides, this whole thing with the lady in the Impala is getting too bizarre for me."

"What are you doin', P.J.?"

"I'm turning around."

"Yes! We're goin' back to the silo," McKenna declared. "We're goin' after the jerk in the Hummer."

"No, we are going back to Interstate 94. I'm going home. I'm really tired, McKenna. That's a concept difficult for you to understand."

"I can't believe you'd walk away from all of this."

"All of what?" Watson protested. "I have no idea what's going on here. I'm a mediocre writer who is worn out. My mind is on overload. I need a break."

"I'll drive. You take a nap," McKenna offered.

Paul James glanced over at the empty passenger's seat in his Chevrolet pickup and rubbed his eyes.

I need some coffee. I need to get home. I need to quit writing for at least a week or two. Maybe Sheila and I could go up to Lake Louise. That would be nice. The lodge has those big old leather chairs by the fireplace.

We could just collapse with our feet up on the ottomans and stare at the dancing flames in that massive log fireplace. They could bring us coffee and tea, and we could talk about when we were young. I used to be young. In those days before writing. I taught history and she taught art at Craig, Colorado. We shoved the kids in the back of the old Buick station wagon and headed for the northern Rockies every summer. We camped for weeks at a time. She would sketch and sketch and sketch.

And I would make up stories for the kids every night around the campfire. Then in the morning I would pull out my notebook and write down what I could remember of the story. Those were pleasant days, Lord. You were close. We were poor. Couldn't afford a motel, so we camped. And the good times were all to be in the future.

We'd crawl into that double flannel sleeping bag at night, the kids asleep around us, and she'd whisper: "Someday, Paulie, you'll get to write your books. I just know you will. You are so creative. I sit in awe every night."

"And someday, babe, your work will hang in famous galleries," I'd assure her.

Then we would whisper, laugh, play, and wait.

Wait for those days to come.

Well, I've written ninety-eight books. Ninety-nine counting Diamond Dandy Disaster, *so I suppose these are the days we were waiting for. How could I have known that those early days were the ones to remember, not these? Everything shined vividly. The sky spread out bluer. Love tasted sweeter. Truth tumbled out crystal clear. And nothing, absolutely nothing, sounded impossible.*

He turned on the CD player and listened to Jimmy Buffett sing "A Pirate Looks at Forty."

"Yeah, Jimmy," he mumbled. "To say nothing about looking at fifty-five."

I really need some coffee.

A lone red, 1957 Chevy pickup rested in front of the Big Timber, Montana, Café and Gas Station. A handwritten sign in the window proclaimed: "Coffee — 1st Cup 10 cents . . . Refills — $1." Paul James Watson pulled the keys from the ignition and ambled inside the building covered in faded gray cedar shingles.

A wide man with a white bib apron straddled a wooden stool behind the counter. A gray-haired man with a clean blue flannel shirt under faded but ironed blue coveralls sat across from him. A cribbage board and deck of cards sprawled between them.

The man in the apron poured a steaming cup of coffee and slid it down toward Watson, two stools from the man in the coveralls.

"Thanks," Watson acknowledged. "That's exactly what I need."

"If you're hungry, I'll be happy to stop this game and cook you up anythin' you want. In fact, I probably ought to quit before I lose more money."

Watson took a sip of the thick, hot coffee. "You in the hole?"

"We're playin' penny a point, and I'm down $3.98," the man reported.

Watson glanced up at the burl wood clock on the wall. "How long you been playing?"

The proprietor glanced at the man in the overalls. "How long has it been, Hibbs?"

"Since Mary Lou died," Hibbs reported. "March 14, 1994."

"We keep a runnin' tally," the aproned man added.

"You've been at it almost ten years, and you're losing less than four bucks?" Watson said.

"Yeah. Well, I led when President Clinton was in office," the large man replied.

"And Al ain't even a Democrat," Hibbs chided.

Watson let another slurp of coffee trickle down his throat. "This is the best dime coffee in North America."

"It ain't bad dollar coffee either," Hibbs added.

"Well, Al, hit me again, and I'll find out."

The man in the apron refilled Watson's navy blue ceramic cup. "You hungry?"

"No, thanks. Just have to wake up a little and get back on the road."

"Where you headed?" Al asked.

"I live in Bridgeport."

"Bridgeport? Do you know ol' Goog Peters?" Hibbs asked.

"Goog died in '89, Hibbs," Al reminded him.

"That's right. I knew that. Well, he's got a boy named Scott," Hibbs announced.

Watson took another sip of coffee. "I know Scott Peters."

"You don't say? Small world, ain't it?" Hibbs nodded. "What's your name?"

"Paul Watson."

Al poured himself another cup of coffee.

"Do you spell it just like the writer?"

"Identical."

Hibbs rubbed his clean-shaven chin. "Do folks ever get you confused for a writer?"

"Not often," Watson admitted.

"I had an old boy in here last week who said he picked up a hitchhiker named Butch Cassidy. Turned out to be a red-headed gal. I reckon more than one person can have the same name. Course, I ain't never met another Hibbs Hornaday."

"What kind of work do you do, Paul?" Al asked.

Watson slid his coffee cup toward the pot and grinned. "Some say I'm a liar and thief."

Hibbs chuckled. "That makes you a politician or a horse trader."

"Or maybe the loan officer at the bank," Al added. "But it don't matter. We don't aim to pry."

Watson rubbed his right shoulder, then stretched his arms. "I've got a question for you two. I was wondering, were there ever any military facilities around here? Maybe north of the river?"

"Military? You mean an army base?" Al asked.

"I was thinking of a Strategic Air Command radar station, or ICBM missile site, or something like that."

"I think most of them was up toward Great Falls. But there always was rumors," Al admitted.

"What do you mean, rumors?"

Hibbs spun around on his stool to face Watson. "Back in the sixties, when ever'one was buildin' fallout shelters and worryin' about H-bombs. The military came on government land and dug a bunch of dummy silos for those big missiles."

"At least they said they was dummy holes," Al said. "I don't think they told anyone. They wanted to confuse the Soviets so they wouldn't know which were armed with live missiles."

"There was one of them up on Big Porcupine Creek," Hibbs declared.

"It was a dummy silo," Al said. "At least, that's what ever'one was always told."

"But me and Al went huntin' antelope one time. We was hunkered down in the sage waitin' for daylight when an army jeep pulled up. Four uniformed men jumped out, unlocked the gate, and disappeared into a tiny toolshed. In a minute or two, four different men came out and drove off in the jeep. Now that don't sound like a dummy site to me."

Al ladled two spoons of sugar into his coffee and stirred. "Anyway, the whole site was abandoned in the early nineties."

"Does the government still own it?" Watson asked.

"I reckon so," Hibbs said. "Who would want to buy a hole in the ground?"

Al drank his coffee one spoonful at a time. "The hippies squatted near there in protest one year, until winter hit."

"When was that?" Watson quizzed.

"1972. They were out there when Nixon beat McGovern. But the army kept them at bay, and the blizzard sent them all to Mexico."

Hibbs stood up and slapped on a Hesston ball cap. "Al, I got to scoot. I got to get the battery changed in the tractor."

"Take it easy, partner. And you go see Doc Kline about that infection."

"You sound like Mary Lou."

Watson glanced over at the older man as he wiped calloused suntanned hands across his eyes.

"I reckon you still miss her."

"Ever' day of my life, son. Ever' day of my life."

Paul James Watson watched the old man amble out of the little café.

When the door clicked shut, Al stuck the cribbage board under the counter. "She was murdered."

"His wife?"

"Yep," Al explained. "She went out to the barn to the calvin' shed and someone shot her in the head."

"Did they capture the killer?"

"Nope. Sheriff said it was probably a transient stayin' out of the cold. She startled him in the dark, and he was packin' a .38 magnum. Some said it was Jonathan Boudary himself."

"The fugitive serial killer?"

"He gets blamed for anythin' that goes unsolved." Al stared out the front window. "Looks like I got a gas customer who can't figure where the credit card goes. Help yourself to more coffee."

"Thanks. I just might do that."

Paul James Watson sat alone in the café that smelled of strong coffee and fried meat.

At least there was some sort of facility up on Big Porcupine Creek. I didn't dream up that part. And I do have Theo's card.

He studied the red-and-blue print on the white business card. "Theodore Revelage, Esq. Confidential Investigations, Old

Coins Appraised, Special Assignments, 438 Parajo Blvd. Marina Del Rey, CA 90291."

Sheila said he moved to Long Beach. So I suppose this number is no longer good. But what in the world was this lady doing with Theodore Revelage's phone number? I'll just have to ask him.

What was that phone number the lady said to call? What was that cryptic answer?

Watson spun the card over with his fingers.

His chin sagged.

His heart raced.

The card dropped to the counter.

The backside of the business card was blank.

chapter five

The Yellowstone River carried only a little mud as it coursed its way through green-leafed cottonwoods and paralleled the interstate. The cab of the pickup felt stuffy. Paul Weston rolled his window down a few inches as he examined the blank backside of the card before tucking it back into his shirt pocket.

"I have the card she gave me but not what she wrote on it. Does that mean I'm only half dreaming this up?" he mumbled.

"Maybe she wrote it in disappearin' ink," Toby McKenna blurted out. "Remember the beach scene in *Maui Mother's Mayhem?* The clue was washed away in the sand at high tide."

"Toby, I don't want to talk about it with you. I think that whole scene of the gal with the Impala was fiction."

McKenna tossed his fedora on the dash and scratched his thick, short hair. "It seemed real to me."

"Toby, I don't want to talk to you right now. Go someplace."

"Go someplace?" McKenna gawked out at irrigated hay fields. "We're travelin' seventy-five miles an hour and you want me to go someplace?"

Paul James Watson waved his hand at the passenger seat of the pickup. "Go visit your pals at the Library of Congress. Go chase waitresses at some café. Go back to some tanning booth, or whatever. I just don't want to talk to you for awhile. You are supposed to be on vacation, anyway."

McKenna plucked up his fedora and spun it in his hand. "P.J., you've got a serious problem."

"Yes, I do. And talking to you might be part of it. I was going to let you ride along in my world, but I seem to be spending my time in yours. Good-bye, Toby."

"Can I just say one thing?"

"No. Bye, Toby."

"Whoa, you are grumpier than an Australian snake."

"I'm not grumpy. I'm tired."

"I think I'll take a nap. I didn't sleep much," Toby admitted. "Me and Barbara Joy, that Miles City Café waitress, you know."

"I trust you spent most of the night

pulling the Corvette off the rocks near the river."

"Oh, yeah, that too." Toby's dimples showed when he grinned wide. "But here's my one question. I know why I can't sleep. I chase around, get easily diverted, and have no responsibilities. . . . I'm a rather worthless lot."

"And your question is?"

"Why doesn't Paul James Watson get any sleep?" McKenna asked.

"I sleep," Watson insisted.

"You haven't slept more than five hours a night in fifteen years. You told me that. You go to bed at 10:00 or 10:30, or even 11:00 o'clock like last night, and you get up at 3:00 a.m. Why is that, P.J.?"

"I can get by with less sleep."

"No you can't. You're tired all the time," McKenna insisted.

"I am not tired all the time."

"Ask Sheila."

"Ask her what?" Watson said.

"Ask her if you are tired all the time."

"She's gone to Kalispell," Watson said.

"Are you sure?" McKenna hounded. "What if you imagined that conversation too?"

"I don't imagine conversations with my wife."

"Never?"

"Not that time. You were with me; you heard her."

"No, you wouldn't let me listen, remember? Besides, I was there when the lady wrote on the card, so that hardly proves anything. But that doesn't answer the question. Why can't you sleep?"

Paul Weston ran his fingers through his hair and gripped the steering wheel tighter. "I have too many projects going on."

"Lots of people are busy, P.J. They seem to sleep. It puzzles me. You tell me of Jesus and the peace he brings, and you can't sleep. Did you ever think about that?" McKenna pressed.

"I don't want to talk about it."

"No, I don't imagine you do." Toby McKenna leaned the electric seat back as far as it would go, pulled his fedora down over his eyes, and sighed. "Is the peace of Jesus only for daytime? I think I'll ponder that awhile."

Like bullets from an automatic rifle, the white lines of the interstate shot past Paul James Watson, mile after mile.

Lord, I'm busy. Maybe I'm too busy, but that's the way life is. I always said I'd rather burn out than rust out. But I can't remember why I said that. Toby's right. I am always tired. But I get a lot done that way. Sheila says I've already done more than most do in an entire lifetime.

I'm just not sure what that proves. Sometimes I'm confused. The Bible says we are to run the race set before us. And yet we are to walk with you. When do I race, and when do I walk?

The truck began to veer right. The loud grind of warning grooves caused him to steer back into the lane. Watson took his right hand and slapped his cheek.

Hard.

He sat straight up.

"That hurt. No more whining, Paul James Watson. Get something accomplished. Call Theo Revelage."

He yanked the card out of his pocket.

But this is his old number. Sheila has a new one in Long Beach. I could wait until we get home. But it will give me something to think about. If anyone can keep me awake, it's Revelage. We never slept at UCLA, that's for sure.

Watson punched a number into his cell phone and turned on the speaker.

The computerized voice drowned into the stuffy cab.

"What state?"

"Eh . . . California."

"What city?"

120

"Long Beach."

"What listing?"

"Theodore Revelage. R – E – V – E – L – A – G – E."

"One moment, please."

Watson pulled a pen from above the top button of his shirt, turned the card over, laid it on his knee, and waited for the number.

"There is no listing for that number."

"It's a new listing," Watson said.

"What state?"

"California."

"What city?"

"Long Beach."

"What listing?"

"Revelage, Private Investigator."

"One moment, please."

"Take your time. I'm driving down the interstate just trying to keep from going to sleep and running off the side of the road. I'm contemplating the meaning of my life, and why at age fifty-five I haven't accomplished more and yet I'm always tired. And why others think my life is much more successful than it really is and why after two weeks of being away from home, my wife takes off and is not going to be there when I arrive, and if the whole incident with the woman in the Impala . . ."

"Please continue to hold."

"Darlin', you might only be a computer voice, but you are talking to the king of hold. I've spent my life on hold while others did things more important. You may not know this, but 'call waiting' was invented for me. Yep, people were afraid of missing important calls while talking to me. Somehow the subject gets changed in the middle of my dialogue."

"Please continue to hold."

"Sure, why not? You know," Watson continued, "I have learned that I don't need a conclusion to my conversations because I'm never allowed to conclude. Maybe that's why I write. So I can actually finish an entire story and wrap it up. It feels good to finish a book. Did I tell you I was a writer?"

"Please continue to hold. The next available operator will be with you shortly."

"It's true. I write books. Paperbacks. Mysteries. Detective stories. That kind of thing. Oh, yeah, sure, I'd like to write something where I could spend more time in character development. But I'm sort of branded with these. It's what people expect. It's OK. I like it. It's my most peaceful time. When I'm buried in a story, it's like I'm at home."

"Hi, I'm Melinda, what listing?"

"Oh, hi, Melinda. A friend of mine recently moved to Long Beach. His name is Theodore Revelage, and he's a private investigator. I'm not sure how he's listed."

"There is nothing under Theo or Theodore or T. Revelage."

"How about Private Investigations, or something like that?"

"No listing. I'm sorry."

"That's OK, Melinda. It was nice to visit with you."

There was a pause.

"Sir, did you know that your conversation can be monitored to improve customer service?"

"You mean you were listening to my diatribe?"

"Yes, I was," she admitted. "I was fascinated."

"Sorry to vent all of that. I was mainly keeping awake."

"Oh, no, it was heartfelt. I was touched. I might get in trouble for this, but can I ask what name you write under? I read a lot of detective stories."

"Paul James Watson."

"Are you kidding me?" she asked.

"Eh, no."

"I just read *Yellow Sea*. It was wonderful."

"Are you serious?"

"I love the way you left Toby heartbroken for the nurse. She should have turned him down. He deserved it."

"Toby didn't think it was so great. Melinda, I know you are on company time, but could you do me a big favor? Could you call me right back at this number?"

"Why?"

"I want to know that you are real and that I'm not imagining all of this," Watson explained.

"Excuse me?"

"Melinda, please call me back whenever you have a chance."

There was a click. Then a dial tone. Watson jammed the phone back into the dash and checked out the strength of reception.

He tapped on the steering wheel and glanced down at the business card on his knee. He turned it over.

Theo, how can you run an agency and have an unlisted number?

The ring of the cell phone raised the hair on the back of his neck. He poked the speaker button.

"Yes?"

A woman's voice filled the truck. "Hi, Paul . . ."

"Spunky?"

"They had their meeting. They decided just to stay with the original cover."

"That's nice."

Spunky Sasser-Hampton's voice softened. "Paul, have you got a minute? I need to talk."

"Eh, sure, I'm just driving home. What do you need?"

"I don't know who to talk to," she said.

He set the cruise control and steadied the wheel in the right-hand lane. "Are you having problems at home again?"

"Paul, I'm a people person. I just can't be the wife he wants me to be. And there is no one at home to talk to."

"Spunky, you knew that when you married the boss."

"He was the boss's son when we got married."

"But you knew. You must have known that you were the trophy on his arm that turned every head in the room. Darlin', I'm just being honest with you."

"Paul, I don't like being displayed anymore. For a year or two, that was fine. But now I'm the trophy in the bookcase. It's cramped and restrictive."

"You got to be receptionist again this week."

"Do you know how many tears I had to shed to get to do this?"

"Have you and Hampty sat down and talked about it, darlin'?"

P.J. yanked up the cell phone and held it to his ear in order to hear her soft voice. "How do I bring up the subject without sounding ungrateful?" she whispered.

"Spunky, what would you rather be doing, besides being the Atlantic-Hampton receptionist?"

"I'd like to have kids." Her voice reminded Paul of a young runaway girl wanting to come home. "And I sometimes think I'd like to go to Columbia and get a degree."

"What keeps you from doing either one?"

"I'm scared to death of failing, Paul."

"Darlin', life is scary. Every advance packs the potential of failure. You have to go for it."

"Which do you think I should do?"

"Sylvia, listen to me . . ."

"Paul, do you know you are the only one I allow to call me Sylvia?"

"I want to get your attention. Hampton loves you. I see it every time I'm in New

York. You just need to find the next step. Why not both? Why not take some classes, and in the meantime, if you get pregnant, that must be the Lord's leading too."

"You see everything as the Lord's leading, don't you?" she asked.

"When I take time to think about it, yes, I suppose so."

"I wish I could see things as clearly as you do, Paul."

He dropped the transmission out of overdrive when he hit the grade and passed a slow-moving semi. "Trust me, Sylvia, you wouldn't want to be in my head."

In the background he heard the classical music that filled the outer office of the publishing company. "I'll bet you'll never guess what I want to take at Columbia," she said.

Watson unwrapped a hard coffee candy and popped it into his mouth. "You want to be an English major, right?"

"How did you know? How in the world did you know that, Paul James Watson? I've never, ever, told anyone."

"Because no one in New York believes that Sylvia 'Spunky' Sasser-Hampton could get a degree in English. The name 'Spunky' fits, darlin'. Go for it. You can do it. In the process I reckon you'll get Columbia straightened out a little."

"Do you really think I can handle that kind of academic pressure?"

"Yes, I do. You've been living that sexy receptionist image so long, you've lost confidence in who you really are."

"How do I convince my honey?"

He sucked on the sweet coffee taste and let his thoughts tumble into a pattern. "Why don't you tell him you know he is proud of how you look. Now you want to make him proud of how you think."

"Should I cry and pout until he gives in?"

"No, Sylvia, that's counterproductive. Instead of acting immature, act extremely mature. Go down to Columbia and sign up for some classes first and then tell him."

"Really?"

"You will regret it if you don't."

"Thanks, Paul. You just might be the easiest man in the world to talk serious with. All the girls in the office know that."

"They do?"

"Oh, yes. We all know you really listen and that you care. Those are wonderful attributes. Sheila is a lucky lady."

"Thanks, Sylvia, that's sweet of you to say."

"Is Toby still with you?" she asked.

Watson glanced at the empty passenger's seat.

"No."

"Good. I wanted to make sure I was talking to the real Paul Watson. Bye, Paul. I don't think I've ever really had a friend like you."

"Bye, Sylvia. You're a smart lady. You'll know what to do."

P.J. plucked up the business card on his knee and shoved it back into his shirt pocket. He passed an old white Buick that seemed to be driven by a barking black Labrador. He stared at the phone for several moments.

If I didn't call information, maybe I should call them now. Perhaps Theo's number is listed, and I was just daydreaming that it was unlisted. If Shelia was at home, I'd just call her and write down the number. Maybe she is home. Perhaps that was just in my mind too.

After passing two sections of a beige double-wide, he pulled into the right-hand lane and punched the speed dial again.

After three rings, a rough male voice answered the phone. "Yeah, what do you want?"

Watson cleared his voice. "Eh . . . is this

the Watson residence?"

"Yeah, so what?"

P.J. stared at the speaker phone. "May I speak to Sheila?"

"Who?"

"Mrs. Watson."

"She ain't here." The voice was as enthusiastic as a taxi driver with his last fare of the evening.

"Who are you?" Watson asked.

"Who are you?" the voice demanded.

"I'm Mr. Watson, and you are in my house. Now who are you, or do I have to phone the police?"

"Just relax, man," the voice insisted. "No reason to get testy. Do you want to speak to Ruth Ann?"

Watson slammed his fist on the dash. "Yes!"

"Daddy?"

"Rudi, who answered the phone?"

"That was Lanny. Isn't he something?"

Watson shook his head and glanced around the empty truck cab. "Who's Lanny?"

"Didn't Mom tell you about him?"

"No. I don't believe she did." When P.J. passed the semi loaded down with lumber, he shook his head as if the driver understood his dilemma.

"He's my guy, Daddy," she giggled.

"Your guy? What happened to good old Chad?"

"That was last summer, Daddy."

"Last summer? It was two weeks ago."

"Anyway, Chad likes Shannon now."

"I thought Shannon was engaged to the Duvall kid."

"Not anymore."

Watson rubbed his temples. "Rudi, you aren't fourteen anymore. You're twenty-three."

"And your point is?"

"I expect you to act more mature."

The giggle disappeared. "Daddy, I'm not a fool."

"I know, darlin' . . . I know. It's just that you didn't date in high school, and hardly went out in college. This is new to me. So, who is this Lanny?"

"He's an ex-steer wrestler. You'll like him. He won the rodeo over in Augusta once. But he doesn't rodeo anymore."

"That is a positive sign."

"He drives this really cool antique Harley, and he lives in Manhattan."

"I presume you mean Manhattan, Montana."

"Of course," she giggled. "And he treats me really, really nice. He always makes sure I wear a helmet when I ride with him."

"Rudi, how long have you known Lanny?"

"I've known him since June, but we've only been going out for two weeks. Pete likes him, Daddy."

"How about Jared?"

"He hasn't met Jared and Marcia yet. Guess what else?"

"I'm afraid to ask."

"He's going to get a heart-shaped tattoo with 'Ruth Ann' on it. Is that too cool, or what?"

"And your mother has met him?"

"Oh, sure. Mom knows Lanny."

"I wonder why she didn't mention him?"

"We wanted to surprise you."

"I'm surprised. Rudi, what did Mama say about him?"

"She said he is very, I think her word was . . . *interesting*."

"Sort of the way she looks at modern art and mumbles 'interesting'?"

"Yeah, that's Lanny! He's a work of art. You ought to see his dreamy eyebrows."

"I can hardly wait."

"Do you want him to stay here until you get home, so you can meet him?"

"No." Watson cleared his throat. "It will

be awhile before I get home. I'm not even to Billings yet."

"Oh, Daddy, this is so incredible; you won't believe this. He's read your books. Really. He's a big fan of yours."

"He's read my books?"

"He checks the audio books out of the library. He's listened to just about every one of the Distracted Detective Series. He says that Toby McKenna is just like him."

Paul James Watson glanced over at the empty passenger's seat in the pickup. "He's like McKenna?"

"Isn't that so cool? He said he thinks of McKenna as sort of an example for him to follow in life. That's how we met in the library. I took some of Mom's art books back for her, and he was sitting there near the book drop with an audio version of *My Time to Fly* and I said, 'That's my dad! He wrote that book.' He said, 'No way!' It's sort of like you introduced us, Daddy. Isn't that cool?"

Lord, when she was sixteen and didn't want to date, I thought it was nice. Now she's twenty-three, acting like sixteen. You're getting even with me, aren't you?

"Does this Lanny have a job, darlin'?"

"Yes, he's been in business for himself since way back in high school."

"How old is he?" P.J. asked.

"Thirty-one, but he doesn't look old. He's really nice to me, Daddy. He scoots the chair in for me at the restaurant."

"Thirty-one?" he gasped. "You're twenty-three."

"And you are six years older than Mom," Rudi blurted out.

"Is he married?" Watson asked.

"Daddy!"

"Rudi, you didn't answer me."

"I didn't ask him if he's married."

"It might be nice to know if he's married or has ever been married."

"OK."

"Ruth Ann? I didn't mean right now."

He passed a flatbed semi loaded with a bulldozer, then dropped the transmission out of overdrive when he came to another grade.

"Daddy, he laughed and said he is not married, nor has he ever been married, but to tell you he has been thinking a lot more about marriage in the past two weeks. Is that sweet, or what? He is so nice, Daddy. He's very strong. I'm really, really happy."

"Well, don't do anything rash until I get home."

"Daddy!"

"You didn't tell me what kind of business he was in."

"He's a plumber," Rudi reported.

"A plumber?"

"He's fixing the shower in yours and mom's bathroom right now. You know how you said you want to get it fixed someday? Well, today's the day."

"That's nice. Tell him to leave a bill. I'll get it paid when I get home."

"Oh, he isn't charging us. He said it was a simple matter. He stopped by to see me."

"Rudi, is Mom home?"

"She's on her way to the foundry in Kalispell. I thought she told you."

"That's right, she did. Baby, there's a phone number I need. She wrote down a couple of notes for me, probably on my desk. One of them is the phone number of my friend, Theo Revelage. Could you get that number for me?"

"Sure. Do you want to talk to Lanny some more?"

"Eh, no. But thank him for the plumbing work."

"You're going to really like him, Daddy. I'm just sure of it. I'll be right back."

Watson rubbed the back of his neck as he paralleled the Yellowstone River. To the south, limestone cliffs sported scattered scrub cedars.

Twenty-three. She's old enough to choose her own life. I hope. Jared's twenty-five. Pete's twenty-one. They all are out on their own. Or do they ever get out on their own? Why do I worry more now than I did eight years ago?

"Here's the number, Daddy."

He yanked the card back out of his pocket and plucked up his pen. "Go ahead."

"562-743-5000."

"Thanks, Rudi." He heard a loud crash and a yell. "What was that?"

"Nothing," she giggled. "I'd better go help. Bye, Daddy."

"Help with what? Ruth Ann?"

When the dial tone buzzed, he turned off the cell phone.

When Watson crossed the river, a gravel frontage road paralleled the interstate. Dust flew from the roadway and drifted across the freeway. He slowed, then glanced over at the car that was stirring up the dirt.

"Look at that," he mumbled.

Toby McKenna sat straight up. His fedora dropped into his lap. "Whoa. I fell asleep. Is that her?"

"It's a green '62 Chevy Impala. I can't tell who's inside."

"It's got to be her," Toby insisted.

"I don't think it has to be. I'm not sure she was there at all."

"That dust is real. You can taste it in your lungs."

"But I can't see who's driving."

The ring of the phone caused both of them to jump.

"You've got to turn down the volume on that sucker," McKenna insisted.

Watson punched the receive button. "Yes?"

"Paul?"

"Yes."

"This is Melinda."

"Melinda?"

"From the phone company. You wanted me to call back. Your line has been busy for almost an hour."

"The phone call was real, wasn't it?"

"Yes, it was. Are you all right?"

"He ain't been all right for thirteen years," McKenna blurted out.

"Did you say something?" she asked.

"No, just engine noise. Thanks for calling back. It was important to me."

"If you need to contact me, call information, then hit the pound key and punch in

2222," she offered. "Bye, Paul."

"Bye, Melinda. Thanks."

Watson blinked his eyes and tried to imagine a face to fit the words and voice.

McKenna poked Watson in the shoulder. "Good grief, she's really movin' fast."

"Not really. She's just a phone operator who's read some of my books. We got to talking about . . ."

"No, not her. I meant the woman in the green Impala."

chapter six

"Whoa!" McKenna shouted. "She had a blowout. Man, did you see that?"

Paul James Watson passed a logging truck and glanced in the side-view mirror. "What are you talking about?"

McKenna waved his arms at the bottomland to the north. "Look at how the car is fishtailin' and spinnin' into the sage."

Watson's right hand gripped the top of the steering wheel. "I've got to keep my eyes on the road. I'm driving, remember?"

"How can I forget. You never let me drive." Toby McKenna tugged down the front of his fedora. "It might not have been a blowout. She could have had her tire shot out. Remember that scene in *Last Time in Tulsa* when that Armenian babe shot the tires on my black Camaro? I almost lost it over a cliff. It's a good thing I spent my teenage years as a stunt driver in Holly-wood. Of course, I can't remember my teenage years, but ever' once in awhile you tell me what I was like. Anyway, that babe was a mile away when she shot my tires."

"She was Abyssinian, not Armenian, and she was a thousand yards away, not a mile," Watson corrected.

"It seemed like a mile to me. Did you ever have your entire life flash in front of you? It was just like watchin' a movie. Of course, there are huge gaps in my memory. Books are better than movies. They have much more character development and plots twists."

"So I've heard," Watson said.

"Say, P.J., I was wonderin' . . . whatever happened to . . ."

"Natalia. She was arrested in Cyprus for plotting to kidnap Marcus Spiropolis and holding him for a five-billion-dollar ransom, remember?"

" . . . to the Camaro?"

"Oh, the Camaro? Remember how she shot out all four tires and you lined up the rims on the railroad track and raced to the Caspian Sea only twenty feet ahead of the Siberian Express? You jumped out into the river just before the train and rammed your Camaro into that stalled tanker truck full of rocket fuel."

"I liked that car," McKenna whined.

"Why couldn't I keep that one?"

"Because Jim Rockford drove a Camaro."

"There's the exit. Pull off," McKenna called out.

Watson hit the brakes just enough to kick off the cruise control. "Why?"

"You're gonna help that lady in the green Impala with the blowout, aren't you? It's the good Samaritan thing to do."

Paul heaved a deep slow sigh. "That lady isn't real. She's fiction. Like you, Toby."

McKenna stared down at his idle hands. "That hurt, P.J.," he murmured.

"I'm really tired, Toby. I don't play well when I'm tired."

McKenna's voice was soft like a light rain turning to snow. "How do you know what's real, P.J.? I mean, what is the definition of real life? Turn off, please?"

Paul James Watson slowed behind a UPS van and flipped on the blinkers. "I can't believe I'm doing this again."

"Maybe you don't think much about real life, P.J. You take it for granted. But me? I think about it all the time. I bet there's a guy in . . . say . . . eh, Dalton, Georgia, that leaves the carpet mill at 5:10 every evenin'. He picks up a number two special at KFC and a half-gallon bottle of Turlock Turkey wine every night and plops down in front of his television. He eats the chicken wings and half the biscuits, drinks the whole jug of hooch, then falls asleep halfway between a rerun of *Hollywood Squares* and a *Seinfield* that he's seen six times. Now, are you tellin' me that's real life and mine isn't?"

"I turned off, didn't I?" Watson said.

"Thanks, P.J. This is as close to real life as I get."

Watson cleared his throat. "I don't know what I'm going to do when I get there."

"Treat her the way you want to in your mind," McKenna advised.

"What do you mean?"

"You live and relive every scene in your mind a dozen times. This time just treat her the way you would in that scene."

"What if it's not her and the little boy?"

McKenna shrugged. "Someone needs help."

The freeway turn exited under the interstate to the south; to the north was only a dirt road. Paul James Watson turned down the dirt road. "This goes out into someone's field."

McKenna surveyed the horizon. "And your point is?"

"We're trespassing."

"If you get stopped, tell them we're

gonna help a lady in distress."

The dirt road led straight north toward the sandstone rimrock that paralleled the Yellowstone River. The fields on both sides had been tilled at one time but now lay fallow, with scattered weeds and resurgent sagebrush. A trail of dust tailed the gold pickup and fogged the inside of the cab.

"Where would she be goin' down a road like this?" McKenna questioned.

"Are you asking me? This was your idea."

Watson slowed down as he approached the green car. The lady and the little boy were parked sideways in the field near an abandoned, rusted corn planter.

"I think she's happy to see us," McKenna said. "She's wavin' at us and shouting somethin'." He rolled down his window and stuck his head out.

Watson parked the truck in the middle of the dirt roadway. "What did she say?"

"Eh, you don't want to know."

"Why not?"

"You know those words you never allow me to say in your books?" McKenna said. "Well, she knows those and some other descriptive words. I've never heard those two words used in that particular combination. She's creative."

Paul James Watson sat behind the steering wheel and stared at the screaming lady. "She cussed me out?"

McKenna leaned back in his seat. "That's a mild way of sayin' it."

Watson opened the door.

"Are you goin' out there?"

"Yes, you told me to do the things that I would do in my mind. So I'm going to help a lady in distress."

"I'm not sure of the lady part . . . or of the distress part," McKenna mumbled. "I think I'll just stay in the rig."

"Get out of here!" the woman screamed.

"Do you need help?" Watson asked.

"Not from you. You don't understand."

"I saw you had a blowout. I thought you might need some help."

"He shot my tire out!" she yelled.

Watson surveyed the countryside. "Who did? Where is he?"

"Oh, he's there. I saw his Hummer."

"Where?"

"About a mile away."

"No one can shoot that far," Watson insisted.

"Get out of here!" she hollered again.

"Will you be all right?"

"No, I won't be all right! But I surely don't need any help from the FBI."

"FBI? I don't work for the FBI."

"Or from the CIA, ATF, or the MSP."

"I don't work for the government."

"Who do you work for?"

"I'm a writer."

"A reporter?" she asked.

"No, I write novels."

"You're a paperback writer?"

"You might say that. Do you know Theo Revelage?"

She grabbed a shotgun out of the backseat and waved it at Paul James Watson. "I'm warning you. If you aren't gone in ten seconds, I'll have to shoot you. He's watching, and he expects me to shoot you."

He strolled toward her. "You aren't going to shoot me."

"I'm warnin' you!"

"Ma'am, you're in a mess of trouble. Looks like to me you could use a friend."

"I need a friend like I need a contagious disease. Get out of here. I'm warning you for the last time." Her voice started to crack. "Please."

"I'm going to mount your spare on that hub. Then you can drive anywhere you want. Put the shotgun down." He looked at the boy. "How are you doing, Toole?"

"That ain't my name, and she's gonna kill you."

"No one is going to get killed today. Your mama's just scared. It's all right to get scared."

The lady stalked north into the sage.

"What's your name today?" he asked the boy.

"Juan Peron."

Watson ambled over to the trunk. "Is she Eva?"

"No." The boy cracked a shy smile. "She's Mama."

"Well, how about you and me changing this tire so we get you and Mama going again?"

"I don't know how to change a tire," he admitted.

"I'll show you. Let's dig out the jack and the spare. Is your name really Juan Peron?"

"No."

Watson unloaded some of the boxes in the trunk, then pulled out the spare tire. "First thing we need to do is loosen those lug nuts. You carry this wrench for me."

"It's heavy."

Watson dropped to his knees and began to crank the lug nuts off the blown-out tire wheel. "So, what is your really, really real name?"

The little boy dropped his chin to his chest. "I don't know," he murmured.

"What do you mean, you don't know?"

"Mama and Daddy wouldn't let me have a real name."

Watson spun off the first lug nut and tossed it into the hub cap. "Why not?"

"Mama said we were different and didn't have to do things like everyone else. And Daddy said if they don't know my name, they can't identify me."

Paul Watson spun off another lug nut. "Does your daddy like being unidentified?"

"I guess."

"What else does your daddy like?"

"He likes eggs."

"That's good. How does he like them?"

"Fried on bread with a slice of onion."

Watson pumped the handle on the bumper jack, and the car lifted up. "Son, what is your daddy's name?"

"Daddy."

"Yes, but what is his name?"

"I just call him Daddy."

"What does your Mama call him?"

A barrage of curses rolled out of the boy's mouth.

"Eh, OK, son. I get the idea. Now we'll pull the old wheel off. That old tire really blew out, didn't it?"

"He shot at us."

"I don't think so, son. Why would he want to do that?"

"Mama says he is crazy. Do you think he's crazy?"

"I don't know him, son. I couldn't say."

"He does crazy things sometimes. Mama told him she didn't flirt with that man hunting quail."

"What man?"

The boy's voice sank to a whisper. "The dead one."

Watson shoved the spare tire on the wheel. "Hand me those lug nuts in the hubcap, son. Thanks. Eh, did your daddy shoot the hunter?"

The boy handed him a lug nut. "No."

"How did he die?"

"I ain't supposed to tell."

"Did that happen back at your underground house?"

The boy handed him another lug nut. "You sure ask a lot of questions."

"OK, it's your turn. You ask the questions." Watson tightened the nuts back on the spare tire.

"Where do you live?" the boy quizzed.

"In Bridgeport."

"What's the street name?"

"Are you aiming to come visit me?"

"How come you won't tell me the street name?"

Paul Watson studied the boy's eyes. "I live on the outskirts of town."

"What's your name?" the boy asked.

"Fidel Castro."

The boy laughed. "No, it isn't."

"You take a guess. What do you think my name is?" Paul slapped the hubcap onto the wheel hub.

The boy flipped his head back to flop his bangs out of his brown eyes. "You're Paul James Watson."

Goose bumps rolled across Watson's arms and neck. He shivered as he crammed the flat tire back into the crowded trunk. "How did you know my name?"

"Mama told me."

"How did she know me? I don't even know her name."

"She has a picture of you in the car."

Watson noticed the shotgun-toting woman hike out of the sage toward the car. "Where did she get a picture of me?"

"Off the Internet. From your Web site. She's been looking for you for two weeks."

The woman shouted something as she approached.

"What did you say?" Watson gasped. He was startled to find himself standing next to his pickup, not the Impala.

"I said, get back in that truck right now and drive out of here, or I'll let you have both barrels right now!" the woman screamed.

Watson clutched the door handle of his truck, and he stared out at the lady and boy next to the Impala with a flat tire.

But I fixed the flat, didn't I? I already lived this scene. I don't want to go back over it again.

"I think she means it, P.J.," McKenna said.

Paul James Watson blinked his eyes.

Lord, this is exactly what I mean. How can I tell what's real and what's in my mind? I'm slowly going insane, aren't I? Is it Alzheimer's? Dementia? Do I have a brain tumor?

"Get in the rig, P.J. She's gonna pull the trigger!" McKenna hollered. "Remember what happened to me in *South Padre Pardon*? It took three chapters to pluck all the buckshot from my backside." Watson slid behind the wheel and slammed the door.

"Step on it! She really is gonna . . ."

Dirt fogged.

Wheels spun.

The 300-horsepower engine roared as the pickup launched backward toward the interstate.

And the shotgun blasted.

McKenna ducked down behind the dash. Like a pail of rock chips, lead shot peppered the pickup.

"Did she hit my truck?" Watson bellowed.

"No time to look. Keep drivin'!"

"I can't believe this, Toby."

"Me either." He pulled himself up into the seat as the truck continued to back up. "P.J., I think you paused a little too long at the door. What were you thinkin' anyway?"

"I helped them, Toby. I changed the tire. I really did." Watson swung out into the field, then turned the truck around.

"I say you were daydreamin' again. You got to live it out, P.J. Don't just think it, but live it out in real life."

"But I did do it. This time I did do it. Besides, you're a fine one to counsel about real life."

"Maybe those of us who don't have it appreciate it more. If you had walked over there, you would have been shot."

"No, when I went over there, she just walked away."

"She didn't this time. Your pickup carries the evidence. Why did you want to stand in her sights so long? You plannin' on leavin' Sheila a widow?"

"No. I have no intention of her bein' a young widow."

"You aren't all that young, P.J." McKenna turned and stared out the back window.

"Sheila is."

"Look at that!" McKenna exclaimed. "That flat is fixed, and they are drivin' north again. How did that happen?"

"I told you I fixed it." Watson stopped the truck and jumped out, then inspected the front fenders and grill. "You see that?"

McKenna rolled down his window. "See what?"

"There is absolutely no damage to the truck! She didn't shoot at me. That was just your imagination, Toby McKenna. I fixed her flat and visited with the boy. I did it. You were wrong. You said I only did such things in my mind. I really did it."

"And here I thought you would just stand there scared to death."

"I was calm and peaceful during the whole thing," Watson proclaimed.

"Are you afraid of dyin', Paul James Watson?" McKenna asked.

"I think I'm more afraid of leaving this

152

earth without accomplishing what I was created to do."

"I was created to entertain and be a diversion for folks with hassled lives. And to come to a meaningful and satisfying conclusion every 346 pages," McKenna said. "What were you created to do?"

"To love and nurture a wife and three children, while I honor God and seek his kingdom, I suppose," Watson reported.

"And the writin'?" McKenna pressed.

"It's an added thing."

"Added? Do you mean that Toby McKenna is not the most important person in your life?"

"That's what I mean." Watson eased back onto the interstate.

"Do you know what it's like to go through life never bein' anyone's most important person?" Toby McKenna challenged.

"I might," P.J. murmured, "but don't blanket me with guilt, McKenna."

"I've been thinkin'. Maybe I don't need to fly back to the Keys. I could just stay in Montana while the Corvette is bein' fixed."

Watson hit the brakes. "Do you want me to let you out here?"

"That's not funny, P.J. I was thinkin' about Jared's room bein' empty. Maybe I'll bunk with you and Sheila Suzanne."

"No one calls her Sheila Suzanne except me."

"Hmmm. Why is that?" McKenna pressed.

"She doesn't like the name."

"Then why do you use it?"

Watson rubbed his temples. "It's a term of affection."

McKenna pulled off his hat and ran his fingers through his hair. "You got a lot to learn about women, P.J."

"Ha, I'm supposed to take advice from a fictional gigolo?"

"Who would you take advice from?" McKenna challenged.

"About what?"

"About you and Sheila Suzanne."

"I don't need any advice."

"Just what I thought. That's good. I don't feel offended that way. You won't pay attention to anyone. It's not just me."

"McKenna, I don't need any advice. Everything is fine with Sheila and me."

Toby leaned his head back against the buckskin leather of the bucket seat. "When's the last time you two had a really good time together?"

"What are you talking about?"

"You know exactly what I'm talkin' about."

Paul James Watson slammed on the brakes and pulled the truck off onto the shoulder of the interstate. Then he stared at the empty passenger's seat. He waited for a break in the traffic, then eased his rig back into the right-hand lane.

He had just passed Pompey's Pillar, where the etched autograph of William Clark lay housed under Plexiglas protection, surrounded by hundreds of other pioneer names, when he pushed the number 2 speed-dial button, then listened to it ring.

"Hello?"

"Hi, babe."

"Paul, honey, are you home already? What do you think of Rudi's new boyfriend? Isn't he something else?"

"I'm not home, darlin'. I'm just about to Billings."

"Oh, you must be doing more research. You need to relax more. Get your mind on something else."

"Like dear ol' Lanny?"

"Oh, so you do know about him?"

"I called home, and Lanny answered."

"I understand he's fixing the shower in our bath," she explained.

"So I heard. What's your evaluation of him?"

"He's rather rough looking but very polite and nice to me and to Rudi. Is that why you called?"

"No, darlin', I was calling to say I missed you horribly and hoped you wouldn't be gone too long."

"That's sweet, honey," her voice softened. "I hope it won't be more than a couple of days."

"A couple of days?" he groaned. "I thought it was overnight."

"They welded 'Rough Day . . .' last Friday and polished on Monday. I'll go over it with a felt-tip pen for flaws and changes tonight. In the morning they will fix all of that and polish it tomorrow afternoon. Friday the patina girls will go to work. Jerre Ann Rueter is going on vacation on Saturday, and you know how I like her work. She said she thought she could do it in one day with two others helping her. You know what a good job she did on the Fort Worth piece. I wanted to be here and make sure they got the patina right and brush the wax into it."

"Saturday? You won't be home until Saturday?"

"Paul, is there a problem?"

"I'm tired, Sheila. You know how my mind plays tricks on me when I'm tired. I was hoping we could just go somewhere and crash for a couple days with nothing to do but rest and play."

"Oh, you are *that* kind of lonesome," she giggled.

"Babe, do you have any idea how good that giggle sounds?"

"I think I might. I think my author misses me."

"Yes, I do. And we have other things to talk about."

"What other things?"

"Darlin', I'm struggling with this reality thing. I just can't turn my mind off fiction."

"Honey, you are so incredible. I've never heard of anyone who has so many stories in his mind at once. You're right. You need a break. How does a week or ten days at Cabo San Lucos sound?" she suggested. "Nothing but lying on the beach and sleeping under a ceiling fan?"

"It sounds wonderful," he admitted.

"I think you should call for reservations right now."

"Really?"

"Yes. Do it."

"But I thought you had a show in Great Falls next week."

"Oh, I do, honey. I can't go. I meant you go."

"By myself?"

"Sure. You deserve a break."

"But I don't want to go by myself."

"Take Ruth Ann. On second thought, that wouldn't be too relaxing."

"It's you I need, Sheila Suzanne."

"You do sound lonely and depressed."

"It's been a crazy trip home. I want to talk to you about it."

"You can tell me about it on Saturday, unless you're in Mexico," she laughed.

"I'm not going anywhere without you."

"Come to Kalispell, honey."

"What?"

"Stop by the house, pick up some clean clothes, and drive up here and stay with me. When the sculpture is finished, we can drive up to Glacier. Let's stay at the lodge in East Glacier."

"And lounge in those huge leather chairs in the lodge and unwind?"

"Yes," she said. "It sounds wonderful."

"You think Rudi and Pete will be all right with us gone?"

"Pete spends every free minute he's not working over at Jared's. And Rudi's twenty-three years old, Paul."

"You didn't answer me."

"I think we'll have Jared and Marcia check on her every thirty minutes," Sheila suggested.

"I could settle things in and drive up to-morrow," he offered.

"Could you come up tonight, honey?" she asked. "You know, I get lonely too."

"Hmmm. Darlin', darlin', darlin', I'll be there tonight. But don't stay with Marty. Get a room at the Inn at White Fish."

"Oh, we're going first-class?" she giggled.

"Yep."

"I won't be through at the foundry until about nine."

"That's fine. Keep your cell phone on. I'll check in with you after while," he said.

"I love you, Paul James Watson."

"I love you too, Sheila Suzanne Watson. Thanks, babe. I really need this."

"I know. I know. Hugs and kisses, honey."

"Hugs and kisses."

Watson was surprised that he muttered the last sentence aloud.

He stared at the low power reading on the cell phone.

I don't only live them out in my mind. Now I'm saying them aloud too. As soon as I get out of the pass, I should have enough power to call Sheila. Then I will see what is really going on. I don't know why I always do that, Lord. I have to practice every scene before I get there. I'm not sure if I can even reach her. But it does seem like fun driving up to be with her. Why didn't I think of that when I called her before?

Paul reached over and punched the speed-dial number 2.

"I'm sorry, all circuits are busy," the computer voice intoned.

"You're not nearly as sorry as I am."

Five minutes later he punched the button again.

"Your party does not answer. The mobile unit you called is not turned on."

"Of course it's turned on. It's always turned on," he muttered.

Ten minutes later, after Interstate 94 merged into Interstate 90 and he could see the refinery smoke at Billings, he punched the speed button again.

"Hello?"

"Hi, babe, it's me."

"Is something wrong, Paul?"

"I'm just missing my girl. Listen, darlin', I have a great idea. Why don't I come to Kalispell. When you are finished at the foundry, we could drive up to Glacier, or even up to Lake Louise for a couple of days, just to relax and . . . well . . . you know, get reacquainted. We could stay at the . . ."

"Paul, I lost your signal. What did you say?"

"I want to come up and be with you."

"What? Why? What's wrong?"

"I'm just missing you."

"Tonight?"

"Yes, tonight. I tried to call you sooner, but I couldn't get through."

"We were visiting, so I turned it off."

Watson's heart sank. "We? Good grief, is someone with you?"

"Brian Albright called at the last minute and wanted a ride to Missoula. He needs to do some research at the university, and his rig is being repaired."

"You're with Brian?"

"Hi, Paul," a man's voice boomed.

"What did you say about coming up tonight?" she asked.

"Never mind. I'll talk to you when you get home."

"Are you all right, honey?"

"Yeah. I'm always all right."

"I know. I was just telling Brian what a rock you are."

There was a long pause.

"Paul?"

"Even rocks sink, darlin'."

161

"What? The signal is disappearing. I'm losing you, Paul. I'll call you tonight from Marty's house."

He listened to the dial tone.

"Yeah, darlin'," he sighed, "we're losing something."

chapter seven

"Lost Cause Conspiracy Consultants and Pacific Palisades Rare Coin Recovery. How may I direct your call?" The voice tittered somewhere between sixteen and thirty-three years old.

Paul James Watson cleared his throat. "May I speak with Theodore Revelage, please?"

The little-girl giggle disappeared. "What extension is that?"

"I have no idea. Put me through to Theo."

"What is your name?"

"Paul Watson."

"What kind of business are you in?"

"I'm a writer, but what has that got to do . . ."

"There is no one here by that name."

"What are you talking about? I received a phone call from Theo. He said to return the call to this number. This is his company. I want to speak to him."

"No one here called a writer," she snapped. "However, leave your name and phone number. I'll ask around. They will return the call, if they choose to do so."

"Look, lady, I'm way too tired to be pleasant. This is Paul Watson. Tell Theo to get on the line, or I'll tell the Treasury Department where they can find a shoebox of forged coins attributed to the Carson City Mint."

"I have no idea what you are talking about," she pouted.

"No, I reckon you don't. But Theo will know."

"You'll have to hold."

"No, I won't. Paul Watson . . . 406-971-5634."

Watson punched the disconnect button on the phone.

"The assertive P.J.? I like it," McKenna jibed.

"Theo is always pretending some great intrigue. I'm tired of it."

"Sort of reminds me of *The Princess Who Kidnapped Herself.* Shoot, I was halfway through the book when I figured out the Serbians just wanted me to think she had kidnapped herself." He leaned back, pulled his fedora brim down over his eyes, and

164

folded his hands in his lap. "She was a spunky gal. When she grabbed my hand and towed me through that makeshift morgue at night, I knew she was going to survive. How's she doin' anyway?"

Watson tried rubbing the cramp out of his right shoulder and neck. "She's living in Toronto, remember?"

"With her uncle?"

"He's not really her uncle."

McKenna kept his eyes closed. "Oh, yeah, he's her brother, the crown prince."

"They are doing fine. They've opened a private museum and can continue to recover the crown treasures under the guise of a museum."

Toby opened one eye and peered over at Watson. "Did she ever get over her . . . eh . . . you know . . . female problems?"

Watson's eyes stayed on the dirt road ahead. "She never had one."

Toby McKenna sat straight up. "Yes, she did. Remember when she told me . . ." he paused. "She lied to me?"

"It was in your best interest."

"Why do you do that, P.J.? Why do you let them lie to me? I'm your protagonist, your bread and butter. Why do you treat me that way?"

"I don't lie, I just withhold some of the

truth. It's sort of a need-to-know basis. It's for your own good, Toby."

"For *my* own good? For Pete's sake, P.J., I'm a fictional character in your mind, not one of your own kids."

"You seem closer than that," Watson murmured. "Like a twin brother at times."

"Yes, but not identical twins!" Toby hooted. "I see you missed the Billings turnoff. How do you expect me to catch my flight?"

"I thought you wanted to go to Bridgeport."

"Are you serious? You're actually gonna let me in your house?"

"You can stay in Jared's old room." Watson lowered his window a couple of inches and felt the fresh air plaster his face and revive his sagging eyelids.

"All right! I'm goin' home at last! Is, eh, Sheila gonna be there?"

Watson glanced in the rearview mirror and studied McKenna's dancing brown eyes. "No, she's in Kalispell."

"Can I use your computer?"

"I suppose; what for?"

"To catch up on my E-mail and chat, of course, and to update my fantasy football teams," McKenna insisted.

"But you are fictional."

"So is fantasy football, most E-mail, and all computer chat."

Watson's broad shoulders sagged. "Yeah, you can use my computer."

When the telephone rang, both Paul James Watson and Toby McKenna flinched.

"You want me to get that?" McKenna offered.

"Sure, go ahead."

"Really?"

"Answer it, Toby."

"Yo! McKenna here. Did you want to talk to me?" McKenna blustered into the dash-mounted black cell phone.

There was a long pause, then a man's voice. "Paul?"

"Do I sound like some mushy-headed paperback writer?" McKenna shot back.

"Is Paul Watson there?"

Toby leaned back in the leather seat and popped his knuckles one at a time. "Maybe yes, maybe no. What's the deal?"

The man's voice grew tight, higher pitched. "I need to talk to Paul Watson."

"Doesn't everyone?"

"He just called my people and asked for a callback. Who is this?"

"And your people gave him the run-around. They insinuated that you didn't exist. What kind of game is that?"

"I need to be cautious when a writer calls and asks for Theodore Revelage," he replied. "I'm involved in some very sensitive investigations."

"Oh, sensitive, eh?" McKenna blustered. "How about that time in *Widow's Wig* when the Arabic princess was arrested in that Paris disco and I had to smuggle her out of the country in the back end of a donkey costume? Now that was sensitive. Especially when they loaded us in that circus train."

"Good grief, man, who are you?"

"Thomas Magnum."

"Listen, Mr. Magnum . . ."

"You can call me Tom."

"Well, Tom, Paul Watson and I are old friends from college days. And we both taught history at Oxnard."

"P.J. taught at Oxford? I didn't know that."

"Oxnard, not Oxford. Oxnard, California. It's by Port Hueneme. Is Paul there?"

"Of course he's here. It's his cell phone."

"Can you put him on, then step out of the room? I need to speak to Paul privately."

"I'm not steppin' out of this room,

buddy," McKenna announced.

"I want to speak to Paul Watson!" Revelage hollered.

"I'll check to see if he's takin' calls."

"This is crazy. Put him on the line."

"Perhaps you ought to leave your name and number, and he can call you back."

"What? He has my name and number! I'm a busy man. I don't have time for this."

"Neither does P.J. I'll put him on, but think about it next time your little honey gives him the runaround. I'll go fetch him."

"This is bizarre. Like a scene from a Quentin Tarrantino movie," Revelage mumbled.

"Relax, Theo, this is Paul."

"Who in the world do you have answering your phone, man? He's a nutcase. What was his name?"

"It was Toby McKenna."

"Never heard of him. Hey, Paul James. I love your new book."

"Which one is that, Theo?"

"You know, the new one."

"What's it about?"

"That detective guy . . . what's-his-name . . . and how he almost got his bell rung, but at the last minute figured out who the murderer was and saved the day."

"Oh, that book? Well, thank you, Theo, that must have been one of the Distracted Detective novels with Toby McKenna."

"Yeah, that's the one, man. Nice work. Is that the character you based on me?"

"Now, Theo, I could never create anyone quite like you."

"You got that right, ol' buddy. But, seriously Paul, get rid of the guy answerin' your phone. He's a pain in the backside. What did you say his name was?"

"Toby McKenna?"

"Sounds like one of those Irish Republican Army expatriates who's hidin' out over here until he can go back and blow up a British police station. Anyway, you ought to get rid of him."

"And just who answers your phone, Theo?"

"That's Heather Hailey. Isn't she a babe?"

"Speaking of real babes, how's Terri?"

There was a pause. Then a weak reply. "I thought you knew."

"Sheila mentioned something, Theo, but I figured I needed to hear it from the big dog himself."

"It wasn't workin' out, Paul. I never could make her happy. After twenty-three years, I was still holdin' her back. She's happy now. She's teaching school in Ojai and last seen goin' out with that dark-haired guy on the interior decorating TV show."

"Are you doing OK with that, Theo? And don't give me any bull."

"I'm OK, Paul. It was tough to admit I was such a failure. Thanks for asking. I know you and Sheila care. Maybe that's why I haven't called in such a long time. I didn't want to face you guys. The two of you make every married couple in America seem like a failure."

"There are no perfect people and no perfect marriages, Theo. You've heard me rant on that subject before."

"That doesn't mean I believe it."

"Now, Theodore Finkle Revelage, what's all this phone calling about? We haven't talked in two years, and then your name gets mentioned twice in the same day."

"Twice?" Revelage pressed.

"What do you want, Theo?"

"Paul, I've got a strange request. You know your way around Montana, right?"

"I've been down most all the roads and trails, but I'm still a newcomer."

"You've been up there for more than twenty years."

"That's what I said, a newcomer," Watson insisted.

"I need you to nose around and see if you can find anything out about a guy without tipping him off."

"Theo, you're the detective. I'm just a lowly paperback writer."

"Exactly my point," Revelage added.

"What point?"

"If I call the authorities or some investigator, the guy I'm looking for will get wind of it, be suspicious, and bolt."

"Are you bounty hunting now, Theo?"

"P.J., it might be much bigger than that. I'll come up and track him down, but I just need a little prelim work done."

"Theo, you know I'm swamped with my writing."

"This will just take a couple of hours. This could be your big story. That's why I want you in on it. It's yours to write. It could make you a household name, like Ozzy Osbourne or Bill O'Reilly."

"I have no desire to be a household name."

"How about successful enough to have to write only one book a year?"

"Now that I could go for. OK, Theo, I know I'll regret this. What's the deal?"

"Are you on a secure phone?"

"There are no extensions for someone to eavesdrop, if that's what you mean. I'm in my truck with my cell phone."

"Get to a pay phone and call me back."

"I'm alone here, Theo. You can go ahead."

"What about that guy . . . you know?"

"The guy in my books?"

"No, the one that answered the phone."

Watson glanced at the empty passenger seat. "He's gone."

"Paul, I need you at a pay phone. Someone has hacked my computer and is tryin' to lock onto my phone system. I can secure a land line, but a cell could broadcast to who knows whom. Where are you?"

"Coming up on Laurel, Montana, just west of Billings."

"Perfect. This is incredible, Paul. You are exactly where I need you to be. It must be one of your divine appointments."

"After all these years, you start believing in the Lord's leading?"

"I've been going to church with Heather for more than a year. I guess some of it's starting to sink in. Remember all those late-night sessions sitting in the sand and debating?"

"I remember you lost every argument

but still wouldn't budge, Theo."

"I guess I don't change quickly. But I do change. Anyway, I don't have time to explain. You need to pull over and get to a pay phone."

"I'm tired, Theo. Why don't I call you from home?"

"Definitely not. I need you to call me right now. Please, Paul. It's that important to me. You're the only one I'd trust with this information."

Watson sighed. "OK, Theo, I'll pull over at the next exit."

"Thanks, partner. Terri always said you were the rock and I was the sand. She was probably right."

Watson hung up the phone and took the Laurel exit. At the stop sign, he turned toward the Texaco station.

"Your buddy, Theo, sounds like a nutcase," Toby McKenna suggested.

"Theo's been a friend ever since golf team days at UCLA. I need to listen to whatever he wants to talk about."

"Is his Terri really a babe? I've never been to Ventura County except that one time in *Blood Red Pacific* when I raced the backhoe to Santa Barbara."

The cell phone rang just as he pulled up to the gas station.

It was Watson who answered the phone. "Yes?"

"Paul . . . I did what you said!"

"Spunky? What did you do?"

"You know, I signed up at Columbia. I'll know by next Friday if I'm accepted."

"Do you need to take a college entrance test?"

"No, they'll check my high school transcripts. That will be a cinch. I was valedictorian — 4.0, you know."

Watson turned off the ignition and pulled the key part of the way out of the steering column. "I didn't know that."

"Twenty-one years ago, Paul."

"Sylvia, I'm sure you're going to do fine at Columbia. You're a smart gal."

"I wish you were here."

"Why?"

"So you could tell my honey."

"Me? Darlin', you need to face up to him and explain how things are. Hampty will understand."

"Can I mention you thought it was a good idea?" she asked.

"Whatever helps you, darlin'. But I don't think the words of Paul Watson hold much weight on Long Island."

"Do you think I should buy some new clothes?"

"How would I know that?"

"What should an English major wear to class?"

"Something warm and comfortable."

"Probably not skirts slit to the thigh."

"Nor plunging necklines, peekaboo blouses, or bubble-wrap vests," he added.

"That was just that one time at the Christmas party. You have such a great memory. You never forget anything, do you?"

"Some things are difficult to forget. I have to go, darlin'. Show him you're serious about this and that it will benefit him," Watson suggested.

"How will it benefit him?"

"You won't be whining around wanting to go back to the reception desk."

"I won't?"

"Sylvia, those days are over. Make today your last. That will impress him."

"Really?"

"Trust me."

"I do trust you, Paul James Watson," she sighed. "Bye, Paul. Thanks for being here for me today."

"You can do it, girl. Just don't go believing your own stereotype."

"Paul, what would I ever do without a friend like you? You are my rock."

"That's what I keep hearing."

"It's true. What can I say? Bye."

"Bye, Sylvia."

He felt his boot for his wallet, then opened the pickup door.

"Whoa, Spunky has a thing for P.J.," McKenna blurted out.

"That's absurd. We've been friends for a long, long time, that's all."

"You are more than a friend to her."

"That's where you're wrong, McKenna. I don't see her more than once a year, and that's at some booksellers convention or publisher's party."

"You mean a whole lot more than just a friend, Paul Watson. She leans on you, P.J., and sooner or later a lady who leans on you will want to hug you. And after she hugs on you awhile, she will want to kiss you. And after she kisses you, she will want you to kiss her back."

"Where did you hear all that nonsense?" Watson challenged.

"*The Lady's Other Tiger*, remember? I was at the bar after getting beat up by the Punjab mafia. That old retired major named Goodnight downed a whiskey and gave me that treasure of advice."

"I made it up."

"You mean, it's not true?"

"I don't know if it's true. It just sounded good."

"You mean you slip in lies and don't tell me they are lies?"

"I'll tell you anything you want . . . after this phone call," Watson said.

"Anything? Even about Sheila?"

"No, not about Sheila."

Paul Watson leaned against the Plexiglas windshield at the pay phone next to the propane refill tank in front of the mini-mart and punched in the phone number.

"Lost Cause Conspiracy Consultants and Pacific Palisades Rare Coin Recovery. How may I direct your call?"

"Cut the bull, Theo, this is Paul."

"What's your phone number?"

"406-789-2323, why?"

"I'll call you back. When I call, don't mention my name, or your name, or where I am, or where you are. Wait right there."

"Theo, are you sure all this is necessary? I'm really tired and I need to . . ." The dial tone interrupted Watson's reply.

This is a game I don't want to play. I have much more important things to take care of. I can't believe I'm standing by a pay phone waiting for a clandestine phone call. Or did I just imagine the whole thing. Maybe I should pull over at a rest stop and sleep . . . for two weeks.

Watson jumped when the phone rang.

He grabbed up the sticky black receiver. "Yeah?"

"Torrey Pines, 1975, Western Regionals, front side. What did you shoot?"

"33," Watson replied.

"How did you do that?"

"Birdie, birdie, birdie, bogie, bogie, bogie, birdie, birdie, and birdie. Why in the world did you ask that?"

"Phones can be tapped. Voice converters are difficult to detect. OK, Arnold Palmer, here's the deal. I'm calling from a disposable phone. When we are done, I destroy the phone. And you drive away fast as soon as we are through."

"All right, Jack Nicklaus," Watson replied. "What is all this foolishness?"

"I think I know the whereabouts of Jonathan Boudary."

"Which means?"

"The San Gabriel Slaughter? You remember . . . the Manson copycat murders of 1979 and also the Colorado Hooker murders in the mid-eighties. Air Alaska flight 404 in '94, not to mention a dozen political assassinations and numerous local unexplained deaths."

"Are you saying it was the same guy?"

"Jonathan Boudary. But there's more."

"More?" Watson asked.

"The Mercury Building explosion in Chicago last March."

"I read that a gas main blew."

"It was bombed. But after 9-11 they didn't want people to panic."

"You think it's the same guy, Boudary?"

"Yep. Arnie, this guy is scary . . . almost demonic. There were six deaths in San Gabriel, twelve in Colorado, twenty-four in Alaska, and forty-eight in the Chicago fire."

"He's doubling up every time?"

"Until he's stopped. A rumor is bouncin' around the conspiracy sites on the Internet that six test tubes of thick anthrax are missing from the Disease Control Center in Atlanta."

"Thick anthrax?"

"It will make 2001 look like kindergarten recess."

"You think this guy has it?"

"He's crazy enough to use it. But so far it's just a rumor."

"Eh, Mr. Nicklaus, why not turn your evidence over to the police?"

"The ten-million-dollar reward generates more than sixteen hundred new tips a day. It will get lost if I don't have solid evidence."

"And what do you want me to do?" Watson asked.

"Check out two places for me."

"In Montana?"

"Yes . . . go nose around Bunker, Montana."

"Where's that?"

"Eh, I thought you'd know."

"I've never heard of it," Watson insisted.

"Search the maps. Ask the old-timers. Maybe it's a ghost town. With a name like Bunker, I'm sure it is in some old mining district. If there's a street, look for 24th Street, or 24 Main Street, or something. Ask around."

"What would I ask for? 'Have any of you murdered a hundred innocent people?' "

"Look for a man of this description: Six-two, stocky, brown hair, fifty-three years old, brown eyes, olive complexion, with a mole on his right cheek. He wears glasses or contacts and is a fan of Bob Wills music. I need a visual sighting before I come up."

"But don't confront him?"

"By all means, no. He is armed and dangerous."

"Even if I could successfully capture

him and could keep the ten-million-dollar reward money for myself, I shouldn't do it?"

"The risk is too great for you, Arnold."

"But you are willing to take it, Jack?"

"It's my job. I'm a professional."

"Does he go by Jonathan Boudary, or does this slimeball have an alias?"

"The last I heard he was using the name Abraham Lincoln."

"Is this a joke?"

"Arnie, he goes by names like John Kennedy, Abe Lincoln, Tom Jefferson."

"You want me to find Bunker, Montana, and look for people with famous names?"

"Yes, but there's more."

"Oh?"

"I got a crank E-mail to my Web site that I'd like checked out. I need you to meet someone for me."

"Now, tell me again, Jack, why am I doing your leg-work for you? Why don't you fly up and check it all out yourself?"

"Eh, negative, Arnie. She doesn't like to fly."

"Who?"

"Heather Hailey. I mean, eh, Margo."

"I think the whole thing is insane. You are nuttier than I am, Jack. Where can I find this so-called informant?"

"She will find you."

"She? How?"

"She said for you to show up at 2:00 p.m. at an airstrip north of Big Timber. Can you get there by then?"

"How do I find this place?"

"Take Wildcat Creek Road to the windmill, then turn north for a few miles. The landing strip is in the sage on the east side of the road."

"Who am I looking for?"

"I have no physical description. She'll find you. She knows your name."

"You gave her my name!" Watson gasped.

"She insisted on it."

"Good grief, Theo."

"Call me Jack."

"This is absurd. I'm going home," Watson insisted.

"Check out the informant, please."

"Have you got a name for her?"

"I know this sounds strange, but she said her name was Jane Fonda."

"A lady named Jane Fonda, a man named Abraham Lincoln, and a kid called Joseph Stalin. This has been quite a day."

"Kid? Someone named their kid Joseph Stalin?"

"I helped a gal and a kid with a flat tire.

The kid said his name was Joseph Stalin, among others."

"You made contact already?"

"I guess. I just stopped to help them. Actually, she stopped me."

"What did this gal look like?"

"Five foot four, medium build, late thirties, thick eyebrows, round flat nose, shoulder-length curly dark brown hair, tan, a bridge mark on the top of her nose from wearing glasses, double-pierced ears with dangling feather earrings, a small scar above her left eyebrow, Levis, a dark green V-necked sweatshirt, off-trail Nikes, and some sort of world championship ring on her right-hand ring finger."

There was a pause on the other end of the line.

"That's incredible, Arnold."

"Do you know her?"

"Never heard of her. But it's incredible how you remember the details about someone."

"It's what I do, Jack. What are you asking me to do?"

"Meet the contact at the airstrip."

"She's already met me. Why didn't she give me information then?"

"Maybe she was trying to get you to commit."

"Commit what?"

"You are supposed to ask her who won the bull-riding at the rodeo."

"And what will she say?"

"Just a minute, let me find this note. It's strange. This whole deal is strange. Here it is. You ask, 'Who won the bull-riding at the rodeo?' and she answers, 'Hank F. Calf.' "

"Hank F. Calf? She said that was what I was supposed to say to you. This is a hokey game, Jack."

"Yeah, sounds like a paperback novel. Eh, not one of yours, of course, I mean, if you were the type to write, which you aren't, because you're a golfer."

"Tell you what, Jack. I'll go to the airstrip. I'll wait a few minutes. If she doesn't show, then I'll go home and search the maps for this town of Bunker. I'll call you from home tonight. That's the end of my involvement. I won't traipse all over Montana. I have neither the time nor the energy."

"Thanks, Pa . . . eh, Pal . . . Arnie. Be careful."

"I'm too tired to be careful."

"You need to get more rest."

"Yeah, that's what everyone keeps telling me."

"Thanks, partner. Now get away from

the pay phone before suits show up in un-marked cars."

"So far there are only truckers in over-alls."

"I knew I could count on you, Arnie. Give Shhhh . . . give that gal of yours a hug. You were the lucky one, pal. We all knew that when you captured her."

"Yeah. That's me. Mr. Lucky. Bye, Jack. I'll go up and meet the woman in the Im-pala."

"What did you say?" Revelage shouted.

"She drives an old Impala. That's all."

"A green '62 Impala?" Revelage choked.

"Yes."

"Oh . . . shoot, Paul . . . this is bigger than I thought," Revelage moaned.

"No more cloak of names?"

"I'm booking a flight this afternoon. Where's the closest airport?"

"Billings. What's the deal now, Theo?"

"Two INS agents were shot and killed at the border near Roosville, Montana, in July 2002 by someone driving a green '62 Chevrolet Impala."

"I never read about that."

"They kept it quiet because they were tracking a Mid-East terrorist connection."

Watson studied the rigs pulled into the mini-mart. A boy in the field across the road was chased by a duck. He rubbed his eye, then let out a long sigh. "Theo, this is getting beyond belief. Is there any attachment between this and reality?"

"Go to the airstrip. I'll call you on your cell phone when I have flight arrangements. Watch out for yourself P.J., Boudary is vicious. This is not fiction."

chapter eight

When Paul James Watson slipped back inside the truck, Toby McKenna munched on potato chips and gulped down a Mountain Dew. His belch started somewhere deep in the diaphragm and exploded into the closed cab of the Chevy pickup. McKenna shrugged and crammed in another chip.

Watson started up the truck, then tugged on his seat belt. "Where did you get those?"

"You want some?" McKenna shoved the bag toward him. "They're the hot barbecue double dipped in black pepper chips."

Watson shook his head and backed out of the parking place. "How can you eat such stuff? That can't be fit for human consumption. That could kill you off."

McKenna grinned. "Fiction heroes never die from what they eat but only because of poor sales. Shoot, I've never even gotten sick from what I ate. One time in *Hong Kong Poison Princess*, I had to eat raw stingray when me and that short little babe with black hair down to her knees were marooned on the island, but even then I could handle it. It tasted like an old tire."

"Did you pay for those things, Toby? Where did you get the money? You didn't have any money."

He smacked his lips, swallowed hard, then pointed to the buckskin jockey box between the seats. "I took some from the brown envelope in the console."

Watson banged on the black leather steering wheel. "But that's my trip money. It's for writing expenses. Every penny has to be accounted for."

McKenna wiped pepper from his lips on the back of his hand. "$7.22, and it *is* a writin' expense. You got to keep your hero happy, P.J. This might look like junk food, but I'm your bread and butter. Do you want a Mountain Dew? I bought two of them."

"You know what Mountain Dew does to me. I get as hyper as . . ."

"As me?" McKenna grinned. "That's what I figured. Don't worry, I'll drink them both. OK, what did that nut Revelage say?"

"He said that I should get rid of you."

"Me?" This time McKenna's belch exploded like a firecracker. "Ah, that's better. Get rid of me? I'm not the paranoid one livin' in a fantasy world."

Paul James Watson stared at the man with barbecue dust on his thick dark mustache.

"OK, technically, I do live in fiction world," McKenna admitted, "but it's the world you created. I don't have any choice. It's always your story, not mine. When did you ever let me tell the story?" He took a big gulp of the pea-green soda. "Maybe some of the time I run the story, like when the twins in *Double or Nothing* drove the Volkswagen bug into Lake Erie and I refused to let them drown, even though you tried to finish them off. But I don't get to control the story very often."

"You are always changing the story," Watson mumbled.

"Only for the better. You'll have to admit that. I do have some good ideas."

Watson unsnapped the sleeves of his blue shirt and rolled up the cuffs. He spun the gold band on his ring finger. "Here's the way the story is going this time. And I won't let you change it. We are going up to some little airstrip to wait for the lady in the green Impala."

"That's what Revelage told you? Wow, do you mean she is real and not someone you created in your mind?"

"I have no idea, Toby. Anytime you are with me, I'm never sure of reality."

"Shoot, P.J., the best times in your life are all with me, admit it."

"Somehow I find that sad but not totally true, Toby. The best times in my life seem like a long, long time ago."

"So Revelage knows about the woman in the Impala?"

"He didn't know her, but he thinks she holds a clue to finding Jonathan Boudary."

"America's most wanted?"

"I think we ran across her by accident. Now he wants me to find out what she knows about this psycho killer."

McKenna gulped down the Mountain Dew. "All right! Now we are gettin' somewhere . . . on the trail of a psycho serial killer. And I thought I was stuck in the hammock in the Florida Keys until you began writin' the next Distracted Detective. Say, aren't all serial killers psycho? I wish I had my .357 magnum."

"I am not writing this story. I'm going to make one contact for Revelage, that's all. We are not going to get involved in this."

McKenna poured the crumbs from the bottom of the bag into his mouth. "That's exactly what LBJ said about Vietnam," he mumbled.

Watson stared at him for a moment.

"What's the matter? You think I don't know any history?"

Watson rubbed the back of his neck. "I just didn't remember telling you that."

"Jyde Nuygn lectured me on the history of Southeast Asia in *Saigon Siren*. Remember when we were locked into the hold of that shrimp boat for three days? We talked a lot about history."

Watson raised his eyebrows.

"Really. We did talk."

"Theo is flying to Montana to chase down some leads. We're going home after this side trip. I need some Advil."

McKenna reached into the glove compartment, pulled out a little white bottle, and handed it to Watson. "Hmmm. Not very involved. Remember how *Distracted in Dublin* begins?"

"I'm surprised you can remember back that far," Watson murmured.

"Of course I remember that. It was the first time I got shot. I was really ticked at you for letting that happen. And now I don't even remember her name."

"Erin O'Neill," Watson said.

"Oh, yeah. The girl with pale skin, red hair, and green eyes. Whatever . . . ?"

"She's married with three children and lives in Belfast now."

"I didn't know that."

"I just made it up," Watson explained.

"Then it's not real?"

"It's as real as you are, McKenna."

"Anyway, I was on holiday in Ireland and sittin' at the pub, when Erin threw a dart into my backside. Next thing I knew, I was solvin' one of the worst crime waves in modern Irish history. And I didn't plan on gettin' involved. I never did get to finish that holiday because the second that case was solved you flew me to Athens."

"We aren't going to get sucked into this deal with the Impala lady. When we leave the airstrip, we'll drive straight to Bridgeport without stopping," Watson said.

"Are you talkin' to yourself?"

"Of course I am."

"I think we ought to stop for lunch." McKenna rolled up a brown strip and shoved it into his mouth.

"Looks like you have enough to eat. What is that?"

"Cajun Buffalo jerky. You wanna piece?"

"No, thanks."

McKenna rolled down the electric window and stuck his entire head out. "So, where's this airstrip?" he hollered.

"North of Big Timber, I think. What are you doing?"

"Tryin' to wear off the Mountain Dew." He sat back down. "How far away is that?"

"About an hour, then north a ways."

Watson eased back onto Interstate 90 and locked the cruise control at seventy-five miles an hour. He passed a long motor home that seemed to be driven by a huge thin poodle sitting in a gray-haired lady's lap.

"Babes dig dogs," McKenna offered. "Did you ever notice that? Maybe I should get a dog."

"Are you calling that little old lady a babe?"

"No, but it reminded me. Remember Dianne Sewgood in *Why Not Now?* She had that Afghan hound that never left her side. Man, she had long legs."

"The hound or Dianne?"

"Both, P.J., don't you remember?"

"I never forget a plot."

"How about the duchess in *Denmark at Daybreak?* She had a rottweiler who fetched her carryout Chinese food."

"She was a marquess from Madrid. It

seems to me, the dog fetched the Chinese boy on more than one occasion too. What's your point, Toby?"

"Both of those ladies were real classy, right?"

"They didn't have obvious vulgar tattoos or pierced body parts other than ears, and their clothes didn't come off the rack at Frederick's of Hollywood. Is that what you mean, classy?"

"Yeah, they were classy. And they had dogs. So, if I had a dog, well, you know, I could . . ."

"You could pick up classy chicks?"

"Just a thought," McKenna mumbled. "I need a cigar."

"You don't smoke, Toby."

"I could start."

"Not in my lifetime."

"What about the dog?"

"That's not a bad idea. Perhaps in the next book."

"What's the title of the next one?" McKenna asked.

"*Backstreet Baltimore Blackmail.*"

"Can I have a dog?"

"I'll think about it."

"Do you have a plot yet?"

"No, and I don't want to think about it today. I'm not working on plots. I'm tired of plots. I just want to sit back in a big old leather chair and let the world pass me by for awhile," Watson insisted.

McKenna unwrapped a PayDay candy bar. "I'll call him Tap."

"Who?"

"My dog. I'll name him after Tap Andrews."

"Tapadera Andrews is a fictional character in Stephen Bly westerns."

"I was considerin' callin' him Stuart Brannon, but no one calls their dog 'Stu.' Tap is a great name for a dog. I'll teach him to respond to my tap commands. Even when I'm tied and gagged, I'll be able to tap signals to him with my toe, and he can run and warn Miss Australia of impending doom."

"Miss Australia?"

"Or Miss Singapore. Or Miss Tahiti. Are you sure you don't want this other Mountain Dew?"

"I'm sure."

McKenna opened the can, took one swallow, and jammed it in the cup holder between them. "I think I'll take a nap."

"How can you have that much caffeine and sleep?"

" 'Cause I'm fictional. Caffeine doesn't affect me. I need a nap. I didn't sleep much."

"I was considering the same thing," Watson murmured. "I never sleep much."

Toby McKenna had his pickup seat leaned back and his fedora over his eyes when Watson felt the truck drift to the right.

OK, paperback writer, stay awake. I'm always this way. Tense for weeks as I finish a book, and then I collapse. I should stay home to write a book and go away to a motel and sleep a week afterward. But writing at home is a zoo. Between the kids, town, church, and correspondence, I'm always swamped.

Lord, this is crazy. I don't know if my mind is a blessing or a curse, or just the result of too many books, too many all-night sessions. I should take some time off. But the readers expect a new book. If I don't produce, they will get hooked on someone else. Where did I lose control of all this? I moved to Montana to relax and write and hide out from the cares of the world. I was going to change the world and enlighten the kingdom of darkness by lobbing out a book or two a year from the safety of my cabin in the mountains.

And now I have a huge log home that needs constant maintenance, a commu-

nity that thinks I'm retired and can volunteer for everything, grown kids who find ways to double my anxiety at a moment's notice, a publisher who thinks I should write a book in a week, fans who expect me to answer every letter and E-mail today, and a wife who . . .

I know, Lord. It sounds like I'm complaining. I'd like a dose of that "peace that passes all understanding," and I'd like it now. Maybe not too peaceful until I get somewhere to rest. No more of this crossing over the white line.

I should call Sheila back. We do need to get away. What happened, Lord? How in the world did we get too busy to spend time with each other? Keep her safe. Keep her in your will, and do the same for me, Lord. And please keep me awake.

Watson reached over and grabbed the open Mountain Dew. He tipped it back and gulped down three-quarters of the can without lowering it. Then he slapped his face.

Hard.

He punched the quick dial and listened to the cell phone ring.

And ring.

And ring.

"The party you are calling does not have

their unit on or is out of range."

"Doesn't have it on?" he mumbled. "Why doesn't she have it on? Is she too enamored talking to Brian Albright?"

Watson took a deep breath and let it out slowly.

"That's ridiculous. I have to be exhausted even to think such a thing. Sheila is much too consumed in her work for me or for anyone. Forgive me, Lord, for even thinking that."

He pulled off at Big Timber and rolled up to a gas station, mini-mart, casino, café, and real estate office combination. McKenna snored in the passenger's seat, so he left the rig unlocked and trudged into the café.

Paul James Watson sat down at the little counter next to a thin man wearing a Levi jacket and sporting a multicolored beard that seemed to explode off his face.

The man nodded and shoved a coffeepot his way. "Looks like you need some java, partner. Who you drivin' for?"

Watson poured the coffee, sloshing some on the sticky counter. "Yeah, I need the coffee. Afraid I'm not a truck driver."

"You come in from the east or the west?"

"From the east."

"There's a big wreck just west of here.

You won't get by it for awhile."

"What happened?"

"One of those Hummers must have sprung a fuel leak or something. I seen it from the top of the hill. It was zippin' along, passin' everyone in sight. Then it just blew up. Just like a fireball explosion. It blocked the highway on the north side. And there's a gulch between east and westbound, so they can't reroute the traffic." His faded baseball cap read "Lansing LugNuts."

Watson sipped on the thick, black ugly coffee. It scorched the tip of his tongue, then like hot lava dribbled down across his tonsils. "Were there fatalities?"

"Had to be. It must have been travelin' ninety miles an hour when it blew. But I ain't heard nothin' official." The truck driver sprinkled Tabasco on his French fries.

"Was it a black Hummer?"

"It's charcoal black right now. It was a dark color, but it was gone before I got close enough to distinguish colors. You might want to go north to Harlowton, and around to Livingston. They surely ain't gonna clear it up real quick. Do you know someone with a black Hummer?"

"I saw one east of here earlier today, up off of Highway 12. But I don't know whose it was." Watson studied the thin plastic menu. "What's good to order?"

"Ever'thin', except the catfish. Don't order the catfish. It tastes like sushi that's been raised in the sewer. I think it was spoiled last July when they first got it in."

"That convinces me."

A young dark brunette waitress sidled up to the counter with a pen and pad in hand. "You ready to order?" With a laundry marker she had written "Kymee" on the white plastic name tag.

"Give me the double bacon cheeseburger . . . with the meat medium rare, the bacon crisp, no mayonnaise, light on the ketchup and mustard, only one thin piece of lettuce, make the tomato thick, put the dill pickle on the side, and make sure the bun is fresh. I don't like stale bread. I'll have potato salad, as long it's fairly dry and without pimentos."

Kymee's chin dropped.

"I don't reckon this darlin's ever had a customer quite that fussy," the truck driver hooted.

"I don't think of it as fussy," Watson mumbled.

The girl disappeared into the kitchen.

"You from around here?" the driver asked.

"I live in Bridgeport."

"Say, do you know the mayor?" the man pressed.

"Stan Blocker? Yes, I do."

"Tell that no-good son-of-a-buck I'll bust his nose if I ever see him again." The man's whiskers twitched like a ticked-off porcupine.

Watson swallowed hard. "You and Stan don't get along?"

"Nope, never have."

"You've known him for a long time?"

"Since I was two."

"Did you grow up together?"

"Yep, in Gold Creek."

"Were you neighbors?"

"Neighbors? He's my dadgum brother."

Watson raised his eyebrows. "Brother? Stan is your brother?"

"Yep. I'm Kenny Blocker. We don't exactly look alike, do we?"

"You look nothing like each other. So you were raised in Gold Creek?"

"Gold Creek, Virginia City, even Bannack. Daddy kept movin' to the old minin' towns in hope things would work out."

Toby McKenna blustered through the

door. "There you are, P.J. You tryin' to slip in here and eat without me?"

P.J. sipped on the coffee and stared straight ahead at the shelf lined with empty Pepsi cans. "I was letting you sleep."

Toby plopped down on a stool on the other side of the truck driver. Blocker turned toward him. "You live in Bridgeport too?"

"Nope. I live mainly in the minds of purdy young ladies ever'where," Toby boasted as Kymee approached. "I got a place in Florida, but I don't get there much."

Watson waited until the truck driver turned back toward him. "Say, I'm looking for a town called Bunker, Montana. Do you know where it is?"

"Bunker?"

"What's good today?" Toby asked the young waitress.

Watson ignored him and continued. "Yeah, I'm looking for a little town called Bunker. But I don't remember ever seeing it."

"Our special is tomato soup and a grilled cheese sandwich for $4.50." She rubbed one smooth calf with her tennis shoe and chewed on her lower lip.

"I think I'll try the catfish, darlin',"

McKenna said with a wink.

She blushed and scurried back into the kitchen.

The driver glanced over his shoulder at McKenna but didn't say anything. He turned back to Watson. "I've hunted gold up and down ever' stream and tailin' in Montana, from Ubet to Polebridge. I don't remember a Bunker."

"I was told to look up someone on 24th Street."

"Twenty-fourth Street? There aren't six towns in all of Montana that have a 24th Street. If there is a Bunker, it surely ain't one of them."

"Maybe it was 24 Bunker Street, I don't know. This guy seemed unsure of the address."

"Are you sure it wasn't Bunker 24?"

"What's Bunker 24?" Watson asked.

"The Air Force laced Montana with underground bunkers, some of which had missile silos. Some were for ordnance storage, and some were just decoys, so the Soviets wouldn't know which ones to bomb. When ol' Clinton cut the military budget, they sold off or abandoned some of them."

"And they had numbers?"

"Apparently. But I surely don't know

what they were. Jake Cooper at Belgrade told me his uncle bought Bunker 10 up near Lewistown."

"There was a 24 on that marker I tossed into that land mine," McKenna reported from the other side of the trucker.

"Good, I'll tell Revelage how to get there. We won't have to go back. We can just head home," Watson insisted.

"But not on the interstate," the trucker cautioned.

Kymee brought Watson his double cheeseburger with runny potato salad.

"Say, sweet pea," McKenna called out, "when you get through takin' care of that ol' man, you want to get me a Mountain Dew? Someone seems to have drunk my last one."

Kymee filled a glass with ice, then slid it and a can of soda toward McKenna.

McKenna studied the teenager. "You weren't in that last Britney Spears television commercial? You know, the one where she has that hot-pink fur collar and is dancin' with a purple poodle?"

"Me?" the waitress gasped. "I never been out of Montana."

"If you had blonde hair, you'd look just like that babe in the white leather miniskirt that steals the Latino tango dancer from her . . . until she offers him some . . . eh, motivation."

"Really? Do you think I look like that?"

"You could be her twin," McKenna assured her.

"I do have a white miniskirt, but it's not leather."

"See? If Britney comes up this way, she'll have competition from Kymee Sue."

"How did you know my middle name?" she giggled.

"I was just tryin' to think of a name as cute as you are, darlin'."

Kymee flashed a wide smile and leaned across the counter. "Britney is so totally awesome."

McKenna leaned closer. "My words exactly."

"Ever since I read her autobiography, I've tried to be like her. She's sort of like a role model to me."

"I read in the *National Enquirer* that she does her own laundry. Just an ordinary girl."

"Do you read the *Enquirer*?"

"Never miss an issue," McKenna said.

"Some say it's all fiction."

"They say that about ever'thin'."

"Do you have her latest album?" Kymee asked. "It came out Tuesday."

"No," McKenna replied. "I've been on the road for what seems forever."

"You want to come out to my car in a few minutes when I take a break, and we can listen to it?" she giggled.

"McKenna!" Paul James Watson called out as he lifted the onion off his double cheeseburger and scraped off the thick mayonnaise.

"Sorry, sweet pea, my daddy won't let me do that."

"He's your father?" she asked.

"He treats me like I was his kid."

"Yeah, that's the way my sister is. So your name is McKenna? That's such a cool first name. My very best friend in high school has a sister named McKenna McQueen. She was named after that detective guy in all those paperbacks."

Toby McKenna raised his eyebrows. "You and your friend read the Distracted Detective Series?"

"No, but her mother does. And my grandmother has every one of them. She says that McKenna is quite the affable rascal."

Paul James Watson thinned down a pile of lettuce and plucked pickles off the double cheeseburger. "I think the cook is calling you," he told the waitress.

Kymee frowned, then scooted back into the kitchen.

Kenny Blocker tossed down six dollars on the counter. "Well, boys, I'm headin' out. Be careful with that catfish," he warned Toby McKenna.

Toby leaned over as the driver pushed out the front door of the café. "What did he mean by that?"

"He doesn't like catfish, I presume. Toby, quit flirting with the teenager."

"I wasn't flirtin'."

"Of course you were."

"I was just keepin' in practice."

"You don't need practice."

"You do. How come you didn't tell her you wrote the Distracted Detective?"

"I didn't want to get started in a long conversation."

McKenna sat back up. "P.J., if you don't push out of that shell of yours, you won't have anyone left to talk to but yourself. A writer who spends the whole day talkin' to himself. Is that pathetic, or what?"

Watson bit into the big hamburger with tough, overcooked meat. "You are exaggerating."

Kymee emerged with a steaming plate stacked with catfish and French fries. "I talked Jerry into giving you a double portion."

"Thanks, darlin' . . . you spoil me."

"I have some work in the back. If you need anything at all, just whistle." She glanced over at Watson. "That goes for your daddy too."

When she had disappeared, P.J. reached out his hand. "Give me the note."

"What note?"

"The one she slipped you with the catfish. I saw it," Watson said.

"It's not a message. Just a number."

"What kind of number?"

"Well, it's either a phone number or the size of her . . ."

"Give me the note."

"You're in a gripey mood today." McKenna shoved the note over to Watson.

Paul James Watson ignored the potato salad and finished his cheeseburger about the time Toby McKenna downed the last of the catfish. Kymee wandered back out and refilled the coffee.

"Tell the cook I like the seasonin'," McKenna reported. "Don't reckon I've ever had catfish that tasted like this."

"That's what everyone says," she nodded.

"When you are done," Watson said,

"we'll go find the lady in the green Impala."

Kymee spun around. "My aunt drives a green Impala. It's like a hundred years old. Really, it's an antique."

"What's her name?" Watson asked.

"Dana Rose Kelly. But I'm not sure what she goes by now. She ran off with this guy, and they've lived in Canada for like forever. For awhile she was calling herself Patty Hearst. Then we heard she was Molly McGuire. Anyway, she might not even have that old car still. But I remember something really funny about it. The back seat is on hinges and you can tilt it forward and crawl into the trunk and never open a door."

"Why would anyone want to crawl into the trunk?" Watson asked.

"We played hide-and-seek in it when we were kids."

"I'm gonna step outside," Toby mumbled.

"Are you all right, McKenna?" she asked him.

He held his side. "I just need to . . . eh . . . stretch my legs, honey."

"You'll phone me, right?" she whimpered. "You can call collect!"

Toby didn't answer but trotted outside.

P. J. Watson stood and handed Kymee a twenty-dollar bill. He waited for her to count the change. "Is Aunt Dana your mom's sister or your dad's sister?"

"She was my mom's sister."

"Was?"

"Mom died in a car wreck when I was sixteen."

"When was that?"

"Two years ago. Mom got a call about midnight that Aunt Dana, well, she was goin' by the name Jane Fonda at the time. Anyway, she called Mom and begged Mom to come pick her up in Great Falls. Mom took off alone 'cause Daddy worked the night shift at the refinery. It was a blizzard. Remember that bad January blizzard that year? Anyway, Mom was killed in a wreck up on Highway 87 by Malmstrom Air Force Base."

Watson sighed. "Sorry to hear that, Kymee."

"Yeah, thanks. I really miss her. We had a big ol' hairy argument that night she was killed. She wouldn't let me get my belly button pierced. And I slammed the door and wouldn't talk to her. How could I have been so stupid?"

Paul James Watson brushed back a tear from his eyes. "Did you ever find out what your aunt wanted?"

"No, we haven't heard from her since. She didn't even show up at the funeral." She wiped her eyes on her mostly white apron. "Sorry."

"No, don't be. There is nothing more important in life than the people we love and the ones that love us. Was your mom in a big wreck? Or just run off the road, or what?" he asked.

Kymee's head sunk to her chest. "It was a head-on crash."

"Did she run into a semi?"

"Actually, it was a Hummer."

"A what?" Watson gasped.

"One of those big old Hummers. It was havin' headlight trouble. The state police said she probably never saw it comin'."

chapter nine

Paul James Watson burst into the Montana daylight outside the café and immediately heard coughing and gagging behind the dumpster that overflowed with a busted olive green couch and a garbage bag of highly used disposable diapers. He ambled around to the weedy edge of the property.

"Toby, are you all right?"

A strong-shouldered man with unbuttoned collar on a black short-sleeved golf shirt bent over the short, metallic guardrail. McKenna wiped his mouth on a blue bandanna. "I lost my lunch," he mumbled.

Watson stared at the tumbleweeds wedged into the railing. "I can see that. I wonder if it was the pepper double-dipped chips, the two Mountain Dews, the Jalapeno buffalo jerky, or the spoiled catfish?"

McKenna stood up, still holding his stomach. "It was spoiled?"

P.J. gazed northwest at the Crazy Mountains. "That was a rumor I heard."

He leaned back over the rail with a dry heave. "Why didn't you tell me it was spoiled?"

"You wouldn't have listened." Watson brushed a white thread from the sleeve of his shirt. "You were too busy flirting with a girl young enough to be your daughter to pay attention to what you ate."

The two hiked to the truck. When McKenna closed the door, he rolled down his window. "I don't think I've ever been that sick. How come you let me get sick?"

"I've sheltered you for too long. In real life, people get that sick."

"I feel better now."

"Good. But you might want to watch what you eat for awhile. From now on, Toby McKenna can eat the wrong things."

"I don't want to talk about food." Toby leaned back against the seat. The brim of his hat pulled low to his eyes. "I don't have a daughter, P.J. I don't reckon I ever will."

"Exactly what subject are we on now?" Watson started the truck.

"You scoldin' me. I'm just statin' a fact. Toby McKenna was created by Paul James Watson to be a reckless and distracted, unmarried detective. No wife. No kids. You won't change that. And heaven knows, I can't."

"Toby, I've never known you to be so melancholy."

McKenna slapped his hand over his mouth, then he belched. "I suppose losin' my lunch gave me time to reflect."

A coy grin snuck across Watson's face. "You mean, your whole life flashed before your eyes?"

"Somethin' like that. But I don't have a long life. My entire existence consists of fifty-three volumes of the Distracted Detective Series."

"Fifty-five. Two are finished, but not yet in print."

"I don't count them because you could still edit them different."

"OK, make your point," Watson said.

"My life consists only of the scenes in those books and whatever memory you choose to give me. It reads like a two-paragraph review in the Sunday edition of the *New York Times.*"

"And you were disappointed with what you saw?"

"It wasn't much." McKenna leaned back and tugged his hat down over his eyes. "P.J., did I have a good childhood?"

"Of course you did. I've told you about some of it, haven't I?"

"You've never let me read the character sketch you compiled before the series began. There seems to be a lot missin'."

"When we get to the house, you can read it."

"Really? Whoa . . . that will be somethin'." McKenna sat up. "You said my mother was a saintly woman who was killed in a yacht explosion when I was twelve. But when I close my eyes, I can't see her, P.J. I'm over forty years old, and I can't imagine my mother. What did she look like?"

"Toby, she looked a lot like Rosalind Russell in *His Girl Friday*, just as vivacious and witty, with a tint of Ingrid Bergman mystique and glamour."

"No foolin'? Wow, Mom was classy, wasn't she?"

"Yes, she was."

"Thanks, P.J."

"You feelin' better now?" Watson asked.

"Yeah, but I still don't have a daughter."

"Are you serious?"

"Look, you get on me because Kymee in there could be my daughter. But I have no concept of being a father or havin' children. So, if I don't think of her as a daughter, it's because there is a void in my mind in that place."

"Toby, you are beginning to make sense."

A wide, dimpled grin rolled across McKenna's tanned face. "I am?"

"I'm going to think about it. Perhaps Toby McKenna needs to settle down just a little in the next book."

McKenna's voice grew quiet. "P.J., if you decide on givin' me a wife, can I have a classy one, like my mother?"

Watson brushed back the tears at the corners of his eyes. "I think that could be arranged."

"You're a lucky man, P.J. You got two fine sons, a vivacious daughter-in-law, a cute daughter, and a very classy wife. Did you know that for most of the rest of us, such a family is just a dream?"

"You mean, those of you in the fictional world?"

"From what I can see, most men in the real world don't have it either. You know it's true."

Paul James Watson let out a deep sigh. "Yeah, Toby. I know that. I forget it sometimes, but I do know that."

"I still don't feel too good," McKenna said. "Think I'll take a little snooze. You can drive up to that airstrip without me, can't you?"

"I think I can manage." Watson backed his truck out of the parking lot and turned onto Highway 191.

Lord, you always do that to me. You always use a wild reprobate like Toby McKenna to speak to me, don't you? He's right. I have what others only dream of having. Too often they are a distraction. I'm happy when they are busy with other people and other projects. But when I get time, I want them to drop everything to be with me. Then I get impatient if they treat me like I treat them.

He fumbled with the speed dial on the cell phone.

It rang several times; then a cheerful feminine voice came on. "Hi."

"Hi, Rudi. It's Dad."

"Hi, Daddy, where are you?"

"I'm still taking the long way home. I'm driving up toward Harlowton to take care of a little errand for Theo Revelage."

"Will you be here for supper?" Rudi asked.

"That's why I called. How about me and you going out to The Buckaroo tonight? Just a daddy and daughter time."

"Daddy, I'm goin' with Lanny to his

mother's tonight. She lives up in Townsend on the lake. We might be late getting home."

"Maybe we can catch breakfast at Myrna's Café in the morning," he suggested.

"Oh, Daddy, you know I never eat breakfast. Besides, I might have the early shift tomorrow at work. If I have to open, I'll just get something to eat there. Did you have something you want to talk to me about?"

I thought maybe we could review your entire life up until this moment and shake our heads and wonder where the time has gone. And maybe talk about the future and how things are really going down in your heart and your spirit. I was hoping to hold your hand and sigh and thank the Lord for blessing me with such a wonderful young woman as a daughter.

"Daddy? Are you there?"

"I'm here, darlin'. It's OK. We'll visit later. Drive safe up to Lanny's mother's."

"He always makes me wear a helmet, Daddy."

"You're going on the Harley?"

"Of course, that's all he has besides his old plumber's truck."

"You could take your car, baby."

"I wouldn't want to insult him, Daddy."

"A 2001 Dodge Neon is not insulting, Rudi."

"Don't worry, Daddy, I'll be all right. We'll talk later, OK?"

"Save me some time, Rudi. Just an hour or two before you turn thirty."

"Thirty? I'm only twenty-three!"

"I know, babe, but time goes by way too quickly."

"Are you all right, Daddy?"

"Oh, you know how I get after I finish a book."

"Mom says you are like a little boy lost in the woods."

"Yeah, that's me."

"Bye, Daddy."

"Bye, Rudi. I love you."

"I love you too."

Paul James Watson had just crossed the Yellowstone River on Highway 191 when a white, late-model Dodge Intrepid marked "Sweet Grass County Sheriff" blocked the highway. A uniformed deputy hiked toward him. P.J. rolled down his window.

The man with the stiff, round-brimmed hat stood more than six feet tall. "Afternoon, mister. Sorry to stop you."

Watson surveyed the road to the north.

"Is there trouble, Deputy?"

He tipped his hat at an old red Toyota pickup that had pulled up behind Watson's Chevy. "Not yet, but we're looking for a man. Just trying to be cautious."

"You have a prisoner escape?"

"Something like that. Actually, he was drivin' a black Hummer, but we're stopping every rig just in case anyone has seen the man or the rig."

"What's the man look like?"

"We have absolutely no description of him. It's strange to have such a wanted man and no description. But we know what the vehicle looks like. Have you seen a Hummer today?"

Watson nodded. "I saw one going east on Highway 12 north of Forslip about three hours ago. But how about the wreck on . . ."

The deputy yanked a notebook and pen from his pocket. "You did? Headed east, was it? Did you get the license number?"

"No, it zipped by going the opposite direction. But how about . . ."

The deputy scribbled on the notepad. "Could you identify who was driving it?"

"No, sir. I couldn't see inside. I don't know if a man was driving it or a woman, or if there were more people. The back

221

windows were tinted. I didn't feel the need to pay attention. Say, did you know that down on the interstate . . ."

"Was anyone else riding in your truck with you at the time when you saw the Hummer?"

P.J. glanced over at the empty passenger's seat. "No, sir. I've been alone all day. But I did hear about a wreck on . . ."

A white motor home with peach-colored trim pulled up behind the red Toyota minitruck.

"Yeah, there are rumors flying all over," the deputy murmured. "Thanks, mister, for that information. That's the most helpful I've heard all day. I'll call it in to the sheriff. Maybe that ol' boy is already out of Sweet Grass County. That would be all right with me. He's violent and crazier than those mountains."

"Who is it you are looking for?" Watson asked.

"I'm not allowed to give out that information. I'm just told to ask if anyone has seen a Hummer."

"What about the one in the wreck?" Watson asked. "Could that be the one you are looking for?"

The tall, thin deputy spun around. "A Hummer's been in a wreck?"

Watson glanced in his side-view mirror and saw an empty logging truck pull up and park behind the motor home. "I ate lunch at a café in Big Timber, and a truck driver reported a bad wreck on Interstate 90 eastbound just before town. He said a Hummer had a fuel leak or something and exploded."

The deputy's eyes widened. "When?"

"I guess about two hours ago, now. He said they closed both westbound lanes. He figured traffic would be backed up for hours."

The deputy rubbed the back of his neck. "I didn't hear anything about that."

"I didn't go that way," Watson reported. "So I didn't see it myself. But I didn't have any reason to doubt him."

"What did the driver look like?" the deputy asked.

"The truck driver?"

"Yeah, maybe it's someone I know. I could follow up."

"His name is Kenny Blocker. I'd say he was about forty-five, a smoker. He looked older. He was five-ten, brown eyes, sun-tanned face, wore a red-and-black Lansing LugNut minor league baseball cap. His hair was mostly dark brown with some gray. It was short but kind of

223

shaggy. He had a full beard that hadn't been cut in a month or combed in a week. It was streaked brown, black, gray, and red and shot out like tumbleweed in all directions. He wore overalls new enough to still have a crease but old enough to be spotted with gear oil, and a green-and-black plaid, long-sleeved cotton shirt. The way it wrinkled, I presume there was no polyester in it. His black boots had square, scuffed, steel-reinforced toes, and he wore the heels off on the outside, so I presume he was a little bowlegged. His hands were as tan as his face but not as calloused as most truck drivers. Either he's new to driving or has the best power steering ever invented. He wore a turquoise-and-silver ring on his right ring finger, and a watchband of coral, turquoise, and silver. It looked like he had two short horizontal scars under his left ear, almost like stripes, but they could have been dirt marks or birthmarks. I really didn't pay that much attention to him."

When P.J. stopped talking, the red-haired deputy stared at him. "That's all you can describe?" he stammered.

"He had dark grease under the fingernails on his right hand but not on his left. I thought that peculiar since we usually get them both dirty, or both washed, at the same time."

"Good grief, mister, where did you learn to describe people like that?" the deputy asked.

"It goes along with my profession." In the rearview mirror, Watson glimpsed a dark red minivan pull up behind the logging truck.

"Are you a barber?" the deputy asked.

"No. Do you need to go check out the story about the wreck?"

"Yeah, wait here."

"Could you ask them how many fatalities there were?"

Paul James Watson watched as the uniformed deputy slipped into his patrol car and used the phone. He stared past the roadblock and spotted a sign pointing east and a road that wound back toward the hills.

That must be Wildcat Creek Road. Then there's a windmill, and I turn north, and in a few miles there is an airport. Not exactly an airport. Just a strip of level dirt. I'm going to sit there and wait for the woman and boy in the Impala. I know the first thing I'll tell her.

"If you had information to give to me,

why didn't you do that back at Bunker 24? Or along the road by Forslip? Or even over in the field where I fixed your flat? You knew who I was, and yet you strung me along."

Undoubtedly she'll stomp around the green Impala with her arms folded across her ample chest.

"Because you seemed clueless to the situation," she'll answer. "I wanted you to say something about Revelage."

"I hadn't talked to Theo yet. You just appeared out of the blue."

"He said he would phone you right away. I assumed you had turned him down and wouldn't help me."

"He called my house, but I wasn't at home."

"You mean someone else knows about this meeting? Someone at your house?"

"Eh, no."

"Absolutely no one?" she demanded.

"Nope. They just said to call Theo. He's an old college friend."

Her round brown eyes gleamed. "You mean, if a meteorite fell on your head right now, no one would know you were out here?"

Watson leaned against the hood of the truck and jammed his hands in his back pockets. "I suppose so. Do you have a fear of meteorites?"

"No, but you should."

"What do you mean by that?" P.J. scanned the weedy airstrip.

"He is a violent man. I'm not sure you've ever faced that much evil in one person."

"Did you say he was going by Abe Lincoln this week?"

She peered at the doghouse-sized boulders around them as if uncovering someone spying on them. "You know too much already," she mumbled. "But you've got his name wrong. Today he will be Millard Fillmore."

Watson covered his mouth but couldn't keep from laughing.

"What's so funny?" she asked.

"Millard Fillmore doesn't exactly instill any great inspirational image to me. I would think he could at least have been Zachary Taylor or James Polk."

"You'll think inspiration if Millard shows up and finds you here."

Watson canvassed the deserted dirt road to the south. "Say, there is one person who knows I'm here."

"Who's that?" she asked.

"Tobias Patrick McKenna," Watson declared.

She tugged on a feathered earring. "The private investigator and international adventurer?"

Watson folded his arms. "Oh, so you know him?"

"I read about him somewhere." She spun around. "Say, was he the one who was with you at the silo?"

"That was Toby."

Her face softened, and she grinned. "He's way more handsome than I imagined."

"Oh, brother," Watson moaned. "This conversation is getting absurd."

"Dreams are that way, you know," she murmured.

Watson let his arm drop to his side. "This is a dream?"

"Maybe it's a hallucination," she replied. "Are you on drugs?"

"What are you talking about?"

"Meta, Ecstasy, you know."

"I don't do drugs," he insisted.

"Never?"

"Never."

"Prescription drugs?" she challenged.

"No."

"Over-the-counter drugs?"

"No."

"Are you drunk?"

Watson shook his head. "I don't drink."

"Perhaps you're having a breakdown. Or maybe it's a brain tumor, and your mind is coming unwired. Do you have severe headaches? A tingling feeling at the base of your neck? Do you forget who you are and what you are doing?"

"I always forget who I am. Now, go away," Watson said as he slipped back inside his truck.

She looked startled. "What?"

"Just go away."

"Don't you want the information I have for you to give to Theo Revelage?"

"Not now. I'll see you at the airstrip. This scene isn't going right. Besides, I need to talk to this deputy," Watson mumbled.

"And I thought Millard Fillmore was weird," she mumbled as she disappeared behind the sheriff's car.

The deputy stalked toward the pickup. "Are you talking to me?" he called out.

"Just mumbling to myself," Watson explained.

"Have you been drinking?" he asked.

"Why do people keep saying that?" Watson asked.

"Just answer the question."

"No, I haven't been drinking. Why would you question my sobriety?"

"There was no wreck on the interstate," the deputy reported. "Yet you had a complete description of a truck driver. And the whole time I was in my squad car, you were talking out loud to yourself."

"No wreck?"

The deputy craned his neck to see what was in the backseat of Watson's extended-cab truck. "There hasn't been an accident on that stretch of the road since a fender bender last April."

"I guess the trucker lied to me," P.J. shrugged. "I don't know why he would do that." In his mirror he spied a man in an old white Ford pickup pull up behind the minivan and get out of his rig.

"Or you lied to me," the deputy insisted.

"Why would I do that?"

"To throw me off the trail."

Watson scratched his ear. "What trail?"

"If you talked me into going down to Interstate 90, that would leave this road open for him to sneak north."

"For who?"

"The guy in the Hummer. Mister, hand me your license and proof of insurance."

"This is crazy," Watson mumbled.

"What did you call me?"

"I didn't call you anything." Paul James Watson reached for his boot wallet.

Immediately the deputy yanked his service pistol and pointed it at Paul James Watson. "Exit the truck slowly with your hands raised and in plain view!" he shouted.

"You're kidding me?" He could see the drivers behind him gather at the Toyota pickup.

"Now!" the officer shouted.

Watson opened the truck door and stepped out.

Lord, is this part real? I must be making this up. Does it matter what I do or say? It's all just a plot for another book anyway. Yet, if it's real . . .

"Put your hands on top of the hood and spread 'em!" the deputy barked.

"I don't understand why you are doing this."

With the gun still pointed at Paul James Watson, the deputy frisked him with his free hand. "What's in your boot?"

"My wallet. I told you that. You asked for my identification and proof of insurance. They are in my wallet. My wallet is in my boot."

"Why is your wallet in your boot?"

"Why do the Cubs never win the pennant?"

"Don't get mouthy."

"Some things have been going on for so long, we can't remember why," Watson said. "I've always carried my wallet in my boot. Do you want me to get out my driver's license and my proof of insurance?"

"Do it slowly."

Watson bent at the waist and tugged up his jeans. "See, there's the wallet. It has a nice little clip on it. It rides at the top of my boot, and I don't have to sit on it. Now may I reach in and take it out?"

"That's cool. You can't lose it that way," the deputy said.

"That's the point." He stood up and handed the deputy the wallet.

"Does it ever get in your way when you are walking? Does it rub against your leg?"

"Nope. I don't even notice it's there."

"Where did you get it?" the deputy asked.

"At Talbot's."

"The one in Billings or the one in Casper?"

"Billings," P.J. explained.

"They come in other colors?"

"Black or brown leather."

"I'm gonna pick one up."

"Can I quit leaning on the hood of the

truck?" Watson asked.

"No, stay right there," the officer called out. "I'm going to run a check on you."

"Why? I've done everything you asked of me."

"Filing a false accident report is a crime."

"I didn't file a report. I merely told you what the truck driver said."

"I don't believe that story."

"Why?"

"No one details another person that way. You made that up. And if you are lying about that, you could be lying about other things."

Watson tossed his hands in the air and spun around. "What are you talking about? I'm a writer. Of course I have detailed character descriptions."

"Down on the ground and spread-eagle now!" the nervous deputy shouted.

Watson eyed the grimy blacktop, then glanced at the half dozen people watching him.

"You heard me, mister! I said drop down and spread 'em, or I'll drop you."

Paul James Watson shook his head. "I don't think so."

"What?"

"This isn't real, is it? I'm a writer, and

I'm just making this up as I go. So, this scene isn't going right. I really don't feel like lying on the blacktop." Watson hiked back to the truck. "Let's take it from when I was still in the truck. You'll ask for my ID, and I'll say, 'My wallet is in my boot; may I reach down for it?' Then you say, 'Sure, just do it slowly.' Or something like that."

"Get back over here! I can shoot you!" the deputy hollered. Most of the spectators snuck back behind the motor home.

Watson stepped right up to the deputy and shook his fist in the man's face. "You shoot me, and I'll write you out of the scene. You will never exist. You'll never make it to the Barnes and Noble bookshelf or the Library of Congress. Now, hand me my wallet, and we'll try it again."

"You are crazier than a fruitcake," the deputy mumbled.

"I like fruitcake. I've always been puzzled by that analogy."

The deputy kept his gun pointed but shoved the wallet at Watson. "Get out of here," he commanded.

"You want me to leave?" Watson headed for the open truck door.

"Get in your truck and drive up to

Harlowton, or wherever. Just get out of here."

"You don't want to try the scene again? Both of us could do it better." P.J. slipped into the truck and closed the door. The window remained opened.

"Mister," the deputy looked at the driver's license in the wallet, "Mister Watson, I never want to see you again." He shoved the wallet through the open window, then paused with his hand on the frame. "Did you say you were a writer?"

"Yes."

"And your name is Watson?"

"Yes."

"Paul James Watson that writes all those Distracted Detective novels?"

"That's me. Do you read them?"

"Nope, but my wife reads every one three or four times."

"That's nice. Tell her thank you very much."

"Say, could I get your autograph? Maybe you have a scrap of paper."

"Better than that, why don't I give her my latest novel, *Over Easy in Omaha*. And I'll autograph it. What's her name?"

The deputy glared back at the line of cars when the folks in the motor home honked. "Oh, that will be great. Sign it, to

Jacqueline Kennedy . . ."

"Your wife is Jackie Kennedy?"

"She doesn't like to be called Jackie."

"And your name?" Watson asked.

"Duward, but everyone calls me Dub."

Within minutes of signing the auto-graph, Watson drove down the crossroad and turned east on a gravel lane marked Wildcat Creek Road. He slowed as the stiff springs on the three-quarter-ton pickup bounced and jarred across the washboard surface. Far to the east a couple of scrub cedars broke up the otherwise buckskin-grass horizon.

Toby McKenna sat up and rubbed his neck. "Whoa, I must have slept. Where are we?"

"Still in Sweet Grass County, north of Big Timber. This is Wildcat Creek Road."

McKenna stretched his arms out and cracked his knuckles. "Did I miss any-thing, or were all the adventures in your head?"

Paul James Watson glanced back over his shoulder toward a deserted Highway 191, then murmured, "I have no idea in the world."

chapter ten

Watson slammed his foot into the brake. The Chevy pickup slid across the gravel and dirt to a complete stop at the fork in the road. "Now, where are we? This isn't the instruction I received. What's that sign say, Toby?"

McKenna squinted. "Do you think it's time for me to wear glasses?"

"What does it say!" Watson repeated.

"Road 7," McKenna reported.

"Road 7? What do you mean, Road 7?" Watson raged. "There's no windmill. Where's the windmill? I was supposed to drive along Wildcat Creek Road until the windmill, then go north. Now here's a road branching north, but there's no windmill. How in the world am I supposed to know if this is the correct road? This is a complete waste of time. I don't even want to be here. I should be home."

McKenna pointed out his open window

at the brush. "Maybe there's a sign down in the weeds. I'll go look."

"Why aren't these roads marked?" Watson fumed. "These roads are made for public use. You'd think they would have the decency to stick a sign at a fork in the road. This is probably Bureau of Land Management property. What do those guys at BLM do anyway? They just loaf around at the office with their Krispy Kremes and draw government checks. I mean, what if this was a crucial trip? What if this was some life-or-death matter, and I needed to make the right choice?"

Toby McKenna combed down his mustache with his fingers. "Relax, P.J. I'll go look for a sign in the weeds."

Paul James Watson slammed his fist on the steering wheel. "Maybe it is a life-and-death situation. What if I get to the airstrip, and the lady and boy have been recently brutally murdered? If I had been there, I could have prevented it. But, oh no, the road isn't marked, and I wandered around for hours before I found it. What if the lady had information to give me of a terrorist plot to assassinate the president of the United States, and because I failed to find the airstrip, I can't send the warning? And what if those radicals in the Middle

East use the president's death to begin a jihad to annihilate Israel, and in order to save themselves, the Israelis drop a nuclear bomb on Baghdad? At which point North Korea sees the world attention elsewhere and drops a nuclear bomb on Seoul and invades South Korea. You see? Who's to say this very bureaucratically caused delay doesn't cost someone's life — or even the world as we know it?" Watson felt his heart beat against his chest.

"Whoa, whoa, whoa, I think your fiction-writin' mind is runnin' around like a penned-up dog in a field of fire hydrants." Toby McKenna opened the door of the gold Chevy pickup. "Paul James, get ahold of yourself. You're beginnin' to sound like a paperback novel. What's goin' on here? This isn't like you. We're talkin' about a Montana back road, not the future of planet Earth. We'll get it figured out. Just relax. It's gonna be all right."

"Relax?" Watson grumbled.

"Just wait in the truck. I'll look for a road sign. Promise you won't drive off without me?" McKenna pressed.

"I'll wait."

Paul James Watson closed his eyes and rubbed his temples. He leaned his head against the steering wheel. He let out several deep breaths. When he rubbed his hands on his neck, they felt cool and sweaty.

When he pried open his eyes, Toby McKenna stood at the open window of the truck door. "Looks like this one that runs northeast is Road 5, and the other is Road 7. Neither says anything about an airstrip," Toby reported. "Are you all right, P.J.? You look pale, and you didn't even eat any of that catfish."

Watson closed his eyes. "I think I'm lost, Toby."

"Lost?" Watson pushed his hat back. "Is that a geographical or a theological statement?"

Watson flopped his head against the back of the truck seat. "Neither. It's a mental statement. Toby, I'm so tired. I think I've lost touch with what is real and what is fiction. I can't tell the difference anymore."

"Join the team, partner; now you know how my life always is. Why now? What happened?"

"Toby, did a black Hummer blow up and wreck on Interstate 90 just west of Big Timber, Montana, or not? The truck driver, Kenny Blocker, said it did. The deputy said it didn't. And it just hit me as I stopped at this fork, that I don't have any idea which one is true. How can I make any decision for the future if I can't tell what was true in the past?"

"We could drive back down to the interstate and take a look. Why is that so crucial?" McKenna asked.

"It's just symptomatic, don't you see? I don't know if the woman and the boy are real. I don't know if Theo Revelage is real. I don't know if Kenny Blocker is real. I don't know why I'm here in the middle of this road, Toby. I don't know if good ol' Lanny the biker/plumber is real. I don't know if Ruth Ann and Sheila are real. I'm losin' it, Toby."

McKenna reached into the truck and shook Watson's shoulder. "You know Sheila and Rudi are real. Get a grip, partner. You have to be the stable one. I can act weird, but not you."

"But I don't know if my conversations with them were real. Look at me. I'm parked on some gravel road in the middle of Montana talking to a fictional character that I created. I think it's too late. I've already lost it."

"Yeah, all of that's true. But I'm real, P.J.," Toby McKenna insisted.

"No you aren't. I invented you. I made

you up. I created you."

"Now wait a minute, Paul James Watson. It's true that I didn't exist before you thought of me. And yes, I am limited to what you allow me to do. But that doesn't mean I'm not real."

"What are you talking about?" Watson grumbled. "You are a fictional character."

"If fiction means I exist as a creation of your mind, then, of course, I am fictional. You thought me up, and I came into being. And just how did you come into being, P.J.?"

"I had a mother and a father, and there was, eh, sex and then . . ."

Toby McKenna leaned against the cab of the pickup. "Is that what you believe? I thought you gave God a little more credit than that."

"What are you talking about?" Watson snapped.

McKenna stepped back and folded his arms. "Wouldn't you say God thought of you and you came into being?"

Watson's voice softened. "I suppose, yes . . . I, eh, agree . . ."

"Then you exist as a creation of God's mind. If so, then you and me aren't much different." Toby pointed his finger like a pistol. "When God stops thinkin' about you . . . you're gone, right?"

"I suppose so."

"When you stop thinkin' about me, I'll still be in the Library of Congress, but not you, you'll be gone."

P.J. stared at Toby's brown eyes. "Is that supposed to cheer me up?"

McKenna leaned inside the cab. "Do you love your wife?"

"What kind of question is that?" Watson exploded. "This is absurd. I don't intend to discuss my married life with you. All I want to know is which road to take."

"Isn't that what real life is all about?" McKenna pressed. "People always wantin' to know which road to take?"

"It's not that simple," Watson murmured.

"Answer my original question."

"Yes, I love Sheila."

"How do you know that? How do you know it's not fiction?"

"What?"

"Answer me," McKenna demanded.

"Down in my heart, there is something that feels her love. It's reinforced with words, actions, gifts, touches."

"But that love is a choice you make every day. It's a mental decision, not from your brain but from your heart. Your love for her is not somethin' material that you can put in a vase and arrange on the dinin' room table."

"Toby, I'm tired. Where is all this going?"

"Because, I say, I'm as real as your love for Sheila," McKenna suggested.

"How do you figure that?"

"Because you choose to make me real. You allow me to affect your life, and you certainly affect mine. You talk to God, and he's not there — not in a physical sense. You talk to me, and I'm not there — not like that rock over there or the dead stump of that cottonwood. Maybe I'm as real as you are."

"I don't know what you are trying to say."

"Maybe you don't have to sort out what is real and what isn't real. Maybe there's not that much difference," Toby insisted.

"I'm not following."

"Enjoy the life God has given to you. Some of it is tangible, and you can touch it, like this leather seat and those snakeskin boots. But some of life is intangible, like your love for Sheila, and your faith that spring will follow winter, and me! It's real too. Enjoy it all, live it all to the fullest."

"Are you implying that even if I am

going crazy, I should just go with it and enjoy it?" Watson asked.

"What I'm sayin' is that perhaps only God knows what is real and what isn't real and that you don't need to spend your life tryin' to sort it out. In the end you will have blown it in some areas, no matter what."

"What about the wreck on the interstate? Did it happen or not?"

"Yes," Toby replied.

"Yes, what?"

"What if both are true?" Toby challenged.

"You can't wreck and not wreck at the same time."

"Why?"

"What do you mean, why?" Watson fumed. "Are you hinting at a parallel universe?"

"Not at all. Talk like that is a cop-out used by college professors and television screenwriters. What I'm sayin' is that life is like one big dumpster. It is a hodgepodge of reality and fiction. We're all mixed in it together."

Watson leaned his elbow on the windowsill and his chin on his hand. "That's a particular comparison I've never heard before."

"Isn't that what the earth is? Just a dumpster until the new heaven and new earth come down? It's a dumpster filled with good things as well as trash. With gems and decomposin' filth. It's a dumpster of fact, fiction, hopes, and dreams, and old tires without tread. It seems like you want to dive into the dumpster and pull out all the items and sort them into their proper categories. But deep down in there it's hard to tell one part from another. And sometimes you just can't categorize them at all."

P.J. sat back and shook his head. "I can't believe I'm getting this lecture from you."

When McKenna grinned, his brown eyes sparkled. "No, I don't imagine you can. But it's true, and you know it."

"Are you saying that down in the dumpster of life is a Hummer wreck and a no-Hummer wreck?"

"I'm saying the pieces have not been properly identified as of yet, so it is necessary to hold onto both until the situation becomes clearer."

Watson's chin slumped to his chest. "Now I know I'm losing it. You make sense."

"Hey, partner, that's what friends are for. You help me when I'm down, and I help you."

Watson sat up. "We are friends, Toby."

"Yep, every day you choose to be my friend, P.J. And that friendship's real, not fiction."

"And every day I choose to have you choose to be my friend. Sounds narcissistic, doesn't it?" Watson added.

"Shoot, how would I know, P.J.? You never gave me that word to use."

"OK," Paul Watson took a deep breath. "What I really want to know is, do I drive down Road 5 or Road 7?"

"Road 5," McKenna declared.

"Why that one?"

"There's a dry creek bed that slants up beside it. That must be the one the locals call Wildcat Creek Road. There is no creek by the other one."

"That makes sense."

"You want me to drive?" Toby offered.

There was a long pause.

"No," Watson murmured. "But I was thinkin' about it. Get in, Toby."

P.J. turned up the northeast road. For several minutes they bounced along the rutted gravel road in silence. The sage and clumps of short brown grass carpeted the rolling hillside as they ascended the ridge of rolling hills that paralleled the Yellowstone River.

Watson cleared his throat. "You made sense, Toby. Thanks."

"You were just tired and not thinkin' clear, P.J."

"I think you're right. And you are right about you being real. You influence my life, just like you affect the lives of all my readers."

"Did you ever notice that us fiction guys affect a lot of lives? Course, some are more influential that others."

"Anyone you have in mind?"

McKenna stretched his arms as he talked. "How many people on the face of this earth have been helped because of that little fictional half-breed known only as 'the good Samaritan'? I'd like to meet him someday. My guess is that because of his highly fictional example, millions of people have been helped."

"You are probably right about that."

"Now I don't claim to be in the same league with him or the repentant tax collector in the temple, anymore than you compare yourself to Jesus, but we can do something real. Both of us. We're a team, P.J."

"Yes, we are. Both slopping around in the same dumpster."

"There it is," Toby called out.

"What?" Watson asked.

"The windmill!"

Only four blades remained on the windmill. The stock tank was at the bottom, and the pipes had been removed. It stood in the weeds and sage like a neglected tombstone, marking the hopes and prayers of another generation. Paul James Watson turned north.

"This is Road 6," McKenna reported.

"Not much of a road. It's hard to believe there's an airstrip up here."

"Why would there be an airstrip in this country?"

Watson shook his head. "That's a good question, Toby. No houses for someone to fly home to. No crops to need a crop duster. No forests in need of firefighters. And no lakes or trees for hunting or fishing camps."

"Are you thinking it's a mysterious airstrip?"

"I'm thinking it's a remote one."

"Remember that time in *Autumn Ambush in Alberta* where I found the airstrip in the middle of the forest that had been built parallel over the remote river? It was painted so that the satellite cameras couldn't detect it."

"That was the time the Hong Kong

mafia was trying to corner the market on spruce trees," Watson said.

"There was a gal about four-eight."

"Tanjee," Watson interrupted.

"She had the biggest . . ."

"Eyes."

McKenna nodded. "And a little cute mole right under her . . ."

"Ear."

"She broke her . . ."

"Right leg," Watson added.

"And I had to . . ."

"Carry her . . ."

"Piggyback, for . . ."

"Four miles."

"If I remember right, she really could . . ."

"Sing," P.J. grinned.

"Yeah. That's her. Whatever . . ."

"She lives in Vancouver, Toby. Her daughter is sixteen."

"No foolin'? I didn't even hear she got married."

"Right after you left her in Banff, she met a . . ."

"Doctor?" Toby interrupted.

"Yes," P.J. said. "He was a heart surgeon from . . ."

"Victoria?"

"Yes, and she was so happy she . . ."

McKenna rubbed his square jaw. "Brought her family over from Hong Kong?"

"That's right. All six brothers and . . ."

"Her twin sister?"

"Yes, eh, no . . . she was a triplet, not a twin," P.J. declared. "Banjee and Danjee are now living in Vancouver, and the sisters have a . . ."

"Home interior business," Toby grinned.

"Yes."

"Is she happy, P.J.?"

"She is delighted with her life. But whenever it snows, she is known to stand by the window and stare out and sigh. She remembers a reckless, strong-shouldered, ruggedly handsome detective who kissed her softly, then packed her up that hill in the blizzard. She remembers how he sat her down on the log, and pulled his own socks off so she could use them as mittens, then carried her the rest of the way to an abandoned ski shack."

"I don't remember the socks thing, P.J."

"Tanjee remembers."

Tobias Patrick McKenna was silent for several moments.

"Thanks, P.J. I needed that," he murmured.

"We need each other, partner."

McKenna pointed to the open prairie. "There's your airstrip, but we still don't know why it's there."

"That's an airstrip? But . . . it has . . . sagebrush and tumbleweeds on it."

"OK, it's dirt and a little overgrown, but a plane could land. Look over on that fence post. There's a battered wind sock on a broomstick. Shoot, it's bigger than that airstrip in *When All the Bridges Burned*. We had to build a log ramp to gain altitude over the pine trees."

"I think you may be right, Toby. This is some sort of airstrip. I'm not sure where to park."

"There are plenty of parking places," McKenna jibed. "Get one up close to the terminal. She might have extra baggage."

Paul James Watson stopped the truck in sage about in the middle of the clearing and turned off the engine. "She has extra baggage all right."

"OK, P.J., how long do we wait? Were you serious about fifteen minutes?"

"We just got here." Watson glanced at his watch. "It's barely two. I reckon we committed this much, so we'll wait until three."

"I think I'll go for a walk," McKenna announced. "You'll be OK, won't you?"

Watson ginned and nodded. "Go on, Toby. Just don't get lost. I don't want to tramp around looking for your tracks. Not that you leave any tracks, of course."

P.J. rolled the windows down in the truck and leaned the buckskin-colored leather seat back until it jammed against the duffel bag in the extended cab behind him. The breeze held a hint of sage. It was a "prairie" aroma that he distinguished from the high desert basin, and even from the juniper smell of the chaparral.

He closed his eyes.

There's something wrong here. I've got to simplify. My life is too scattered. I have to leave town to have enough quiet to write. Twenty years ago Sheila and I moved to Montana so we would have a quiet place for her to do her art and for me to write. We wanted a big old log house with a studio for her and a study for me. We were going to keep a low profile at church and a lower one in the community. We would follow those unique talents the Lord gave us. We would do those things that we could uniquely add to our world. Is Toby McGuire my unique contribution to humankind? Maybe so.

He let out a long, slow sigh.

I'm dissatisfied, Lord, and I don't even know what I'm dissatisfied with. Maybe it's the growing realization that Pete's right. I will always be a minor celebrity. Always a mediocre writer. But what troubles me more is that I'm afraid of becoming a mediocre husband, father, and disciple. Days go by too fast. OK, maybe not this one. One week, then two, then a month is gone, and a season. Each one is crammed, but are they crammed with the right things?

Sleep sounds so good. It's the only time my mind relaxes. I wish I could sleep for a week straight, Lord. I do believe I'd wake up fresh and ready to tackle anything. Next time I'll stay gone three days after the book is done and just sleep. Yeah, right. I can't stand being gone from her this long, and now she won't even be there.

Paul James Watson, you are a pathetic, insecure, mediocre paperback writer. The prospects don't look good for much else. So you might as well just accept it and enjoy what it provides. You are jammed in down there, about in the middle of the dumpster. You are a good mediocre writer. I doubt if there are six mediocre writers in the country any better than you. It's your calling. Someone has to have modest book sales.

Lord, maybe I don't need more sales. Just more satisfaction. And fun.

Toby's right. Don't worry about what is real or what is fiction. Just enjoy them all as gifts from the Lord.

I not only talk to myself. Now I'm preaching to myself.

If I get any more complex, I'll be a society unto myself without need of anyone else.

Sheila's smile came into view. "Yeah, right," he blurted out. "I'm about as self-sufficient as mistletoe growing on an oak tree."

Watson sat up and surveyed the rolling prairie landscape of short gray scattered sage and brown grass. No cars. No houses. No cows. Nothing.

No Toby. No sound. And no lady in the green Impala.

Watson glanced at his watch. 2:13 p.m. He leaned back and closed his eyes.

The telephone ring slapped him in the face like a taut branch pulled back on the trail and purposely released. He sat up on the second ring and blinked his eyes open, somewhat surprised to be sitting in the cab of his truck by a clearing in the sage. He

255

punched the green button on the phone.

"Hello?"

"Hi, honey, it's me. You were sleeping, weren't you?"

"Hi, Sheila, darlin'. Eh, yeah, how can you tell?"

"Hmmm, I wonder. After all these years, Paul James Watson, I not only know when you are sleeping, I can probably guess what you were dreaming."

"Oh?"

"Let's see. Toby McKenna is rescuing a lovely Irish lass from a shipping tycoon who kidnapped her and is planning on forcing her to live on an isolated island where she is chained to a computer and obligated to run his Internet gun-running operation."

"Whoa, good plot, darlin'!" he laughed.

"Yes, it is. I believe that was your book *Avery's Arms*."

"I knew I had heard that somewhere."

"Where are you, honey?"

"It's crazy, Sheila. I called Theo, and he wanted me to meet some informant out here on the prairie north of Big Timber. So I'm sitting up here waiting for some lady to . . ."

"Oh? Waiting for a lady?" she giggled. "Be sure and behave yourself."

"Look who's talking," he laughed.

"What did you mean by that?" she pressed.

"Eh, nothin'. Why did you call, darlin'?"

"You did too mean something. I'm in Missoula. It just dawned on me that you might be trying to call me, and I left my cell phone in my jacket, then forgot my jacket."

"Are you saying you don't have a cell phone?" P.J. asked.

"That's what I'm saying."

"Does Brian have a cell phone?"

"Brian who?" she asked.

"Brian Albright."

"How would I know? Do you need to call him?"

"No, I thought you . . ."

"Isn't this the week that he and Jerry Gaten were going fishing in Alaska?"

"It is?"

"I think so," she replied. "Anyway, I suppose I was lonesome driving up here by myself and wanted to hear your voice. Sorry I won't be there when you get home, honey. Paul, are you there?"

It was as if his joints were like a stick figure held tight by string tension, and the button on the bottom was pushed and every joint went limp all at once.

"That was a big sigh," she giggled. "Do you miss me too?"

"Yeah, babe. I'm going through one of those 'simplify, simplify, simplify' stages."

"Honey, don't get tied up worrying today. Enjoy having a book done. I'll be home by one o'clock tomorrow."

"I thought you had to stay for the patina girls to finish?"

"Oh, no, darlin'. This is just where I'm going to customize some of the wax pieces, add brands and details before they make the hard mold."

"I'm glad you called, Sheila," he said.

"So am I. It's nice to know you get as lonesome as I do. You are so self-sufficient, Paul James Watson. I get worried at times that I'm superfluous in your life."

"Are you kidding me? My world centers around you, babe."

"You are one smooth-talking author."

"Yeah, that's me, Mr. Smooth."

"Well, Mr. Smooth, I'll call you tonight from Marty's, if I get a chance. Bye, honey."

"Bye, babe. You have no idea how important this phone call was for me."

"Get your business done for Theo, and get home for some rest. I've got all sorts of things planned for you when I get home."

"You do? I thought we could have some time together, alone."

"That's exactly what I'm talking about," she giggled.

The wind picked up, blowing dust swirls, when he heard the truck door open. He peeked one eye at Toby McKenna.

"There's a rig comin' up the road. Must be a couple miles away, but it's throwin' up dust like a dirt bike on the Mojave Desert."

Watson sat up and raised his seat back.

"You took a little nap?" Toby asked.

"Yeah, I actually fell asleep until the phone woke me up."

"The phone?" McKenna pointed at the dash-mounted black cell phone. "I'm surprised you get reception out here. Anyway, I thought your cell phone didn't work unless the key was turned on."

"No, it doesn't, but I must have . . ." He glanced down at the cell phone face that was turned off. "Maybe I just dreamed I had a phone call."

"Did you enjoy it?"

P.J. smiled. "Yes, I did."

"You see, fiction isn't a bad place to live."

"You're right, Toby. Sometimes it beats real life."

The dirt that preceded the speeding green Impala was so thick that Watson rolled up the windows, and he waited for her sliding stop. The woman leaped out of her car and sprinted to the pickup.

P.J. rolled down the window.

"Who won bull-riding at the rodeo?" she asked.

"Hank F. Calf," Watson replied.

A wide grin broke across her round face. "I'm glad to see you. I figured you would be dead by now."

chapter eleven

Watson opened the door and eased out of the truck. The warm drift of wind surprised him. "Why would I be dead?"

The lady paced the yellow-brown dirt in her once-white tennies. "He knows who you are."

"Who knows who I am?" *Why doesn't she want to mention the name of Jonathan Boudary? It's a strange game we are playing.*

"Never mind who." Her eyes pierced into his. "If you don't know his name, they can't beat it out of you."

Is she really worried about me? P.J. jammed his hands in his pockets and surveyed the short trees at the end of the weedy airstrip. "Who's going to beat it out of me?"

"Them." The word dropped and splattered like a plum in October.

"Are you talking about creatures from

outer space or what?"

"You wish."

"How long have you been playing games like this?"

"What are you talking about?" she questioned.

"You know what I mean. How long have you been underground?"

Her shoulders sank, her eyes sagged. "Since I left home . . . a million years ago."

Watson glanced into the Impala. "Where's your boy?"

"I'm back here," a muffled voice filtered out from the back of the car.

P.J. surveyed the backseat. "Are you in the trunk?"

"Yeah. I'm hiding."

"Who are you hiding from, partner?"

"Him and them."

"Are you OK?"

"It's quite comfy," the boy called out. "Do you have any pizza?"

"No, sorry."

"I like mine with extra cheese."

Watson leaned his back against the pickup and studied the woman's face. *I wonder when they ever have time for meals. What do they eat, anyway?* "I'll remember that."

"I need to leave. I can't stay in one place

too long," the lady said. "The satellite will spot me." She surveyed the deep Montana sky. "Do you hear an airplane?"

"No."

"Are you sure you don't have any pizza?" the boy called out from the trunk.

"I'm sure, Attila. I don't have a thing to eat." He turned to the lady. "Just for the sake of argument, let's say that Millard Fillmore doesn't kill me, and that 'they' don't beat it out of me. What am I supposed to do?"

"How did you know he was Millard Fillmore?" she pressed.

"Because it seems like I've been here before."

"Yeah, that happens to me all the time," she murmured.

"And I am not Attila the Hun," the boy shouted. "You can call me Pol Pot."

"Sorry, little pal. I don't like that game anymore. No one should be called those names. From now on, I'm calling you Duke. You might as well get used to it." He turned to the woman. "Have you got a name? I'm tired of calling you the lady in the Impala."

She leaned close enough that he could smell woodstove smoke on her clothes. "You can call me Nicole Kidman."

How can they have a bath or a shower underground? Maybe the army had some advanced facilities down there. "OK, Nicole. Now why am I here, and what am I supposed to tell Theo Revelage?"

She stepped closer until she was almost leaning against him. "I want you to show him something." She reached under her sweatshirt.

Watson scooted away. "What are you doing?"

"Getting you this." She pulled a black object out from under her sweatshirt and handed him a very warm floppy diskette.

P.J. stared at the unmarked computer disk. "I'm supposed to attach this to an E-mail and send it to Revelage?"

"Yes, but use his secure line. You'll need to hook your computer up to a pay phone, somewhere they can't trace you. Then destroy your computer when you are done."

"What?" The word had just escaped his lips when a hawk screeched overhead, and they both looked up.

"Your call will be traced," she insisted.

"Who? The CIA? The FBI?"

"Dream on. That would be the least of your worries."

Watson glanced back at his briefcase in

the pickup. "I don't intend to destroy my computer."

"What's a thousand-dollar laptop computer compared to this?" She tapped at the disk.

"I have no idea what 'this' is."

"That's exactly my point. You don't know squat, and you've assumed it's not worth a laptop."

"My computer has way too much valuable information on it, Nicole. You'll have to find someone else to send it to Revelage. I'm not destroying it."

"Find someone else? You don't have any choice in this matter. You don't understand."

"Of course I don't. I don't understand anything that's going on. I'm lucky to remember my name. Now I think I'll head home. I'm tired. I'll tell Theo it just didn't work out."

She grabbed his arm. "If you aren't in on this, I'll have to kill you myself."

Her fingers felt sweaty, sticky as he pulled his arm away. "I'm leaving."

"You can't run. I know where 2214 Tomahawk Drive, Bridgeport, Montana, is. It's the big log home surrounded by fir trees. The master bedroom is on the west end of the house, isn't it? Your wife's studio is the room with the cathedral ceiling."

Watson glared. "You know my house?" The air suddenly felt as oppressive as being trapped in a full-body vise.

"I know that you sleep on the side of the queen-sized bed closest to the bathroom and that your CD-playing alarm clock is set at 3:15 a.m., and that you have it set to Buddy Holly's 'True Love Ways.' But you always wake up before it goes off. You are in way too deep, Paul James Watson."

His neck stiffened. His heart raced.

Lord, I'm not going to take this anymore. That's it. This is crazy. "I'm going to the authorities," he blurted out.

"Hah!" Her laugh seemed to rumble up from the bowels of hell. "You wouldn't know an authority if you saw one. You thought that guy down on the blacktop was a deputy sheriff. You are a paperback writer, P. J. Watson. You deal in fiction. And no one on earth will believe your story. You are in this, Watson. The battle is deeper than this world. You probably think dear old Lanny is really a biker/plumber. You don't know anything of importance, that's for sure. You either do this, or you are a dead man. Do you understand?"

In every book that Paul James Watson

266

had written, there came what he called the "defining moment." It was a line, a paragraph, or a page that explained to the readers why the book had to be written and why they needed to read it.

He never knew where that defining moment would happen. He never planned to insert it, never thought about it ahead of time. But, like an unexpected but welcome visitor, it suddenly appeared and brought every other scene into focus.

"I said," she growled, "you either do this, or I will kill you."

Somewhere deep down in that place where his spirit clutches to faith in God, moral absolutes, and self-respect, the words exploded out of him like the defining moment in his novel. "Nicole," he grabbed her shoulder hard. "I'm sick and tired of these threats to kill me!" he shouted. "Now, shut up, get in your car, and leave! If I hear one more lame threat, I'll hog-tie you and toss you in the trunk with little Joseph Stalin. Do you understand?"

"My name is Duke," a voice filtered up from the trunk.

She jerked loose from his grip. "What did you say to me?"

Watson grabbed the collar of her sweatshirt and almost lifted her off the ground with his left hand. "I said, you don't seem to understand that it is only by the grace of God that I don't break your nose with my fist. And if you mention my family, or my home again, or threaten to kill me again, I'll break more than your nose. Do you comprehend what I'm saying? Or do I need to be more graphic? You are absurd. I will not be threatened anymore. You're like a pimple on prom night: no matter what I do, I can't make you go away."

She opened her mouth to speak, sucked in several deep breaths, then threw her arms around his neck and began to sob.

P.J. released his grip on her sweatshirt, looped his arms around her, and patted her thick, matted dark hair. *This was not the reaction I expected.*

"Did you hit my mama?" the boy called out.

"No, Duke, I didn't hit your mama."

"If I come out to see, are you gonna hit me?"

"No. Come on out."

The back cushion in the backseat swung forward, and the boy blinked his way out into the Montana afternoon. He crawled up to the front seat, then leaned out the window. "Mama, are you all right?"

She continued to clutch Watson and sob.

"She's OK," P.J. explained. She finally released her arms and stepped back, wiping teary eyes on the sleeves of her forest green sweatshirt. Her eyes dropped to her shoes.

He patted her shoulder. Without looking at him, she reached up and gripped his hand.

"Are you scared, Nicole?"

Her voice was so soft, he had to lean forward to hear her. "I've lived in terror for twenty years. Hell couldn't be any worse. But I don't know anything else."

"Does he beat you?"

"I can take that part."

"Let's get to some real authorities," Watson suggested.

She glanced up in terror. "Oh, please, no. No! It's more complicated than that. He has her with him."

Watson scratched the back of his head. "Who?"

"My sister," Duke called out from the front seat.

"Sister?"

"He never goes anywhere without taking one of them. He knows I'll have to do what he says, or he'll kill them." She began to sob again.

Watson turned to the boy. "Duke, get back in the trunk."

"What?" the boy said.

"You get back there for a few minutes, and I'll buy you a pizza with extra cheese," Watson promised.

"You will?"

"As soon as I find a pizza place. Now go on."

When the boy disappeared, Watson took Nicole's arm and led her away from the car.

His voice was soft, yet insistent. "Are the children his children too?"

She nodded.

"Do you think he would actually harm them?"

She bit her lip so hard it began to bleed.

"Nicole. Has he hurt them already? *Oh, please no . . . no.* I won't go to the authorities until we get all your children back. We don't want them hurt anymore."

"It's too late for that," she whimpered. "I will never get them all back."

Paul James Watson found himself gasping for breath. "What are you telling me?"

"He took my baby, and I couldn't stop him," she sobbed.

He hugged her shoulder. "Can you tell me about it?"

"He took my little baby girl. I was still nursing her. I begged him to take one of the others, but he took her. So I called the Montana State Police and turned him in." She spoke in a forced, shocked monotone.

"What happened?"

"They couldn't find him. But he found out that I turned him in. He killed her and buried her and won't even tell me where." Tears tumbled down her cheeks. "I don't even know where my baby is buried!" she sobbed.

Lord, I know our battle is not against flesh and blood, but this seems like teetering on the brink of the abyss. "Nicole, we're going to get this thing figured out. Let's take it one step at a time. What will he expect you to do? Are you supposed to be waiting for him at Bunker 24?"

She held her cheeks with the palms of her hands. "Yes, unless I was being followed. I can never get away from the bunker when he is there. So I gathered some things and took off. I left a coded message that someone was following me and showed up at the bunker. I told him I loaded up the important things and would meet him here. At least, I think it was here."

"What do you mean, you think it was here?"

"He changes the code names for these places every two or three days. This is either Iraq or Iran this week. I can't remember for sure."

"Where's the other one?"

"At Carrol Creek."

For the first time he noticed how large and round her eyes were. "In the Bridger Range?"

Her voice lost all of its former harshness. "Yes."

"Do you think he'll buy the story of you being followed?" Watson asked.

"Yes, I think he will. That's why he'll be looking for you. I gave him a description of your truck."

P.J. kicked at the loose dirt with the toe of his boot. "My truck?"

"Revelage told me what kind of truck you would be drivin'. But when you didn't know the code response, I figured Revelage had changed his mind. So I thought I'd get you to follow me up to the bunker. He would see the tracks and know someone had followed."

"What if he had been there?"

"He would have shot you."

"So I either help you escape, or he tracks me down and you blame everything on me?"

"That's the way I figured it. I know it sounds awful. But I'm fighting for my children's lives as well as mine."

"I'm not real fond of being the stooge, but I do know you are scared. What's Theo Revelage have to do with all this?"

"I hope he's my insurance. If I can get this information to him, I'll have an ace-in-the-hole that might save my daughter's life."

"Theo is supposed to sit on it and not use it on his Web site?"

"He said he would give me two weeks to make a break for it before he made it public. Do you think he can be trusted?"

"Theo knows when to speak up and when to be quiet. So in your mind what is to happen now?"

"You've got to get this information to Revelage."

"I can see that he gets it. But I won't destroy my computer."

"That's up to you," she said. "I'm warning you; he's vicious. Almost Satanic. And he knows computers better than Bill Gates and Steve Jobs put together. He'll track you down."

"Thanks for the caution, Nicole. I'll take this one step at a time. If I take off to get this to Theo, what will you do?"

She stared back down the long dirt road that led to the airstrip. "I'll stay here and wait for him and little Helena."

"Her name is Helena?"

"This week. Last week it was Cheyenne."

"How old is she?"

"Four. My baby would have been two." Her words tumbled out emotionless, as if well practiced.

"How did you link up to Theo?"

"On his Web site. Lots of people think his conspiracy theories are off-the-wall, but he is right sometimes. He was the only one that would take me seriously."

"Do you have a phone line out there at the bunker?"

"No line, but we have a satellite phone. All those bunkers have satellites beaming down at them. He rigged up an outfit where we could pirate satellite space."

"How did you keep him from knowing you were in touch with Revelage?"

"He knew. He's the one that told me to watch that site. So every time I went to Revelage's site, I was doing what he asked."

"Isn't there any way he would leave both children with you for awhile?"

"Not that I can think of."

"Then you will be no better off when he gets here. And if you don't do something, Revelage will post what's on this floppy, and your lives will be in danger. Let me think of something."

"What do you mean?" she asked.

"Can you stall him?"

"I don't understand," she said.

"What if you leave a coded note here, and say he didn't show and you went to the other site, the Carrol Creek one. Tell him you saw the two guys in the gold pickup watching cars down at the interstate and you are taking a long way to the site. Tell him to take a long way there too, and whatever he does not to go back to the bunker, because 'they' have unmanned surveillance planes flying over it."

She nodded. "He'll believe that."

"I thought he would."

"What do I do at Carrol Creek?"

"Phone me before you get there. I'll come up with a plan by then."

She stared at him from head to toe. "You are awfully confident for a paperback writer."

Watson grinned. "I have lots of experience making up plots."

"But do you ever try them out to see if they work? Do they really work?"

"Yep. I know if they work by the reaction of the readers. If I've convinced them they are real, then they work."

"But the people in the books aren't real," she protested.

Watson took her hand and led her back over to the Impala. "They are as real as you are."

Nicole stared at his eyes for a moment and clutched his hand. "You know, don't you?"

"Yeah, I know," he whispered. "I know the line between reality and fiction is so thin that at times it disappears completely and that the real battle is always the forces of darkness."

"Can I come out yet?" a young voice pleaded.

"Come on out, Duke. I owe you a pizza."

The seat flopped down, and the boy crawled out. "When do I get it?"

"I am going to stop at the very next pizza place I find and buy one. Then I'll deliver it to you next time I see you."

"What if I don't see you again?"

"You'll see me. Ask your mama."

"Will he come back, Mama?"

"Yes, he will," she mumbled. "This kind always comes back. I haven't forgotten everything." She clutched P.J.'s arm. "You're a believer, aren't you?"

"Yes. What made you ask?"

"They are the only ones that see everything. Everyone else is too busy." She nodded at the boy. "We'll leave first. You follow in five minutes. That way the tracks will look like you are still following me. He's a good tracker."

"When you hit the blacktop, turn north. I'll turn south to the interstate. Give me at least a couple hours before you call my cell phone."

"What is your number?" she asked.

"If you know my bedroom and my house layout, you have my phone numbers."

Nicole grinned. "Yeah, I know it."

"Now, how did you . . ."

"An Internet survey." She drew a large peace symbol in the dirt. Then wrote "I-2" beside it.

"I don't remember doing a survey. Is that the note you are leaving him?"

"Yes, he will know. It was your daughter, Ruth Ann, who told me. I was monitoring all the chats in Montana . . ."

"You can do that?"

"I told you, he knows computers.

Anyway, in a chat room she mentioned her dad being a writer. So I broke in and asked her to take a survey." She got in the car and started the engine.

He leaned down into the passenger-side window. "I have one question. Is Lanny a plumber/biker or something else? Is he scamming my daughter?"

"Oh, he's a plumber/biker. I just said the other to try to scare you. But your daughter thinks he is 'something else,' that's for sure."

Paul James Watson watched as Nicole and Duke drove away. He rubbed the back of his neck and stretched his arms. There was no pain in his neck. No pain in his shoulder. He wasn't sleepy or particularly tired. He glanced at his watch, then slid into the seat. He turned on the ignition and turned on the CD player.

He listened to Jimmy Buffet sing something about "savin' the world on his own."

I'll leave at the end of the song. I have no idea what I'll do if some psycho-killer shows up, Lord. It might be interesting just to sit here and wait for him. I can't believe I said that. I can't believe I meant it. Maybe I have been writing fiction too long. Am I becoming Toby McKenna? Or have I been Toby all along? Either way, I will accept every dilemma that confronts me as an assignment from you. Whether it's fiction or real, I will attempt to solve it in such a way that good triumphs over evil. That's all I ever wanted to do. It's my message. My sermon, I suppose. Keep doing good, no matter what the circumstance, no matter what the repercussions, no matter how tired, no matter who or what the enemy, no matter how lonely it gets. Keep doing good. Over and over and over and over and over. I don't know any other way.

The rap on the passenger window caught him by surprise. A chill ran down his back as he whipped around. Then he relaxed.

"The door's locked, P.J.," Toby called out.

Watson hit the unlock button. "That never stopped you before."

McKenna brushed the knees and cuffs of his trousers before he climbed inside the truck. "You looked lost in thought. I'm the same way when Buffet is singin'."

"That was a long walk you took, Toby. What did you do, roll in the dirt?"

"I dug a little bit with my hands. You'll never guess what I found. Someone buried a cache of supplies down at the end of the runway by that little grove of scrub cedars."

"How did you discover that?"

"I was diggin' for gold, and I . . ."

"You were doing what?" Watson asked.

McKenna dug into his pocket and pulled out a big coin, then handed it to him.

"A silver dollar?" Watson said.

"Look again."

"A double eagle?"

"A twenty-dollar gold piece," McKenna announced. "I kicked at a clod and that's what turned up."

"So you dug for some more?"

"Yep, I thought maybe a strongbox or something had been lost up here. Anyway, I decided that I would only dig down a foot since I just had a tent peg to dig with."

"Where in the world did you find a tent peg, Toby McKenna?"

"In those squatty-lookin' cedars." He pointed to the east.

"That was convenient."

"My life is always convenient, did you notice that, P.J.? It's one of the delights of being a fictional character. My life is an amazing string of coincidences, half of them get me into trouble and the other half of which provide an escape from trouble. Remember that time in *Renegade Rembrandt* I was in Bonn . . ."

"Berlin," Watson corrected.

"Where I was surrounded by twelve . . ."

"Six."

McKenna waved his hand as he continued. "Lithuanian dope smugglers . . ."

"They were Latvian."

"And they chased me out the back door of the cabaret."

"It was a cheap saloon," Watson insisted.

"I had to swim the river . . ."

"It was a canal."

"In my tuxedo."

"You were wearing a black turtleneck."

"And there was a Turk with a machine gun."

"He was Greek . . ."

"Greek? But they hate Turks."

"Trust me," Watson said.

"And, suddenly, submerged in the water, I discovered a twelfth-century sword."

"Fourteenth-century."

"And I chopped off his head."

"You stuck him in the rear end, and he ran off. But what does this have to do with tent pegs?" Watson laughed.

"I was explaining how nice it is to be fictional and always stumble onto exactly what I need, when I need it. As I was saying . . ." Toby paused as Watson turned the pickup down dirt Road 6. "Where are you goin'?"

"Down to the blacktop and the interstate."

"Aren't you gonna wait for the lady in the Impala?" Toby prodded.

"She came and left."

"What?" McKenna gasped. "How can that be?"

"You were busy digging, I suppose."

"Maybe it didn't happen, and you were just imaginin' it."

"And your point is?"

"Paul James Watson, you are finally getting it, aren't you?"

"I think so."

"What happened? What did she want to give Revelage?"

"A floppy disk."

"What's on it?"

"I have no idea."

"You didn't ask her?"

"Nope."

"Then that's it, we're all through with her? And we can go on to something else?" McKenna asked.

"Nothing is over. If we play this right, Tobias McKenna, we can come face-to-face with a psychotic mass murderer. The absolute face of evil."

"Whoa, like the long-legged Swiss blonde in *Deception in Geneva*?"

"Similar, but the Swiss gal didn't have long legs."

"She most certainly did," McKenna insisted.

"I did not give Candice long legs."

"P.J., you didn't give her any legs at all."

"Of course I did."

"No, there was not one place in the entire book that you said a word about her legs. So the readers and the fictional hero can make up anything they want for your creative neglect."

"As long as it's consistent with the rest of the description of the character."

"Oh, it was consistent. I choose to give her long legs. If you don't give complete descriptions, we get to fill in the rest. That's one of the rules of fiction. Anyway, she was wacko, a loony. I never knew any woman or any man for that matter that could operate a chain saw in each hand. I suppose she learned that tight grip from milking goats. This guy can't be any worse than the butcheress of Berne. Besides, we have more important things to examine."

"For instance?"

"There is a cache of supplies buried at the end of the runway, including a Japanese flag and a bunch of rotten pamphlets in a tin box."

"What did the pamphlets say?"

"I don't know. They were all written in Japanese. Did I ever study any foreign languages, P.J.?"

"You took French when you were in high school."

"I don't remember that."

"No one does."

"Anyway, I think these pamphlets were in Japanese. There were also bits and pieces of a decomposed rubber raft. Why would anyone up in these hills bury a rubber raft?"

"I don't know, Toby. Were there any more gold coins?"

"Not that I could find. Aren't we gonna check it out?"

"Nope, my life is too complicated as it is," P.J. explained.

"You're just walkin' away from it?"

"Driving away, to be precise."

"Why?"

"Because I get to be a part of a fight between good and evil, if I go this way. And I have no idea how a decomposing rubber raft and a Japanese flag fit into that fight, so I will eliminate that choice for now. It could be just a side plot that goes nowhere."

"But, but, how can you do that, P.J.?"

284

"I've had years of experience of leaving diversionary ideas by the side of the road."

"Side of a runway. P.J., do you ever forget good story ideas?"

"Never. It will show up somewhere, Toby. For now we might have some lives to save."

"What in the world did that lady tell you?"

"Nicole had quite a story."

"Her name is Nicole?"

"Nicole Kidman."

"That's Nicole Kidman?" McKenna gasped. "I always figured she was, you know, thinner."

"Not that Nicole Kidman. Now just sit still and let me tell you her story."

Watson had just finished briefing Toby McKenna when they reached Interstate 90 at Big Timber, Montana.

"You actually yelled at her?" McKenna gasped.

"Yep."

Toby shook his head. "What's got into you, P.J.? You used to be so peaceful. And you told her she was like a pimple on prom night? That sounds like somethin' I would say."

"Yes, I regret the use of cheap similes. I think for a moment I forgot I wasn't you."

McKenna leaned forward, his elbows on his knees, his chin resting on his palms. "I can't believe I missed all of that," he mumbled.

Watson pulled onto the freeway in the westbound lanes.

"I can't believe you picked her up and threatened to bust her nose."

"I was angry," Watson admitted.

"I reckon you were, Mr. P. J. Watson. No wonder she burst into tears."

"I just refused to be threatened or to have my family threatened."

"What made you do such a thing?" McKenna asked. "It's not like you."

"I just thought to myself, *What would Toby McKenna do?*"

"Really?" McKenna grinned.

"Yep."

"You're right. That's what I would have done. Then when she hugged me and sobbed, I would have . . ."

"I didn't do that," Watson insisted.

"Do what?"

"Whatever it is you had in mind."

"I was merely gonna hand her a clean handkerchief."

"Oh, yes, I should have remembered that," Watson said.

"So what is your big plan for protecting her and her two remaining children?"

"I have no idea at all. I should probably pull over and think this through."

Toby pointed up ahead on the freeway. "No reason to pull over. Looks like traffic is backed up like johns at a stage door."

"What's goin' on?" Watson mumbled.

A burly, bearded trucker with a semi-load of milk wandered back to the pickup. "Looks like at least thirty minutes more delay, buddy," he said.

"What's the deal?" Watson inquired.

"A rig caught fire and burned up on the highway."

"Anyone hurt?"

"No one saw the driver escape. Must have caught the fuel line. They say it exploded like a bomb."

"I didn't know diesel exploded like gasoline," P.J. mumbled.

"How did you know it was diesel?"

"Hummers run on diesel, don't they?"

The trucker studied him. "You can tell that to the FBI," the trucker said.

"FBI?"

The trucker rubbed his beard and

287

pointed west. "They have a roadblock at the accident site. The FBI showed up within twenty minutes and started interviewing everyone in the westbound lanes."

chapter twelve

As far as Watson could see, traffic congested the westbound side of Interstate 90. Many of the drivers loitered beside their vehicles in the dry fall midafternoon Montana breeze. Paul James Watson rolled down the electric window in the gold Chevy pickup.

Watson yanked his wallet from his boot before the man in the dark suit reached his pickup.

With no show of emotion, the man said, "Excuse me, sir, I need to see your driver's license."

P.J. handed him the license. "Do you mind if I see some ID from you?"

The man leaned closer to the pickup. There was a strong aroma of spice aftershave. "What did you say?"

P.J. tried to peer at the man's eyes. "You see, sir, I can tell those men over by the burning vehicle are Montana State Police. Then there are several county sheriff vehicles and uniformed officers combing that field for something. And I can tell the firemen and the EMTs. But I don't know who you are. Could you show me some identification, please?"

The man pulled a leather case from his belt and opened it up. "Agent Smith, Federal Bureau of Investigation."

"Smith, huh?" Watson replied. "Just like the movie? Maybe you guys need to work on names more."

"You got problems with my name?"

"No, sir. It just reminded me of something else," Watson sighed. "Sorry about that, Agent Smith. It's just that I have several files of names at home. I collect them. Maybe you guys should do the same thing."

The agent studied his driver's license. "Where are you headed, Mr. Weston?"

"Watson. Paul James Watson. See, it's right there on the license, although the picture isn't real good. I had a migraine that day. I'm on my way home."

The agent continued to study the license. "And where is your home?"

"It's a little smeared, but it's correct on the license. One time my wallet tumbled off the shelf into the washer. The wet dye in the leather left a permanent mark.

That's the time I ruined that cute picture of my daughter, Rudi, when she rode the paint pony. I've regretted that ever since."

"Just repeat your address for me."

"2214 Tomahawk Drive, Bridgeport, Montana."

"And the zip code?"

"Are you planning on writing to me? No, probably not? It's 59725. By the way, why is the FBI doing automobile accident investigations in the middle of Montana?"

"We're not investigating an accident. Where are you coming from, Mr. Weston?"

"I've been out in Miles City for a couple of weeks. And, not that it matters, I suppose, but my name is Watson, sir. Is it true that a federal crime has to be committed in order for the FBI to investigate?"

Agent Smith studied the long line of traffic stacked up behind Watson and shook his head. His voice continued a monotone. "Business or pleasure?"

"What?"

He leaned down to the open window; his voice boomed. "Were you in Miles City for business or pleasure?"

"Agent Smith, you must not ever have been in Miles City. No one goes to Miles City, Montana, for two weeks for pleasure, except perhaps during the bucking horse sale. But that lasts only a week. I was there on business."

"What kind of business?"

"I'm a writer," Watson announced.

"What kind of a writer?"

"A paperback writer."

Agent Smith looked again at the driver's license. "I've never heard of you, Mr. Weston."

"In this particular case that's probably just fine."

The agent handed Watson his driver's license. "The driver of that rig ahead mentioned you knew the burning vehicle was a Hummer. Can you tell me how you knew that since it is now burnt and blown apart beyond recognition?"

"I ate lunch at the Big Timber Café. A trucker came in and said he was traveling eastbound when he saw a black Hummer explode."

"What was his name and what did he look like?" Agent Smith asked.

"He said his name was Kenny Blocker. I gave the deputy at the roadblock on Highway 191 a complete description of him."

The agent looked surprised. "What roadblock? Which deputy?"

"When the trucker said the Hummer

was blocking traffic, I went north to look at the countryside."

"Why?"

"I told you, I'm a writer. I am always hoping to find a new setting for a story."

"Where did you go?"

"Up Road 6. Or was it Road 7? I can't remember. It was the one by the windmill."

"Did you find anything up there?"

"Yes. I thought up a plot for a new book about World War II goods stashed at a remote airstrip. It's a secret Japanese invasion of Montana that gets sidetracked by two old prospectors. No one knew about it until last year when a letter postmarked September 2, 1945, showed up in Tokyo. One of the invaders explained the entire operation and how he decided to stay in Montana after the war and run a drive-in theater."

The agent pulled off his glasses, and his eyes were as dark as his thick eyebrows. "What? Are you serious?"

"I made all of that up. I'm a writer. That's what I do. You are the very first to hear my new plot."

The agent jammed the dark glasses back on his long, thin nose. "That's the world's stupidest plot."

Watson nodded. "Thank you. I always try to stay ahead of the others. Like you, I appreciate an honest answer."

The man lowered his voice to a whisper. "Have you ever heard of a man named Jonathan Boudary?"

"Who hasn't? I once saw a television show about him. If I remember correctly, you've been looking for him since 1979? And now you have a roadblock in the middle of Montana? I don't think Boudary would ever allow himself to be snagged in a setup like this."

"Do you know him?"

"No, but I saw some of your composite drawings on *America's Most Wanted* one time. Frankly, Agent Smith, it looked like half the men in the United States. Is that the best you can do? If I made character sketches that poor, I'd never get a book published."

"I don't appreciate your attitude, Mr. Weston."

"You'll have to excuse me. This has been a rather strange day of mixing facts and fiction. I haven't determined which you are. I can't believe you are stopping all the traffic in Montana to ask these kinds of questions. You'll have traffic backed up for days. By then someone like

Boudary could drive to Panama."

"Mister Weston, are you telling me the kinds of questions I should ask?"

"Yes. I think you should be asking about the nationality of the deceased."

"Who said anything about anyone dying?"

"You see that white suburban? That's a state vehicle. I think it belongs to the office of the Montana State Coroner. He didn't show up just to count scorched hubcaps."

"Why is it important to find out his nationality?"

Watson winked. "What if he is Japanese?"

"What are you talking about?"

"And you laughed at my theory about the Japanese secret invasion of Montana."

"Weston, I think you're a loony."

"It's just a plot I'm working on while I sit here. I find it a lot more fun than getting stressed out over a traffic delay."

"Wait right here. Don't move. I need to verify some of this," Agent Smith demanded.

Watson gazed at the team of officers combing the sage and grass near the wreck. "I wonder what they are looking for."

"Nice goin', P.J. I think you sufficiently

offended the Federal Bureau of Investigation."

Watson looked over at Toby McKenna. "He can't be FBI Agent Smith? Give me a break. I saw those movies. I think this is just one of the plots I'm dreaming up in my mind."

"What if it isn't?" McKenna cautioned. "Remember that time in *False Truth in Frisco* when I caught the Singapore illegal arms dealer by leakin' info that I was plannin' a sting on his operations by pretendin' to be an ATF agent? Then I tipped off the real ATF agents. Maybe the real FBI is wantin' this to look like a phony FBI operation."

"That's even too complicated for me," Watson replied. "But this Agent Smith guy is tough to take seriously. I think he's fresh out of fictional stereotype school. In a novel they would never let me create a guy like this."

McKenna rolled down his window. "There's one way to find out how serious they are."

"I don't really care whether they are serious. I just want to get down the road."

Toby McKenna leaned out the window. "Let's see if this gets any attention. Hey, Agent Smith! Matrix, dude!" McKenna shouted. "How come you didn't ask P.J. about the woman in the green '62 Impala?"

"What are you doing?" Watson gasped. "We don't even know who these guys are! What if they are in the league with Boudary himself?"

Six men in dark suits, with guns drawn, sprinted toward the pickup. McKenna pulled back inside the cab. "Obviously, they know who the woman is."

"What do I do now?"

"This might be a good time to step on the accelerator," McKenna insisted.

"You mean, just drive off?"

"Quick, P.J.!"

"But, but, but . . ."

"Pull forward, P.J."

"No, I'm not running . . ."

"Who said anything about runnin'?" McKenna questioned. "I just said pull up there so the state police can question you. See, he's waving you up there."

A uniformed MSP officer motioned him forward. "You mean I was dreaming all that up?"

"All what up?" McKenna asked.

Watson pulled his truck up to the uniformed state patrolman and opened his wallet.

"I need to see your driver's license, sir."

P.J. handed the man his license. The silver name tag on the officer's uniform read "Myerskoff."

The officer ran a handheld scanner over the license and handed it back. "Thank you, Mr. Watson. You may proceed. If need be, we will follow up with a phone call or a visit."

"That's it?"

"Yes, sir. We don't want to hold you up any longer than necessary."

"Was anyone killed here, Officer?"

"One fatality that we are sure of. But the way the rig blew up, it's hard to tell if it was a man or a woman. Thank you for your cooperation. Please move along now."

Watson eased away from the accident scene. "I've got to stop doing that — living a scene before it arrives."

"Have you figured out a plan for Nicole and the little boy?" Toby quizzed.

"If Boudary was in that rig, her problems are over. He's toast."

"And if he wasn't?" Toby asked.

"Then it's an amazing coincidence. How many Hummers could there be in Montana?"

"Let's call that red-haired girl in Denver. You know the one with the funny name and the wide . . ."

"Smile? Her name is DeWalla Coltrain."

"In *Rocky Mountain Misery* she had access to every vehicle record in the United States, Canada, and Guam," McKenna said.

"But she's a . . ." P.J. stammered.

"Don't say it."

"I created her and . . ."

McKenna folded his hands behind his head and leaned back in the seat. "Look, do you want to know about Hummers or not?"

"I don't have her phone number."

"Make one up," Toby said.

"What do you mean, make one up?"

"You created DeWalla, so whatever phone number you give her, that's her number. Make one up, P.J."

"This is really weird."

"Of course it's weird; you're a paperback writer. Everything you do is a little weird. What's her number?"

"Denver? 303-817-1944," Watson mumbled. "But I can't see how this will work."

Toby reached over and punched numbers. "You want me to leave it on speakerphone?"

"Sure, I forget what she sounds like," Watson said.

"You gave her a very sultry voice for a rather, eh, big-boned lady."

"I did?"

"Yeah, on page 137, don't you remember?"

After two long rings, a voice came on. "You have reached the office of Goldstein, Schmidt, and Hanover Research Associates. If you know your party's extension, please dial it now."

"What's her extension?" Toby asked.

Watson shrugged. "How would I know?"

"Quick, make one up."

"This is incredible, Toby. This not the way real life works."

"The number, P.J."

"Eh, 751," he blurted out.

Toby McKenna jabbed the number. "Cars, trains, and semi-trucks. This is Ms. Coltrain, how may I assist you?"

"DeWalla, darlin', your voice is just as sexy as ever!" McKenna rocked back and forth in his seat.

"Oh . . . oh! Toby, honey, is that you?"

"Hi, darlin'."

"Baby, baby, baby, where have you been?" she purred. "I've really missed you."

"Oh, you know, it's been hectic solving one disastrous crime after another," Toby reported. "The mysteries roll around faster than a gutter ball at the bowling alley."

"Are you in Denver, cupcake?" she purred.

"No, I'm up in Montana, darlin'. I desperately need somethin' that only you can give me."

DeWalla giggled.

It was a sultry giggle.

McKenna lowered his voice and whispered at Watson. "She's very good at rubbin' my back. She has strong thumbs."

"I don't remember writing that about her," Watson said.

"You didn't," Toby grinned. "DeWalla, I'm workin' on a new case up here, and I need to know how many black Hummers are registered in Montana. Is there any way I can find that out?"

The voice turned didactic. "I am very sorry, sir, such information cannot be released."

Toby turned to P.J. and whispered, "Just wait."

"That's OK, darlin'. I certainly don't want to jeopardize your position or do anythin' illegal. Thanks for clarifying that. Say, on another subject, DeWalla, are you still runnin' cows in Montana?"

"Yes, Toby, I am. You know me. I like to

own a few head at all times."

"Do you still have black angus, sweetie? Those are the ones I like best."

"Yes, I do."

"How many head are you grazin'?"

"On government land or on private land?"

"Private."

"Let me check the tally sheet. We only have six at the moment."

"In the whole state of Montana?"

"Yes."

"That's not a very large herd."

"Oh, I know it, Toby, honey. But they are presold."

"Any of them sold to unusual people?"

"Well, I even sold one to Abraham Lincoln."

"That's too bad. She's probably the cow I wanted," McKenna said. "What's the ear tag number on her?"

"37H-261."

"Do you have a phone number or address? Perhaps I can contact them about buying the cow."

"Sorry, no phone, and the only address is Bunker, Montana."

"Abe Lincoln in Bunker, eh?" McKenna mumbled.

"Yes. Do you know where that is?"

"I think so. Thanks DeWalla, darlin', you are a prize! Don't be surprised if your Toby phones you up in the middle of the night sometime."

"That's a promise I've heard before. But it still sounds wonderful. You just made my day, my week — shoot, my whole year. Bye, baby."

"Bye, sweet thing."

McKenna glanced over at Watson and shrugged. "What can I say? I get along well with the ladies."

"I can see that."

"Six black hummers in Montana, and one sold to Abraham Lincoln," Toby reported. "We even got the license number."

"The fictional license plate number."

"Do you have any indication that this scenario is real?" McKenna probed.

"Yeah, one tangible fact." Watson rubbed the left shoulder of his black shirt. "When she hugged me and started sobbing, her tears soaked the shoulder of my shirt. It's still damp."

"Whoa, P.J. Do you mean I might actually get to be a part of a real mystery?"

"It's possible we might both be a part of a real mystery."

The cell phone startled both of them.

"I bet it's DeWalla callin' back," Toby

suggested. "I'll take it." Toby poked the receive button. "Hi, darlin'! Thanks for that license number."

"Paul? What number? Your voice sounds different."

"Spunky?" Watson blurted out. "Eh, I thought you were someone else. A friend in Denver searched a license number for me."

"I can get that kind of info for you," Spunky announced.

"You can?"

"Silly boy, don't you remember who my brother is?"

"I thought he wasn't allowed back into the country."

"He runs it all from Bermuda now," Spunky replied.

"But why did you call?"

"You sound better than last time. Did you get a nap?" she asked.

"Thank you, but no, not yet."

"Paul, I told my hubby about signing up for the classes at Columbia."

"And what did Mr. Hampton III say?"

"He stormed around like Martha Stewart with a collapsed soufflé. Paul, it was awful."

"Really? I don't know why he wouldn't be proud of you. I certainly am."

"Here, you talk to him," she said.

"What?"

A click, a buzz, and a man cleared his throat.

"Watson?"

"I'm here, Hampty . . ."

"Did you incite my wife to sign up for classes at Columbia?"

"It wasn't my idea, but I do think it's a good one," Watson responded.

"It's an absurd idea!" Hampton blustered.

"Are you saying that because you don't want a smart wife?"

"She's setting herself up to fail, Paul. You know Spunky."

"High school valedictorian doesn't sound too shabby. She can handle Columbia. Give her a chance at it."

"Valedictorian?" he stammered.

"You didn't ask her about her 4.0 average in high school?"

"But, but, but that was years ago. You don't understand, Watson. She'll be ridiculed. It will crush her."

"Hampty, you and I both know that Sylvia Sasser Hampton is as tough as nails. Who are you kidding? There's no one in Columbia that could touch her tenacity."

"I don't understand why she can't be

content just being my wife."

Watson slowed the pickup as one logging truck struggled to pass another. "Hampton, she's crazy about you. Every man with an ounce of testosterone in New York City is jealous of you. But, if she heads off and gets a degree, it will prove that you are even smarter than they thought."

"How do you figure?"

"Right now they just think you are rich and lucky. The sexiest lady not on Broadway is hanging on your arm. But Mrs. Hampton with a master's in English literature? Hampty, you'll be thought of as a genius. The man who could look past the thigh-high slit in her red silk dress and see a smart, if somewhat insecure, lady."

"Never thought of it that way. I suppose we could keep it on the hush. Not many would have to know."

"Just the opposite. Tell everyone you meet how excited you are and how proud you are of Sylvia."

"But, but, but, what if she does fail?"

"Hampty, if you publicly stand by her on this, without hesitation, then that gal will be at your side until you breathe your last breath. She will never forget it. Hampty, you're in a win-win situation. You always were one lucky publisher."

"You know, Paul, people always tell me that. I've made some smart choices they don't give me credit for."

"Tell Sylvia if that's what she wants, to go for it. Tell her you think she should get a doctorate. Dr. Spunky. It has a nice ring to it."

"I can't believe I'm taking advice from a . . . a . . . ."

"Paperback writer?"

"Thanks, Paul. Eh, by the way, don't I have a manuscript due on my desk by Monday?"

"It will be there."

When Watson punched the stop button, he noticed Toby McKenna was grinning at him. "What? What is it?"

McKenna spun his fedora around in his hand. "I just realized I'm sittin' at the feet of the master."

"What are you talking about?"

"P.J., that was one smooth line you fed him."

"I wasn't joking."

"I know, I know, that's what made it so smooth. You're the best there is, P.J. I can't believe you haven't won a Pulitzer Prize."

"Hah, now you are the one dreaming."

"Still, it was nice what you did for her."

Watson continued to stare down the road. "I think everyone deserves a chance to see how far they can go."

"I'm glad you said that. I've been thinkin' about goin' to med school," Toby blurted out.

Watson burst out laughing.

McKenna grinned. "Yeah, I was just teasin'. I don't think I did very well in college, did I?"

"Captain of the rugby team."

"I mean in academics."

Watson signaled and took the next exit. "You didn't spend a lot of time studying, Toby. You could have done better. But you had a good time, especially when you and those other guys rented that big old mansion up in Laurel Canyon."

McKenna sighed. "I surely wish I knew more of my past." He glanced out the window. "Are we pullin' off in Livingston?"

"Yes. I'm supposed to send the contents of this diskette to Theo Revelage, remember?"

"I thought he was flying up here. You could just hand it to him."

"In the meantime, I think the contents need to be stored somewhere besides this one little floppy. So I'll send it to him. All I need is a telephone line," Watson insisted. "Livingston is a fair-sized town for Montana. Sheila and I come over here for the summer theater series. They put on some nice plays."

"Did that guy from New York ever make a play out of *Pirates of Battery Park*?"

"No, his financial backing dried up after 9-11." Watson slowed down as they came to a commercial district. "There's got to be somewhere I can hook up."

"They should have an Internet café somewhere," Toby said.

"No, but an agreeable insurance office will do. Or a hotel lobby. Or a friendly waitress with a phone behind the counter."

"P.J., you are such a smooth talker when you want to be. How come you been hidin' that talent? Why, I can hear you now: 'Hi, darlin', you have such a beautiful phone line. Why don't we hook up sometime?' "

Watson ignored the comment.

Toby pointed to a huge silver building. "We can stop at that grain elevator. Maybe they have a telephone."

"It's a big town. There will be some place. Maybe a library."

"How about the Caterpillar Tractor dealer? Whoa, there's the Last Loop Saloon. Looks a tad run-down. You think they have a phone?" McKenna said.

"I don't know if they have indoor plumbing."

"The train yard is big," Toby said. "Is there anyplace there?"

"I doubt it."

"Remember that train yard in Kansas City?" Toby blabbed. "What was the name of that book?"

"*Blue Days, Red Nights.*"

"I never did understand that title."

"Obviously from sales, neither did anyone else," Watson mumbled.

"Anyway, I'll never forget openin' that freight car, expectin' to find a fugitive who skipped bail, and I discovered the Vietnamese family livin' in there. And the one . . ."

"Janie."

"She had the prettiest eyes I've ever seen in my life," McKenna proclaimed.

"I'm glad you remember that."

"And I remember they had a crate of brand-new computers."

"Fake computers. They were rigged to explode every time someone turned on the solitaire game."

"Yes, but she saved my life."

"Twice," Watson added. "Once, by not letting you play solitaire, and once when she threw you off the moving train."

"She knew about the sabotaged tracks?"

"She knew." Watson studied the buildings that lined the main street. "Maybe the bank would let me hook up . . ."

"I got you one better, P.J. Look over here!"

"Park County Internet Café & Espresso Bar? You got to be kidding me!" Watson groaned. "In Livingston?"

"What did I tell you? Modern times have come to Montana."

Watson pulled up in front of the old, two-story green building. "This is unbelievable. I've been to Livingston often. This wasn't here before."

"Must be providential. Do I have time to check E-mail?" McKenna asked.

"No, I just want to run in and out."

"Then I'll wait in the rig," McKenna said.

"It will just be a minute." Watson pulled his black computer case from the back of the extended cab.

McKenna leaned his seat back. "Why don't you just use one of their computers?"

"I'm told this is sensitive matter. I don't want it stored on some computer where there is public access."

"Now you sound like Revelage."

"He could be right about some things."

"I suppose that's a possibility."

A bell jingled as Watson entered the place. To the left were two tables and chairs and an espresso bar. Three computer stations lined the east wall, and a large open doorway led to a side room with another half-dozen computers. He couldn't spot any customers.

A young Asian-American man, about twenty, straddled a tall stool at the counter, glued to a monitor and keyboard. "This Siberian is sick," he mumbled.

"Excuse me?" Watson asked.

The young man looked up.

"This is quite a setup," Watson said. "I'm surprised that Livingston can support such a place."

"Yes, every once in awhile we actually have a customer."

"I need to use . . ."

"Use any machine you want. Two dollars for every fifteen minutes. Six dollars for a full hour. Or ten dollars for an hour and a tall double shot mocha and almond biscotti."

"I just need two minutes. Can I hook up my machine to one of these phone lines?"

"Sure, in the side room. Use the red phone jack at the empty station against the wall." The young man in the white T-shirt remained glued to his computer. "Never play chess with a Siberian," he advised.

Watson plopped down on the cold white plastic chair and opened up his laptop, leaving it in the black nylon carrying case. He plugged in the phone line and waited for it to boot up. A hand-scribbled yellow sticky note read, "For a good time, check out Chat Room 666. Look for Beelzebub.'"

He rapped his fingers on the tabletop. *Someone is trying to be funny. At least, I think they are trying to be funny.*

He typed in his server code, and when the Internet came on, he slipped the diskette into the computer. The second the diskette engaged, his screen turned crimson red.

"What is this?" he mumbled.

A picture of a mule's rear end appeared, and the computer started making a grinding noise.

"What's going on?" P.J. shouted. "What is this!"

The red screen resurfaced, and the computer began a horrible screeching sound like a choir of fingernails on chalkboards. "What's happening?"

The Asian-American young man sprinted into the room. "You got a virus, man! Yank it . . ."

"What?"

The man grabbed the phone line and pulled it out of the laptop.

"A virus?" P.J. mumbled. He pointed to the red screen. "But it's still doin' something."

"It's eating your memory, man! It's the floppy. Get that floppy out of there."

The man hit the eject button but jerked his hand back. "It's melting!" he hollered. "What did you shove in there? Your computer's toast, man. I'm glad you didn't use one of mine."

"What can I do?" Watson yelled.

"Buy a new computer."

"What? This can't be happening to me."

"You've lost everything on that computer, dude."

"My book! My manuscript!"

"You wrote a book?"

"It's in there!" P.J. moaned.

"You got a backup, don't you?"

P.J. reached into the black nylon case and yanked out a diskette. "It's hot too!"

"Get away from your computer!" The man tugged on his arm. "It's radiating something."

"Radiating? What do you mean radiating?"

"Like, radioactive, dude. Get back!"

Watson jumped back and watched his laptop smoke. "What . . . what . . ."

"Man, where did you get that floppy? Chernobyl? Let me see the backup. Let's make sure you still have it."

"It can't have a virus. It wasn't hooked up."

"I'll test it for you in that machine down at the end. It's a solo machine, too old to network with the others. I won't mind replacing it. Isn't the aroma of fried computer lovely?"

"I . . . I can't believe this," Paul James Watson moaned.

"I'll try it here," the man said. "It won't come up."

"It what?"

"It won't open — file errors. Whoa, are you sure this is your backup?"

"Of course I'm sure. I've been using it to back things up for a month."

"Well, it distorted from the heat, I suppose. I hate to be the one to tell you, but this disk is useless. You'll never retrieve this."

Once, when Paul James Watson was five years old, he fell out of the back of his father's moving pickup and bounced down the gravel road for three hundred feet. He was in the hospital for eleven days, and it took several months for him to regain his strength. He was sure every square inch of his body was severely bruised. But never in that time of extreme pain did he feel as bad as he did at this very moment.

He stared at the black computer screen. "Are you telling me my book is gone? That 450 pages of *Diamond Dandy Disaster* is destroyed? That months of work is lost forever?"

The Asian-American man shrugged. "No, man, I'm just telling you your computer is trashed, and this diskette is empty."

chapter thirteen

At eleven years old, Paul James Watson vacationed at his grandparents' house located along the Pacific coast, near Carpenteria, California. He hiked out by himself in the misty fog early one morning to the rocks at low tide to check the marine life stranded in the tide pools. After fifteen minutes of wonderful discoveries, he climbed the rocky cliff to watch the waves come back. His flip-flops caught on a jagged rock. He tumbled down a fifteen-foot cliff, landing in the packed wet sand and rocks below.

Later he calculated that he must have been unconscious for fifteen to twenty minutes. He surmised that the cold, salty tide had revived him. Somehow he staggered up to his grandparents' house. He climbed all seventy-two steps from the sand to their house on top of the cypress-crested cliff. All young Paul knew was that when he awoke the next morning in his bed in their guestroom, he had a splitting headache, was short of breath, and had no knowledge of how he got there.

He now experienced a similar feeling.

Watson staggered back out onto the Livingston, Montana, sidewalk. For a moment he stood by the truck, leaning his hand on the hood and holding his head with the other.

His heart raced. Then stopped. Then seemed to explode when it started beating again. Beads of sweat oozed from his forehead. His knees wobbled. He could barely stand. He struggled to the truck door and threw himself onto the seat.

Toby McKenna had turned a potato chip bag inside out, licking off the salt. "Hey, I'm gettin' my appetite back. P.J., but you don't look so good."

"Shut up, McKenna."

I don't know where I am. I don't know how I got here, and I have a headache that would make a migraine feel like a neck rub.

"A little ticked off at the Rocky Mountain Internet Café? I suppose the equipment isn't what you expected." He wadded up the potato chip sack and tossed it into the gear behind the seat. "Remember that time in *Hawaii Reins* when the stun gun didn't arrive and I had to make one out of two paper clips, a chalkboard eraser, and a hundred-foot extension cord? Sometimes you just have to improvise with the technology available to you."

"Shut up, Toby."

"Hey, where's your laptop? Get back in there and get your laptop."

"Get out, McKenna," Watson growled.

"What?"

Paul James Watson glared at the fictional detective. "I don't want you in the truck. I don't want you with me. I don't want to talk to you. Get out, or I'll throw you out."

"Throw me out? You're a little out of shape for that."

"McKenna, with the stroke of a pen, I can have worms eating your guts out one bite at a time. I can have a meteorite strike you in the head and compress your entire body to the thickness of toilet paper. I can have you slip and fall into a cesspool behind those grain bins and drown — slowly. Now, get out of my truck!"

McKenna grabbed his brown fedora and pushed the door ajar. "P.J., are you sure you know what you are doin'?"

"I haven't known what I'm doing since you showed up in my truck at the motel this morning. My computer and backup disk were just fried in there. I have no

bar
319

book. I have worked months for nothing. Do you understand? There is no *Diamond Dandy Disaster.* No number fifty-five in the series. It was your story as well as mine, and it is gone forever. Have a nice non-life. I might see you again. Or I might not."

"What are you talking about?" McKenna closed the door. "You can't lose a whole book!"

"I just did. The computer and the backup were destroyed by sabotage. How much clearer can I be? I don't want to talk about it, and I don't want to see you again." Watson started the truck. "All I wanted out of this day was to go home with a completed manuscript. Now I have no book, and I'm still on the road with you. I just can't take this. Go away."

McKenna stepped out and closed the door. "P.J.? What's the deal? Too much stress, partner. You need to relax more. I think you really may have lost it this time."

"Yeah, I lost it all right!" Watson hollered as he pulled onto the street and headed west. "I lost it, and I'm not going to get it back."

With his head throbbing, Watson turned north on U.S. 89. The sign read, "Wilsall, Ringling, and White Sulphur Springs." He paralleled Shields River and stuck it on cruise control at fifty-five. His shoulders slumped. He was barely aware of the empty two-lane blacktop road.

Lord, I don't know what to do. I don't know where I am. I don't know who I am. I lost an entire book back there. Almost three months' work. One-fifth of my yearly income. I will never get the book back. It's dead. They killed my baby. They killed my baby in the womb.

No. No, that's not it. It wasn't a baby. It was a full-grown daughter. I was about to walk her down the aisle so she could have a life of her own. And they slaughtered her. In her pretty white dress and flowers in her hand, they killed her.

No one will ever read those scenes. No one will ever know those characters. Or the plot twist. Or the snappy dialogue. No one will laugh at the humor or cry at the sorrow. I can't believe it.

They murdered my book, my story, my very own creation.

An oncoming red 1956 Chevrolet pickup honked. Watson pulled back to his side of the road.

I'll kill them.

I'll kill the lady in the Impala. I'll kill Jonathan Boudary. They killed my book. They don't deserve to live.

He grabbed his chest and heaved.

He jerked the truck off the road and parked next to the river.

I can't do this anymore. I can't live this kind of life. I don't have the strength or the will to rewrite that book. I don't want to write any more books, Lord. I don't want to do anything. I just want to go to sleep and never wake up.

I don't know what to do. Do you understand, Lord? They killed it before it was ever read. How could you let this happen? I don't need a best-seller, Lord, I just need my book in print. Someone has to read it. It validates my effort. It validates my life.

He turned off the engine and lowered his seat back as far as it would go.

He leaned back and closed his eyes.

Lord, I want all this to go away. I want to wake up in a Miles City motel. I want to drive home and be with my Sheila and show her my new book. I want her to look at me and shake her head and say, "You are some writer, Paul James Watson." I don't care what the critics say. I don't need an award. I just want it alive! In print. Published. I want it to have a chance to live and see what it can accomplish in this world. Oh, Lord, I can't believe it. Why? I just can't believe it.

Watson sucked in several deep breaths.

No. You're right, Lord. I know you're right. This is different. No one lost his life. No sinner was killed before a chance to convert. No baby stolen from her home and brutally murdered. No sinless Savior dying on the cross. I know in my mind that it's not that big a deal. But somehow my heart doesn't believe my mind.

Watson beat his clenched fist against his knee as he mumbled. *Lord, if you wanted me to stop writing, you could have told me some other way. Writer's block, Lord. Writer's block lets a man quit because he's out of stories. That's the way it should be. If you have nothing to say, be quiet. But I have a dozen stories in my mind all the time. I can write until you return and not run out of stories.*

Which is the point, I suppose. Maybe this is the time you want me to stop writing.

Why did you let this book die? I just don't understand.

Watson leaned back against the seat and closed his eyes. The cab of the pickup was comfortable and the sunlight blocked when he fell asleep.

It was stuffy inside, the sun barely above the mountains in the west when he woke up.

He sat straight up and wiped sweat from his neck.

"OK, enough of this," he murmured. "Sitting here accomplishes nothing. I can go home, mope, and hide in my shop and never write another word. Or I can track down this psycho, Jonathan Boudary, and make sure *Diamond Dandy Disaster* did not die in vain. He might have killed the book, but he's ticked off Paul James Watson. That is his fatal mistake."

Watson gunned the engine. "Where's McKenna when I need him? I dumped him. Where would he go? To a café? One with friendly waitresses."

He turned the pickup around and drove south toward Livingston.

OK, there is no *book, and for the rest of the day I am not a writer. I am a man on a mission. Boudary must be stopped. And if it costs me my life, what a way to go. It beats driving my truck off a cliff because I was depressed about frying my book.*

He punched in a number on the phone.

A gruff male voice came on the line. "Yeah, what is it?"

"Lanny, why are you still at my house?"

"Who is this?"

"Mr. Watson. Did you get the plumbing fixed?"

"I fixed that hours ago."

"Then go home."

"What?"

"I said, go home. And you do not have permission to answer the phone again. Do I make myself clear?" P.J. barked.

There was a pause. Then a weak response. "Uh, yes, sir."

"Thank you. Now put Ruth Ann on the phone, please."

The voice was a puzzled giggle. "Daddy?"

"Hi, Rudi, I need you to . . ."

"What did you tell Lanny?" she asked.

Watson rolled down his window and sucked in some fresh air. "I told him to go home."

"Why? I wanted you to meet him," she whimpered.

"I won't be home for awhile, so send him home."

"He doesn't really have a home."

"What are you talking about? He has a business," Watson fumed. "He has to have a home."

"He lives in a little fifth-wheeler parked

behind the plumbing shop out on the highway behind Cecil's Like-New Transmissions. He's saving his money to buy his own shop instead of leasing one."

"Then he does have a home. Send him to the fifth-wheeler."

"Really?"

"Rudi!"

"OK," Rudi sighed. "I don't think you understand."

"You can tell me when I do get home. But don't wait up for me. I'm having a rather dramatic situation here."

Her voice softened. "What are you doing?"

"A radioactive diskette just wiped out my laptop and obliterated the book I've been writing. Now I'm headed up into the Bridger Range to find America's most wanted fugitive, Jonathan Boudary, and bring him in dead or alive. So I might be late. Or I might not make it at all."

Rudi Watson exploded with laughter. "Daddy, daddy, daddy, you are so good at creating stories. I never know when to believe you."

"You know, I have the same problem. Now don't wait up for me. Tell Pete and Jared I'm going up to Carrol Creek in the Bridger Range. They know where that is. If

I'm not home by ten o'clock in the morning, have them come look for me."

"Daddy, that isn't funny."

"No it isn't, darlin'. Just do it. I need Aunt Marty's phone number at the shop. I want to try to call your mother."

"It's 406-786-3298."

"Thanks, Rudi. I love you, and I'll see you later."

"I love you too, Daddy. Are you all right?"

"I'm doing very well, for the circumstances. Now tell Lanny he has to be out of the house in two minutes."

"Daddy!" she squealed.

"Put the plumber on."

"What?"

"I want to talk to dear ol' Lanny."

The deep voice was now hesitant. "Eh, this is Lanny."

"What are you still doing there? I think I made it plain for you to leave."

"Yes, sir. But I was just waiting to say good-bye to Rudi."

"Let me tell you a secret, son. You won't have a chance in the world of seeing my daughter again if you don't learn to mind her father. Now, if I say I want you out of the house in two minutes, I don't mean three minutes. I don't even mean two-and-a-half minutes. But if you do what I ask, I will personally invite you over for steaks after church on Sunday. Is that a deal?"

"I leave in two minutes and you invite me back?" Lanny repeated.

"No, you have to leave in one minute now, because you wasted one minute talking to me on the phone."

"Daddy?" Rudi said. "What did you tell Lanny?"

"Is he still there?"

"No, he jogged right out the front door and drove off," she whined.

"I invited him over for steaks on Sunday after church."

"You did?"

"Yep."

"Why did he run away?"

"He's in a hurry for Sunday to get here, I reckon."

"Daddy, do you like him?"

"I believe he's a quick learner. I like that."

"He has dreamy eyebrows. Did I tell you that?"

"I think you might have mentioned that. Bye, baby."

"Bye, Daddy. Have a grand adventure."

When he hung up, he punched in Marty Steerwalt's phone number.

The voice was perky, with a musical tone. "Sunshine Pottery."

"Hi, Marty, this is Paul. How's my favorite potter?"

"Oh, hi, Paul. I'm a mess right now. My hands look like they've just emerged from primal ooze. Where have you been? Sheila tried to call you."

"My phone's been off. I'm in the midst of tracking down a notorious criminal."

"Paul, Paul, Paul. Your mind is marvelous. Always working on the next book. I hear you just finished one."

"That's the rumor," he replied.

The proprietor and sole employee of Kalispell's Sunshine Pottery bantered like a fifty-year-old who refused to grow up. "Is the latest number fifty-four or fifty-five in the Distracted Detective Series?"

"Both, probably. Can I talk to Sheila, Marty?"

"She's not here, Paul." Her voice turned serious. "She's over at the foundry. When she checked with them, there was some sort of mini-crisis that needed her immediate attention."

"What kind of crisis?"

"I think the stallion in the statue came out of the mold as a . . . eh . . ."

"A gelding?"

"Something like that. She said to tell you she'd call when she got back. You are at home, aren't you?"

"No, it's a rather complicated story. Tell her to try the cell phone. If it's off, I'll call her. If I don't call her, tell her I love her and check with Pete and Jared. They will know where I'm supposed to be."

Marty's voice got a little higher. "That's all very cryptic."

"The best I can do, Marty. Tell her just the way I told you."

"Oh, I know, Paul. You don't want to give away the ending."

"Marty, I don't even know how it ends," he sighed.

"That's what Sheila tells me. It's so amazing. You have an incredible mind."

"There is a short distance between incredible and extremely confused, Marty. But thanks anyway."

The sun hung no more than a thumb-width above the mountains when he pulled into Livingston. Pickups and a few SUVs lined the streets. He cruised past several cafés and finally halted in front of one called Lydia's Lounge & Grill.

The red Naugahyde-padded front door had a small diamond-shaped window and swung easily into the smoky interior. It was dark inside, but he recognized the back of a brown fedora and the broad shoulders of a man in a black golf shirt.

Watson scooted a chair next to Toby McKenna, then straddled it. "I've been looking for you."

McKenna dove a greasy curly fry through a pool of thin red ketchup, then shoved it into his mouth. "Well, if it isn't ol' dump-your-best-friend-and-drive-off Watson!" he mumbled.

A redheaded waitress, past her prime but pleasant looking, strutted over to the table. "Is this the pond scum you told me about, Toby, sweetie? The slimeball that turned on you and drove off?"

McKenna cleared his throat. "Actually, he's a jerk at times but not exactly a slimeball."

She reached over and held McKenna's hand. "Those were your exact words, darlin'. I think you called him a 'mealy-headed, gutless wonder of slimeball, a paperback writer no better than pond scum'."

"Did I say all that?" McKenna gulped.

She patted his hand. "Yes, you did."

Paul James Watson burst out laughing. "McKenna, it's lucky for me I never let you curse, or you would have said things a whole lot worse. I needed to get away and think things through. I don't share grief well. Sorry about that, partner. I wasn't thinking straight and deserve every word of it."

"Partner?" McKenna plopped a bread-and-butter pickle on his tongue like it was a pill, then swallowed it without chewing. He winked at the waitress. "I hate those pickles." Then he turned to Watson. "So you need ol' Toby now, do you?"

"I need you, Tobias McKenna. We have some detective work to do."

"Wow, are you a world-famous detective like my sweet Toby?" the waitress asked.

Watson studied the way she bounced when she mentioned McKenna's name. "No, darlin', I'm afraid Toby is the famous one. No one's heard of me."

She leaned over the counter.

He could smell the lilac perfume. "That's OK, honey. I'm a nobody too. Except . . . ," she stood up and winked. "Except maybe at the Nighthawk Saloon. But don't believe what the boys at the Nighthawk say about me. It's only mostly true."

He studied her name tag. "I imagine the boys at the Nighthawk fight over Miss Nadine."

She grinned and revealed two sweet dimples and cigarette-stained teeth. "I've been known to turn a few heads."

"That's nice perfume."

"Thank you. Some men never seem to notice," she glanced at Toby. "It's called Midnight Desperado. Lynda Dawn, that's a friend of mine who lives out on a ranch west of here, told me about it. She said it was the best October perfume made."

"P.J.'s a happily married man," McKenna mumbled.

Watson shook his head. "Toby, that's the first time I've ever made you jealous. Look, partner, I'm sorry I overreacted. I just didn't know how to handle losing a whole book. I've lost chapters from time to time but not an entire manuscript."

"You can rewrite it, can't you, P.J.?"

"Oh, in theory, I can rewrite it. But it will be different, and many of the lines I liked so well are gone forever. It's not a matter of rewriting; it's a matter of having the heart to do it. Lose a chapter or a book and something dies inside of you. It's a period of grief. I don't want to talk about it. I don't want to think about it for awhile. Don't mention the book, the computer, or any of that for awhile."

McKenna glanced down at his feet. "You

got it, partner." Then he looked back up. "Now what's this about needin' me?"

Watson leaned closer and lowered his voice. "We're going to take on Jonathan Boudary face-to-face."

"We are?" McKenna whistled. "Ain't that like takin' on ol' Hannibal when he's in a hungry mood?"

"We'll stop Boudary, Toby. Now how much is your supper? I'll pay since you didn't have any money anyway. I'm surprised you felt like eating."

"Yeah, I reckon I recover fast. Nadine was buyin' my supper."

"Well, kiss Nadine good-bye and come on. We have to get to Carrol Creek before the sun goes down."

Watson paid the tab and waited at the door. A grinnin' Toby McKenna strolled over, carrying a large brown paper sack.

"I was teasin' you about the kiss, Toby."

"Nadine wasn't. What a sweet lady. She wanted to give me a little something to remember her by," he explained.

"I can see that. That's a generous doggie bag," Watson said.

"Oh, this? Well, it's actually . . . I mean . . . well . . ."

"Don't tell me what she gave you. I don't want to know what's in the sack."

"Oh, OK," McKenna sighed.

One block to the east, Watson pulled into an empty parking lot.

"Pizza?" Toby asked. "Are you hungry?"

"I promised a little boy a pizza."

"What if we don't hook up with them?"

"Then we have breakfast taken care of."

The aroma of a family-size, thin-crust, Italian-sausage-with-double-cheese pizza filled the cab as they drove out of town on U.S. 89. The afternoon shadows stretched long to the east. When they dropped behind the hills, the sun disappeared.

McKenna reached into the glove compartment and pulled out the fingernail clippers. "What's the plan, P.J.?"

"We'll drive toward Carrol Creek and wait for Nicole's call."

McKenna clipped his nails. "What if she doesn't call?"

"That means either she's safe or dead. But she will call."

"Do you really think this guy, Boudary, will show up looking for her?"

"Yep. She's got the data and records from Bunker 24. He'll be frantic to get them back. And he won't want to lose her."

"You think he loves her?"

"Not the way I use the word, but he won't want to lose her on principle. He's convinced that he can do anything he wants anytime he wants. In his mind he rules the world. If she leaves him against his will, it's a stark reminder that he has limits."

McKenna used the tiny file to smooth his squared-off fingernails. "Does anyone know what this dude really looks like?"

Watson shook his head. "No."

"That might be a good question to ask her. I'd kind of like to know him when I see him."

"You're right. Be thinking of other questions to ask her."

McKenna leaned back in the truck seat and tugged his fedora down in front.

P.J. stared at the Shields River and the spot where he had slept earlier.

I don't understand it, Lord. A couple of hours ago I was parked over there, wishing I could shoot myself. And now I'm driving north, anxious to tackle America's most wanted. I'm not sure what happened, except you gave me the strength to find control. I've been jumping through other people's hoops for so long, I lost all sight of my own life. No more. Whether my years be short or long,

I must do the things I'll regret not doing.

And right now, catching Jonathan Boudary is what must be done.

When he destroyed a paperback writer's book, he had no idea what he stirred up. He would have been better off dropping a bomb on the Statue of Liberty.

Beware the wrath of a writer deleted!

I've been living my life through others for so long I think I forgot how to be me. It's sort of like waking up from a coma, Lord. Now I'm alive again. I don't know how long I'll have before I slip into that coma again, so I'm going to live every last minute to the fullest. Help me do the important things.

"Is this a town? What is this place called?" McKenna asked.

"Clyde Park."

"It looks like a small convention of single-wides," McKenna muttered. "Where is Carrol Creek?"

"We go up past Wilsall and turn west on Flathead Creek Road. We'll drop down on Highway 86, past Sedan, then turn right on Seitz Road. The boys and I used to fish up on Carrol Creek, Fairy Creek, and Cache Creek."

"Are we gonna need guns?" Toby asked.

"We don't have a thing. We'll just have to overpower him with our wits."

"He's outwitted the FBI for twenty years. What do we have that they don't?"

"The reckless courage of Toby McKenna and the incredible creativity of Paul James Watson."

"You could always stop and write a scene with me carryin' a gun."

"That's a scary thought."

"What are you talkin' about? You have me with a gun in all the books."

"Yes, and I'm not in all the books. Well, not directly, anyway."

"Do you have a voice-mail hookup with this cell phone?"

"You mean like an answering-machine service? Maybe. I don't know. I never use it. It's a fairly new phone. Rudi gave it to me for Christmas last year."

"Since you are expecting a call from Nicole and the phone has been off awhile, perhaps it would be a good time to try to find the voice mail," McKenna suggested.

"I don't have any idea how to find it, if it's there," Watson admitted.

Toby studied the control face of the dash-mounted cell phone. "Why don't I push this *retrieve* button?"

"It has a retrieve button?" Watson gasped.

McKenna pressed it. After a moment of silence and buzzing, a lady's voice purred. "Hi, Paulie! Hurry home, baby. I want you to unwrap your Valentine's present. I didn't know your new phone had voice mail. Hugs and naughty kisses, sweetie."

"Whoa," McKenna gasped. "Was that Sheila?"

"What's that doing on there?"

"Well, Paulie, if you'd ever check your voice mail, you'd know. You didn't miss out on the Valentine's present, did you?"

"Eh, no." Watson blushed. "I didn't know I had a voice mail."

"Obviously," McKenna grinned, then pushed the button again.

"Paul? Stan Blocker, here. Listen, can you make the Planning and Zoning Meeting on August 12? I'll be in Switzerland on business. Thanks, partner."

"Did you make that meeting?" McKenna asked.

"Yeah, Stan left a message on the home machine too."

McKenna pressed *retrieve* again.

This time it was a garbled voice of a man in a crowd. "Yo! P.J., hang on, pal. Just a minute. 'What? Salt Lake City?

Whatever.' Eh, look, Paul, the FAA has closed down all the airports in Montana. Some kind of wacko bomb threat. Which makes me think he's really up there. If Boudary is on the move, maybe he's instigating all this. Anyway, it's a lot more critical than I thought. I'm at LAX and am going to fly to Salt Lake, it looks like. If things are still shut down, I'll rent a rig and be at your place as quick as I can. Don't try anything until I get there. This guy is a fruitcake, and today he seems to be carrying bombs."

"Are you gonna wait for Revelage?" Toby asked.

"No, that would jeopardize Nicole and little Duke. We'll do what we can without Theodore Revelage. I figure no one can stand against McKenna and Watson."

"Top billing, huh?"

"You deserve it."

"There's one more message." McKenna hit the button again.

"Hi, Paul. What did you say to my husband? He came into the reception room bragging about how his wife is going for a doctorate at Columbia. He's beaming and charming. I owe you, Paul James Watson. If you were here, I'd hug you and kiss you. Call me when you can. You are a prince. Does your wife know how lucky she is?"

"Hmmmm," McKenna pondered. "The sensitive, kind, helpful Paul James Watson has the cutest babe in New York drooling over him."

"Spunky is not drooling over me."

"Well, she can drool over me if she wants to," McKenna chuckled.

Watson slowed the truck and signaled left.

"What is this place?"

"Wilsall."

"It's not much different from Clyde Park."

"You were expecting West Palm Beach?"

When the phone rang, Watson pulled off to the side of the narrow, two-lane blacktop road.

"Yes?"

"Paul, it's Nicole. Are you all right? You haven't seen him, have you?"

"I'm fine. Haven't see him. How are you and little Duke?"

"He's asleep. Did you hear about the wreck?"

"Yes, we parked at the wreck site awhile."

"We?" she asked.

"I have Toby McKenna with me. He's like . . ."

"I know who he is, Paul. Remember, I

do know what's going on."

"I know you do."

"Were there any fatalities?"

"MSP reported one person died," Watson said. "They couldn't identify the person yet."

"A man or a child?" she asked.

"They said they really couldn't tell. There was only one."

"Thank goodness. That's horrible to say. But if he had wrecked the rig, there would have been two bodies. It's all a ruse."

"Are you saying he wrecked the Hummer and killed someone in it just to throw them off his track?"

"It wouldn't be the first time. You watch. The dental records will match his. But you just wait. He's still alive."

"If that's the case, then we'll need my plan. Where are you right now?"

"Bozeman, in the parking lot next to Applebee's. I'm using their pay phone."

"Do you know how to get to Carrol Creek from there?"

"I think so. North on Highway 86 until Seitz Road?"

"Yes, but don't go east on Brackett Creek Road. Hang a left and stay on 86," he said.

"Then what?"

"I want to confront him straight on, Nicole."

The laugh was more like a yell. "That's your plan?"

"I'm going to be the bait. When he comes after me, he'll have to leave your daughter. You grab both kids and hop in my truck and take off west into the mountains."

"I thought the road dead-ends up there."

"You'll need the high center and four-wheel drive of the pickup, but keep going. It will take you right over the Bridger Range and Colby Gulch Road, leading you to Bridgeport. He might try to follow, but he won't make it on that road. Besides, I don't plan on letting him win."

"What will you do?"

"Beat him to a pulp, then tie him up and haul him to the sheriff. I'll use your Impala, then meet up with you at my house in Bridgeport."

"It's a crazy plan. You know he will kill you if he gets a chance."

"I know, Nicole."

"Why are you doing this?"

"Because it's the right thing to do. Good has to triumph over evil."

"Who told you that?"

"Jesus." He paused a moment. "I'm the

one in the position to do it."

"But we are . . . I mean, this is only a . . ."

"It's real to me, Nicole. Is it real to you?"

"Oh, yes! And my real name is Dana. I don't think there is anyone alive who knows that, except you and him."

"And your niece."

"You know Kymee?"

"Yes, I do. I'll see you at the campground at Carrol Creek. Let's hope we get there before he does. What will he be driving?"

"If his Hummer is gone, he'll have an old green Volkswagen bus, I suppose."

"Good. There is no way to catch you in the mountains with a VW bus."

"I thought you were going to see that he didn't follow."

"You're right. He could have a helicopter, and I'd still capture him."

"He does have a helicopter," she murmured.

"Doesn't matter. He's not going anywhere. Now, I'll see you at Carrol Creek."

"I can't believe you are doing this for me. No one has stood up for me in years. Are you for real, Paul James Watson?"

"That's an interesting question. I'm glad I can answer it. Yes, Dana, I am for real."

chapter fourteen

Toby McKenna grinned ear to ear as they pulled back onto Highway 86, headed west. The evening shadows made his white teeth contrast dramatically with his thick bushy mustache.

"What?" Watson questioned.

McKenna twirled his fedora in hand and shook his head. "I didn't say anything."

P.J. stared straight ahead at the mountain range. "You were thinking it."

McKenna leaned back in the seat. "I just hadn't realized how smooth Paul James Watson was with the ladies. My oh my, he could teach Cary Grant a lesson in charm."

"Smooth? Charm? Dream on. You're the ladies' man, Toby."

"I'm an amateur," Toby faked a loud sigh, "sitting at the feet of the master."

"That's absurd."

"Spunky purred over you. Dana's pinin'

over you. It comes natural to you. You need to school me better, P.J. What's your secret?"

"No one ever asked me that before."

"I'm askin'."

Watson rapped his fingers on the steering wheel as he continued to drive west. "OK, sort of a father-to-son lecture. When you are visiting with a lady, listen to more than her words. Seventy-five percent of what a woman wants to say is never put into words. Listen to her heart, her tone. Pay attention to her posture. Study her eyes. Don't ever take her literal words as the whole story. It never is."

McKenna sat up and slapped his knee. "Whoa, I should be takin' notes."

"You asked, partner. I can stop, or do you want more?"

"No, go on, what else?" McKenna prodded.

"OK, Watson's second tenet: treat every lady nicer than she thinks she deserves — politer, kinder, more encouraging than she expects."

"You mean manners?"

"I mean manners, behavior, tone, actions, what you say about her to others when she isn't around."

"And just how do I know what she

thinks she deserves?"

"That was tenet number one, re-member?"

"All right, is there more?"

"Don't demand anything from her, and don't expect anything in return for your behavior. Give her the freedom to do whatever she wants. Just enjoy the friendship. Let her see you aren't after anything."

"You are nailin' me with that one, aren't you? Dadgumit, P.J., I feel like a fifteen-year-old kid just gettin' his first lesson out behind the woodshed."

Watson began to laugh. "It's not your fault, Toby. I created you much too shallow and stereotyped. Maybe that's why *Diamond Dandy Disaster* was lost. I'm going to rewrite it with more depth of character. You'll have inner turmoil and struggles."

"Don't go overboard, P.J. That doesn't sound all that fun."

"You have to come to grips with some important things, Toby — God, marriage, a purpose for your life."

McKenna rolled his window down and sailed his hand in the breeze. "All in one book?"

"No, maybe not," Watson grinned. "But you are going to get started. I'm anxious to get going on it. Soon as I get home, I'll hide out in the shop and flesh out the new plot."

"Something's got into you, P.J. You came back from that tizzy about losin' your book, and, well, there's a confidence I've just not seen before."

"You're dreaming, McKenna."

"Nope. Hey, P.J., did you know that fictional characters don't dream? I mean, I can dream if you write me into a scene where I dream, but that's not really my dream but your dream. I wonder what it would be like to have my own dreams? I know dreams aren't real, but then . . . so what, right? Did you ever ponder that real people spend some of every night in a fictional world? Hmmm. Did you know that even though I'm a fictional character, women dream about me? Is that cool or what? Too bad I can't actually be there in their dreams . . . on second thought, maybe it's best that I can't. You know what I mean?"

"No, I probably don't. But I do know that you're doin' a lot more pondering. That's good." He glanced over at McKenna. "What happened to your knuckles?"

Toby examined his hands. "What?"

Watson nodded his way. "On your right hand, your knuckles look skinned up."

"Oh," McKenna rubbed his hands. "I was a little ticked off when you drove off and left me, so I punched the Plexiglas on the phone booth."

"I hope you didn't break anything."

"No, my fingers are fine, or did you mean break the Plexiglas?"

"Both. Toby, I am sorry about driving off like that. I got an inflated idea about my writing. I needed to back up and see it from the Lord's point of view. I'm a paperback writer, Toby. I'm not a world-famous novelist. Not a Pulitzer Prize-winning author. I'm a paperback writer, just like in the old Beatles song. But I'm good at it. And it's my place that the Lord has provided.

"They don't study my novels in English lit. classes at Stanford. But there's a single mom, struggling to make ends meet working as a clerk-typist in the admissions office, who tucks those preschoolers in late Friday night in that one-bedroom apartment #421 on 16th Street in Palo Alto, and then curls up on the faded pea-green sofa she inherited from her granny, pulls a tattered afghan over her feet, and reads my book until she falls asleep about three in the morning. And for five straight hours, she isn't worried about car payments, or alimony checks that never arrive, or little sissy constantly getting sick at day care, or the jerk at the office who brushed up against her backside in the elevator, or her mother's comments about her marriage failure, or the fact that she's gained six pounds since Christmas. For those few hours it's just her and Toby McKenna, having one incredible adventure after another.

"She will fall asleep with a sweet dream of a dashing, though distracted, detective. She'll wake up in the real world, but for a few hours, Toby, we gave her mind and body and soul a break. She got to live in your world. And because of that, she'll tackle the new day with just a little more strength, courage, direction, and, I hope, more faith.

"Oh, the critics don't think much of my books. But the critics don't have to carry a three-year-old up two flights of steps every evening at 5:45 and twice on Sundays.

"That's it, partner."

"That's you and me."

"A paperback hero and a paperback writer."

"You make it sound almost noble," McKenna said.

"My books aren't gilded carriages, Toby. Not vehicles made for the rich and famous. They are wheelbarrows. Utilitarian. Lots of folks have to go though life never riding in a gilded carriage, but sooner or later they will all need the services of a wheelbarrow."

"P.J., remember that horse-drawn carriage in *High Tea, Low Life*? The lady in the white chiffon dress had a Kalashnikov under her flowin' skirt."

"Which you were clever enough to discover."

"I have a trained eye for that kind of thing," McKenna added.

"I believe I will train your eyes on higher goals in the next book," Watson said.

"So you aren't quittin' the series?"

"No, but it might take awhile to get it written. I think I'll start from scratch." Watson pulled off his sunglasses and jammed them in the center console of the truck.

"Say, about your computer . . ."

"I don't want to talk about it, Toby." P.J. pulled out a pair of gold-rimmed regular glasses and shoved them on his nose. "I'm doing real well as long as I don't think about it too much."

Toby threw up his hands. "Sorry."

The sun dropped below the Bridger Range when Highway 86 turned due south. They breezed through Sedan, which contained little more than its namesake. The old blacktop on Seitz Road crumbled to gravel about a half-mile after they turned west. It was washboard gravel by the time they reached the picnic table at the Carrol Creek bridge. A green Impala was parked among the cottonwoods.

McKenna's window was already down. "Do you see anyone else? Is Boudary here yet?"

Paul James Watson strained to survey the brush as if looking for a Boone and Crockett buck on the first day of hunting season. "I don't even see Dana and Duke." He parked the truck and continued to look for movement.

"What happens now, P.J.? Have you lived this scene out already in your mind?"

"No, I'm trying to quit doing that. It doubles my stress. Going though it once is enough. I wonder where they are?"

Toby leaned over and mashed on the horn.

Watson pushed his hand away. "What are you doing?"

"Finding them. There they are." Toby pointed to a woman and boy hiking out from behind a battered outhouse.

Watson left his door open and his keys partway in the ignition, far enough out to silence the warning buzzer. "What if Jonathan Boudary had been here?"

Toby McKenna pushed open the other door. "Then we'll take him on, face-to-face. Isn't that what you said?"

"I hoped to plan a little strategy first."

"I tried strategy once," Toby said as he walked around to the front of the pickup. "Remember in *Last Digit to Go*, I concocted that intricate plan to catch the murderer? Then the teenage girl hit me in the back of the head with a baseball bat, and I woke up the prime suspect in a double slaying. I've never trusted strategy since that day."

"Amber was eleven," Watson reported.

"Oh, yeah, well, she hit hard for bein' eleven. I'll bet she's a teenager now."

"She's twenty and studying criminal law at the University of Texas."

The boy ran toward them. "Hi, Mr. Paul James Watson!"

Paul Watson squatted down on his haunches. "Hi, Duke."

"Who's he?"

"That's none other than the famous detective Toby McKenna."

Duke stopped right next to Watson. "I never heard of him."

Toby strolled over to them. "And that's the way I like it, son. Low profile. Just slip in and solve the crime and slip out without bringin' lightnin' down on my head, do you know what I mean? I shun notoriety, just like P.J. shuns gigantic book sales."

"He's funny!" Duke grinned. He put his arm around P.J.'s shoulder. "Hey, guess what? I know my mama's real name."

P.J. glanced at the lady in the green sweatshirt and jeans who approached them.

"Can you guess?" the boy challenged.

"How about a very pretty name like Dana Rose Kelly?"

"Wow, that's a very good guess. Can you guess my name?"

"Do you know your real name?" Watson asked.

"Yes," the boy nodded.

"Eh . . ." Watson rubbed his chin. "Ronald Reagan?"

"No," Duke protested. "But my mama rode his horses one time."

McKenna glanced over at Dana. "Really?"

"It's a rather long and tedious story. Reagan wasn't president then. Just governor. I was a little girl."

"My real name is Duke!" the boy blurted out. "Mama said you had guessed it. And my sister is really Diana. Isn't that nice? Dana, Duke, and Diana."

Watson glanced up at Dana. "Good choices."

"Did you bring me a pizza?" Duke asked.

"It's in the truck. I had to get one with extra cheese; I hope that's all right. Toby, help Duke tote the pizza over here. Mama might want a piece too."

As the two headed to the truck, P.J. sidled up to the woman. "How are you doing, Dana?"

"I'm scared to death. But I've been scared for years. I'm tired of it, Paul. I want my children and a chance to run away."

"The keys are in the truck. At the first opportunity, grab your daughter, shove Duke in the truck, and head straight into those mountains. You'll need the four-wheel drive up on top, and watch for the boulders, but you can make it. Don't stop until you get to my house. You know the address."

"What do I do then?"

"Theo Revelage will be there. He'll take care of you."

"Are you really going to offer yourself as bait?"

"I told you I would. Toby will help you get away, then come back. We'll take Boudary on."

"You don't have a chance. The entire FBI can't stop him. How are you going to do it?" she challenged.

"He's never faced the team of a paperback writer and a paperback hero. They are almost indestructible."

She took his arm. "Paul, he will kill you if he can. Why are you doing this? You know I have to let you try it. It might well be my only chance."

"I guess I'm doing it because I need the practice."

"Practice?" she questioned.

"Practice standing up for what is right, even if no one stands with you. Evil has to be opposed wherever we find it. Not just evil in general but the evil one. And I've never known anyone more evil than Boudary. In real life, I don't get many chances to do something like this. So I reckon I'm kind of like Gary Cooper in *High Noon*."

"Cooper had Grace Kelly . . . and you?" Dana challenged.

"I've got Toby McKenna. He isn't nearly

as pretty as Grace, but he can brawl like a bobcat."

"That won't help much. Boudary's not a brawler. He's a sniper at a thousand yards, or he'll tie you to a tree and shove your mouth full of dynamite, or just roll a coffee can full of plastic explosives under your truck. There won't be enough left of you to find a DNA sample. And he doesn't stop there. He'll go after your family, your parents, and your first-grade schoolteacher. Do you still want to go on with it?"

"I'm committed, Dana. It's too late now to back out of it, don't you think? You told him I was the one following you."

"Yes, and I'm sorry for that. He's psychotic and brilliant. He has never changed his mind about killing anyone. Everyone he has ever thought about killing is dead. Think about that, Paul. And now he's thinking about killing me and Duke."

Watson glanced back at Duke and McKenna eating pizza on the tailgate of the truck. "And me. If we stay back in those trees, it will eliminate the sniper shot."

"It's getting dark, but he has infrared night scopes," she cautioned.

"Does he think I will be here?" Watson asked.

"I don't know."

"What if Toby and I stay out of sight until he arrives? We drive up, divert his attention, and you hop in my truck with the kids."

She bit her lower lip. Her voice drained of emotion. "He has no reason not to shoot me and Duke when he first drives up."

"Then you two hide. Hide in the trees, behind the boulders, somewhere. He would expect you to hide if someone were following you, right?"

"Yes, I suppose so."

"Hide in the trunk. All you need is to slow him down until I drive up. He will want to kill me more than he wants to kill you. I'll chase him into the trees, or he'll chase me into the trees. Either way, you'll have a second or two to grab Diana and Duke and head up into the mountains."

She folded her arms across her chest and sighed. "Are you sure we can make it over the ridge?"

"Trust me, Dana."

"I've had men tell me that since I was fourteen. Why is it you're the only one I've believed?"

"Because at this minute you're desperate to believe me."

"Maybe. Maybe that's all it is. I think we'd better hide now."

Watson hiked with her over to the pickup. "You were supposed to save some of that for Mama. Listen, Duke, I need you and her to hide in the secret trunk of your car."

Duke wiped tomato sauce on his sleeve. "Why? We're waiting for Daddy."

"He might be upset with you for not being at Bunker 24. It would be best to lay low and see what his mood is, don't you think?"

Duke curled his lower lip. "He better not hit Mama again."

"We won't let him do that, will we?"

"No. Can we take the pizza?"

"Of course." He glanced at the distracted detective, who rolled up an entire slice of pizza, then ate it in two bites. "Toby, hike out to the road and see if you can see a rig headed this way."

Watson helped the boy box up the remaining pizza. "Remember to save your mama a couple pieces."

"What if I'm still hungry? Do you have any other food?"

"Toby got a doggie bag at the café. Grab

that brown paper bag."

The boy struggled with the sack. "It's heavy."

"Good, then you won't be hungry."

Watson had Dana and Duke hidden behind the seat in the green Impala by the time Toby returned. "No one coming," he reported. "Are they tucked away?"

"Yep. Let's go up to the road and see if we can find a place to wait for Boudary to show."

"Did you ever try to eat pizza in the dark?" a young muffled voice called out.

McKenna strolled to the trunk. "One time in *Cairo Customs Charade* I stumbled across triplets in a dark closet. They were tryin' to feed me grapes and . . ."

"Toby!" P.J. interrupted. "Get in the truck."

The two men ambled to the gold truck, one shaking his head, the other grinning.

Toby slammed his door first. "Whatever happened to . . ."

"One is married to the Egyptian minister of finance. The second lives in Geneva and is married to a Swiss banker. The third worked in New York for a Mideast financial consulting firm and died on the ninety-first floor of the south tower of the World Trade Center when it went down on September 11."

"Ah, P.J., why do you make up tragedies? Why couldn't she be terribly happy and working as a cabaret singer in Athens?"

"Because no one is happy being a cabaret singer in Athens."

P.J. backed the truck toward the gravel road.

"So it's just hide in the bushes and wait?" Toby added.

"Basically, yes."

"Do you think he will show?"

"Toby, I'm not even sure there is a Jonathan Boudary. I have no idea what is going to happen next. I haven't gotten it planned out."

"It's scary to be in a story when even the writer doesn't know what is goin' on."

"You should be used to it."

It was almost dark when Watson hid the truck behind a thicket of wild apple trees that had sprouted along the roadside.

"I wish I had a gun," Toby mumbled.

"You said that before."

"I wish it more now."

"I'm just hoping he shows up while I still have the nerve."

"Remember that time in *Mexicali Melee* when I had to lay in the attic above the bakery and wait for those twin gals with long black hair who were drug runners?"

"You are daydreaming in multiple siblings today. I believe their names were Juana and Julia."

"Yeah, I never did learn how to tell them apart."

"Good."

"Anyway, I remember I fell asleep durin' that wait, and you gave me some nice dreams that time."

P.J.'s elbow rested on the windowsill, his chin on his hand. "If I recall, you dreamed about being a young boy."

"I was fishin' on a lake with my grandfather, and there was a soft summer breeze, and we were catchin' one rainbow trout after another. And we had a big bag of M&Ms. And we were drinkin' grape sodas from long-neck bottles. Grandma was back at the cabin fryin' chicken. It was June 22, wasn't it? Because grandma was complainin' about it being the longest day of the year."

"I'm surprised you remember all that. That book has been out of print for ten years."

"I don't have many memories of childhood, P.J. It's not crowded. Is that sort of what heaven will be like?"

"I don't know what it will look like,

Toby, but I'm guessing the peace and joy and deep satisfaction of that dream is a hint of how we will feel in heaven. I do know that it is Jesus' home, and we will feel at home there."

McKenna was silent for a moment. His voice softened. "Remember what you said this mornin'?"

"About what?"

"That maybe you ought to create a fictional heaven so I'd have a place to go."

Watson grinned. "I do remember that I mentioned creating two places."

"Why don't you write it so I make good choices and end up in heaven?"

"I can do that. Of course, it just takes one good choice."

"You're talking about Jesus?"

"Yep."

"I've been ponderin' that too," McKenna murmured.

Watson kept his eyes focused on Seitz Road and where it turned off from Highway 86 in the east. He spotted the headlights of several rigs, but none of them coming his way.

I wonder how long we should wait here before we decide he won't show. He's got to show up. Dana and Duke are gone, and so are some of the incriminating computer files and records. But he doesn't know it's fried. He has to show up. Unless it turns out he was in the Hummer wreck.

Lord, it's like every moment I wait, I get a little more unsure of things. Of course, it might help if I weren't so sleepy.

"You still ponderin', partner?" Watson asked.

He waited.

Then he reached over to McKenna's shoulder. "Wake up! That's a little too distracted."

"Oh, man," Toby mumbled. "I must have dozed off. It's pitch dark now."

"Look. That rig is slowing down at Seitz Road. Maybe . . ."

"He turned east."

"Hmmm. OK, stakeout duty isn't all that exciting," Watson admitted.

"It was exciting that time in *Tragedy in Toledo* when I was hidin' in the neighbor's apartment watchin' for the counterfeiter to come home. The neighbors turned out to be those four flight attendants who thought I looked a lot like Tom Selleck."

"They weren't quadruplets, were they?" P.J. chided.

"No, but if you squinted, they sort of

looked alike, except for the color of their hair and their height."

Watson brushed his hair off the top of his ear. *I need a haircut.* "If the dog hadn't barked, you would have missed catching that counterfeiter." *I'll get one next week, provided there is a next week.*

"Are you really gonna write me a dog in the next book?" Toby blurted out.

"I think so."

"Now that gives me somethin' else to ponder."

For several moments nothing was said. Every time Paul James Watson blinked his eyes open, there were no cars headed their way.

"Hey, partner, here comes someone!" Toby called out.

Watson flinched when McKenna's hand grabbed his shoulder.

"You must have been the one sleepin'."

"Just had my eyes closed, that's all," Watson explained. He put his hand to the key, but didn't start the engine.

Both men rolled up their windows.

"What's the plan?" Toby asked.

"Separate the jerk from little Diana, then draw him off toward those cedars. Get him to follow us into the trees."

"Then what?" Toby asked.

"We overpower him with our superior intellect and brute strength," Watson proposed.

McKenna focused on the oncoming headlights. "I hear he's a genius."

"Then we have to rely on good old brute force," Watson said.

"It's a Volkswagen bus all right."

"Are you sure?" Watson pressed.

"Remember *Texas City Tornado*? I had to drive a VW bus in that entire book. I can tell by how narrow and low the headlights are."

Watson watched as the rig pulled in toward the picnic table. As soon as it turned away from the road, he started the pickup. The headlights automatically came on. The three-hundred-horsepower engine spun gravel as he lunged out from behind the brush. They sped right at the VW bus that was parked near the creek, far south of the Impala.

"He's getting out!" Toby shouted.

"What does he have on his shoulder?" Watson asked.

"A rocket launcher."

"You got to be kidding me. He can't do that!"

The blaze from the launched rocket caused Watson to stomp on the brakes.

The pickup slid to a halt just as a fireball exploded the green Chevy Impala.

"He blew them up!" Toby shouted. "He blew up little Duke and his mama!"

"No! No!" Watson screamed. "He can't do that! I'm the writer. He can't do that. That's not in the story."

"Step on it, P.J. He's turnin' it toward us," McKenna blustered.

"But, but handheld rocket launchers only hold one rocket. It's not a lever-action Winchester."

"Don't tell him that!" McKenna shouted. "Jump, P.J., jump!"

"No! No! This isn't right. This is wrong!"

With a dive across the cab, Toby McKenna shoved himself and P. J. Watson out the door. With Watson's foot off the brake, the truck rolled forward just as the rocket exploded from the launcher.

The blast and fireball from the truck surpassed that of the Impala.

P.J. felt his singed eyebrows as he rolled in the dirt beside McKenna. "No! No! No! This is wrong. This is horribly wrong! I won't accept it!"

"Get to the trees, P.J.!" McKenna shouted. "He's got an Uzi!"

"No, no, this is wrong. This isn't the way I wrote it."

"P.J., this isn't your story," McKenna screamed. "We've got to go now!"

McKenna raised to his knees and grabbed P.J.'s shoulder. "Now's the time to run, Paul James Watson. Do it for Sheila, for Rudi, for the boys, for Dana and Duke!"

The burst of automatic gunfire was simultaneous with the dull thuds and red streaks in Toby's shirt as he dropped on top of Watson.

"But Dana and Duke are dead," Watson insisted.

McKenna shook his shoulder. "No, but they will be if you don't wake up and follow that VW bus."

Through the tangled brush of the wild apple trees, Watson saw the vehicle turn into Carrol Creek picnic area. He started his truck and lunged across the dark gravel road.

"I was sleeping?" Watson mumbled.

"I'm hopin' you were planning strategy," McKenna replied. "Let's roll."

chapter fifteen

The man who leaped from the Volkswagen bus wore a camouflage slouch hat and T-shirt. A 9-mm pistol pointed at the headlights of the approaching truck.

McKenna ducked down behind the dash. "P.J., he's got a gun."

Watson stepped on the gas and lurched the truck forward. "At least it's not a rocket launcher."

McKenna peeked up. "What's that supposed to mean? What are you doing?"

Watson felt every nerve ending tense. He clenched the steering wheel. "I'm facing evil head-on, Toby McKenna. Stay down. We're taking this guy out."

The gun flared. They heard an explosion, but no glass shattered.

"Are you going to run over him?" Toby shouted.

"I hope so," Watson hollered.

The short, bearded man in camouflage

turned and sprinted toward the trees as the truck barreled after him. He fired the gun wildly over his shoulder.

"Toby, the girl should still be in the van. Get Dana and Duke and the girl and pile into the truck. You go with them," Watson ordered.

"You're crazy, P.J. What's gotten into you?"

"Do it," Watson hollered.

As the man dove into the scrub cedars and brushy cottonwoods, Paul James Watson slammed on the brakes and jumped out of the truck. "Go!"

Head-on, Lord, this time I tackle evil face-to-face. I'll draw a line in the dirt at Carrol Creek. Boudary has to be stopped. Satan will be defeated right here. Right now.

He scrambled out of the piercing light of the headlamps and rolled into the brush. He could hear McKenna shout and Dana and the children scamper behind the truck.

Maybe Boudary didn't see me slip in here.

The bullet sprayed dirt in his eyes. He rolled deeper into the brush.

OK, he knows I'm here. Now what? I can't hide. I've got to keep him coming at me, or he'll shoot them first. What would Toby McKenna do?

Watson crawled on his belly back out toward the headlights.

He can't shoot at me unless he sees me, so I'll have to make sure he sees me.

"Boudary, I'm over here. You are the most overrated weirdo in America. It doesn't take brains to slaughter innocent people with a bomb or a sniper's bullet. All it takes is moral depravity. You're a gutless psycho who doesn't have the courage of a slug."

Two more shots rang out. The bullets buzzed close to his head.

He scurried around to the edge of the brush. "Is that your best shot, Boudary? You're not only dumb, you're incompetent!"

It felt like lightning when it sliced his arm. Warm blood dripped down to his palm.

"Over here, you jerk."

The pickup spun dirt as it backed out of the campsite. In the headlights Watson saw the man in camouflage break out of the brush and dash for the truck, firing the pistol. Watson struggled to his feet. He tackled the man just as the truck hit the gravel road. Its headlights pointed west, darkening the campsite.

A warm gun barrel slammed against his head. His roundhouse right fist cracked into the man's jaw. Watson scrambled in the dark toward the cars while a shot blasted dirt behind him. His arm burned. His temple throbbed.

They got away, just like I planned. But now what?

He crouched behind the Volkswagen. The motor roared, and lights beamed. The vehicle backed toward him.

He's trying to run over me!

Knocked to his feet, Watson grabbed the back bumper and was shoved into the rocks. With his bleeding left arm, he opened the engine compartment at the back of the rig. In the dark he grabbed at wires and tried to yank on them, but his grip was too weak. He grabbed the wires with both hands just as the van lunged forward. His grip held, and the deadweight of his body yanked the wires loose.

The engine died.

The headlamps faded to darkness.

Jonathan Boudary shouted curses that raised every hair on Watson's neck.

Two gunshots preceded Boudary to the back of the van, but Paul James Watson had scampered around to the front of the rig and now circled behind him. When Boudary spun around in the Montana darkness, a softball-sized boulder smashed into his wrist, and the gun tumbled into the shadows.

Watson grabbed the man's collar with one hand, his chin with the other. He slammed Jonathan Boudary's head into the van's back window.

"What are you doing!" the man screamed as he struggled with one hand to pull free. "Don't you know who I am?"

"This is for Dana." Watson slammed Boudary's head into the glass again.

"Who?" the man hollered.

"And Duke!" Again Watson slammed Boudary's head into the side panel of the van.

"I don't even know Duke!" Boudary bellowed.

"And Diana." Paul James Watson was surprised at the strength in his injured arm as he cracked the man's head into the van again.

"Diana? I don't know Diana. Who are you?" the man pleaded.

"I'm Paul James Watson!"

Slam.

"A paperback writer."

Crash.

"And a minor celebrity."

Bang.

Boudary could hardly raise his arms to fend off Watson. "Stop, you're killing me!"

"How many have you killed, Boudary? And what about the baby? This is for the baby," Watson yelled.

This time he dented the van panel with Boudary's bleeding head.

The voice was almost inaudible. "I . . . didn't . . . kill . . . the . . . baby."

Over and over and over, Watson slammed him into the van — until America's Most Wanted lay unconscious at his feet.

"He didn't kill the baby?" P.J. gasped. "What did he mean he didn't kill the baby?"

Watson dropped to his knees. In the dark he searched for Boudary's pulse. *Lord, keep him alive. You've got to keep him alive. Where's the baby?*

Watson struggled to the Impala and started the motor, then turned on the headlights.

I've got to tie him up and get him to a hospital. He can't die now, not until I find out what he meant about the baby.

Still gasping for breath, Watson sorted though a cardboard box in the trunk. Most of the trunk looked like a blanketed nest, but jammed against a jack handle was a half-used roll of duct tape.

Toby's right. There is always just what you need.

He shoved aside some of the boxes and left the trunk open, then hiked over to the unconscious man. When he had Boudary's hands, arms, legs, feet, and mouth taped, he staggered to the car with the man on his shoulder and dumped him into the trunk.

He climbed into the front seat. The car smelled somewhere between musk incense and garlic. He turned right on Highway 86 and headed south. There were no cars on the road. Only the stars lit the countryside. He reached Interstate 90 just west of Bozeman and turned toward Belgrade.

Lord, I'm learning things about myself that only you knew. I can get mad enough to kill. I really wanted him dead, and now I really want him alive. I don't know what to say, except I'm not much of a prize. I've never focused my anger on one person like that. I think he deserved it, but that's for you to say, not me. I scared him. I put fear into a psycho-serial killer. I scared me. If he hadn't mentioned the baby, I'd never have stopped. I might still be up there smashing his head against the car.

He ran his fingers through his greasy, dirt-covered hair.

I'm glad I stopped.

He glanced into the backseat.

At least, I think I'm glad I stopped.

When he reached Logan, Watson pulled off the interstate and took the frontage road into Bridgeport. The sign at the bank flashed 11:45 as he turned down Tomahawk Drive and left the blacktop.

Lord, I don't know how long that fight took, but I hope to see my pickup parked in front of the house. I haven't been across that pass in a couple years, and I'm hoping it is still open.

There were no lights on in the big log house, but the streetlight revealed a white Oldsmobile parked in the driveway.

Watson paused in the middle of the gravel street and studied the car. A tall, thin man wearing a red alpaca golf sweater and golf hat pulled himself out of it.

Watson drove in next to the Oldsmobile.

The man waited for him to get out.

"Well, if it isn't Jack Nicklaus," Watson called out.

"Nice car, Arnie! Do you have the woman?"

"She's headed this way in my truck."

"By herself?" Theo Revelage asked.

"Toby's with her and the kids."

"I thought you fired that guy."

"Did you fire Heather?"

Theo Revelage shook his head. "Look, Paul, thanks for all your help. Did you get the info from her?"

"Oh, I got it, then lost it when my computer fried."

"You lost my data?" Revelage groaned.

"I lost my book, Theo, and my backup disk."

"Well, at least we stopped Boudary."

Watson glanced at the trunk of the Impala. "How did you know?"

"I've got friends at the FBI, remember?"

"Yes, but how did they know so soon?"

"They identified the body."

"Body?"

"It was Boudary in the Hummer wreck," Revelage announced.

"No, he faked his death. I've got . . ." Watson murmured.

"No fake this time. It seems his bomb exploded prematurely and blew up his own Hummer . . . and himself."

"What?"

"Yeah, he was headed this way with a coffee can full of plastic explosives when they detonated. He died from the blast.

The rig caught on fire after the bomb exploded."

"But it wasn't Boudary," Watson insisted. "He just wanted you to think that."

"They positively IDed him this time, P.J."

"How can they do that if the body was incinerated?"

"Not incinerated. Exploded. Not all of him burnt up," Revelage declared.

"I don't understand."

Six-foot, six-inch Theo Revelage folded his arms and leaned against the white rental car. "When the bomb went off, it blew bits and pieces of him all across that field. Then the rig burned to the ground. They got a positive ID from the bits and pieces, not from the wreckage."

"But, but, how . . . ?" Watson stammered.

"Don't ask. It's gruesome."

Watson tugged at his ear. He surveyed the darkened neighborhood and felt a cool Montana breeze drift from the river. "But if Boudary was blown to bits," he finally murmured, "who do I have in the trunk?"

"You got a body in the trunk? Whoa, P.J., I'm proud of you. Let's take a look." Revelage pointed to his arm. "What's with the bandanna on the arm?"

"I, eh, got a slight wound." Watson pulled off the bandanna as they ambled to the back of the Impala.

"It must be really slight. I don't see anything," Revelage said.

Watson held his arm up to the streetlight.

No blood.

No wound.

Not even a scratch.

"But he shot at me. The bullet . . ."

"Who shot at you?"

Watson pointed at the trunk. "Him!"

Theo Revelage opened the trunk. "Eh, P.J., there's no one in here, just some blankets and garbage."

Paul James Watson dug through the trunk as if to find Boudary hiding in a sack. "But, but, but I . . ."

"You tossed him in a trunk? Now you are sounding like one of your paperbacks." Revelage rummaged through the trunk. "I'm sorry that data got fried. It would have been helpful in writing up this story when it's done. Is there anything to eat back there? Everything in Bridgeport's closed. Where do the locals go to get a late-night snack?"

"Their refrigerator," Watson mumbled.

"But there was a fight and gunshots, and I tried to kill him."

"Is there pizza in that box?"

"I can't believe I made up that whole fight scene," Watson mumbled. "Eh, the pizza's gone. May be something in the paper sack, though. I think Toby had some leftovers."

"Nah, nothing in here but a laptop and a couple of disks," Revelage said.

Watson peered into the sack. "A what?" He pulled the black laptop from the paper sack. "It's my computer."

Toby must have retrieved it. And my backup disk. Why did he go after these?

"He saved my disk?" Revelage said. "All right, P.J. I'm glad you didn't fire him after all."

"But they were all fried — the computer, both disks, my book," Watson insisted.

"Turn it on," Revelage replied. "Let's double-check."

"No, it's burned up and . . ."

Revelage toted the laptop to the front of the Impala and opened it.

"Theo, be careful. I think there's radiation there."

"Radiation? In a laptop? Where did you come up with an insane idea like that? Come on, let's see. There's a disk in here."

"That's yours, but it's melted."

Revelage pulled it out and held it up to a streetlight. "It looks fine."

Watson grabbed at the disk. "It can't be."

Revelage shoved it in his coat pocket. "Open up one of the files on your disk."

"What do you mean?"

"The computer booted up just fine. Open up one of these documents, P.J."

Watson clicked on "D.D.D. Chapter 1." With white pages and black print, a document opened. "My book! My book is still there, Theo!"

"Now let me open up my disk."

"No! I don't want to lose my book again."

Revelage shoved the disk inside and opened it.

"Too late. Wow!" he gasped. "The Chicago bombing was a conspiracy?"

"You mean your disk works?" Watson asked.

"This is wonderful, P.J.!" Revelage pulled out the floppy and shoved it back into his sweater pocket. "I owe you big time. Was it hard to secure?"

"I've been through a lot today," Paul Watson mumbled.

"This is incredible."

"Let's go inside," Watson suggested.

"I've got to take off, P.J. I've got to make contact over at Big Timber as soon as I can." He held up the diskette. "I've got to get this posted tonight. This is fantastic, Paul. Boudary has been stopped, and I have an exclusive on his story. I'll post it on the Web site, and then you can write the book."

"Thanks, Theo, but I have all the book plots I need for years. By the way, where was Boudary headed with that bomb? Maelstrom Air Force Base?"

"The bomb was too small for that. You don't want to know where he was headed," Revelage said.

"What are you talking about?"

"The bits and pieces. You know, hand . . . finger . . . shirt pocket. They think they have an address of where he was headed."

"Where?" Watson pressed.

"2214 Tomahawk Drive."

"My house? He was coming to bomb my house?" Watson gasped. "I didn't know anything. Why would he do that? Why me?"

"She must have told him you were after her or something. The FBI will probably be contacting you tomorrow."

Watson studied the big log house stretched out in the Montana night. "He was going to bomb my house?" he muttered again.

"Not anymore." Revelage slid behind the wheel of the Olds. "I'll call you tomorrow, Paul. When I get this posted, Matt Drudge will die of envy!"

"Are you sure it was Boudary who was blown up?" Watson pressed.

"Positive. There are some body parts a guy can't fake, P.J."

Watson held up his hands. "I don't want to hear."

"I didn't think so."

Watson was still watching the street when he heard a rig pull up from the turn onto Tomahawk Drive. He recognized his gold Chevy pickup.

Dana was the first out, then Duke and a girl a tad shorter than him, then a grinning Toby McKenna. "Boy, am I glad to see you. I was thinkin' I was stuck in the Library of Congress the rest of my life."

"It was good for you to be on your own, Toby," Watson said.

Dana reached Paul's side. "Is he?"

"He's dead, Dana. Jonathan Boudary is dead."

"I can't believe it," she sighed.

"You killed him?" McKenna asked.

"No. In the end, it was one of his own bombs that blew him up. It's a long story."

"What happens now?" McKenna asked.

"Go to my truck and get DeWalla Coltrain on the phone," Watson ordered.

"At midnight?"

"Yeah. She has access to more information than any person in the country."

"I don't have her home number."

"It's 720-409-5600."

"You just made that up," McKenna challenged.

"Of course I did. Call her."

"Have you got anything to eat?" the boy asked. "Diana and me are hungry."

"Nothing out here, Duke. Go in the front door, turn to the left, and you'll find the kitchen. Help yourself to the fridge." Watson took Dana's arm and led her over to the pickup as the children scampered up the sidewalk.

"What's this all about?" she asked.

"Toby has a friend who can find out anything."

"What are we looking for?" Dana asked.

Watson silenced her with a finger to her lips.

Toby cleared his throat and punched on the speaker.

"Yeah?" The voice was sleepy, not sultry.

"DeWalla, darlin', it's me."

"Toby? Why aren't you here? Baby, I'm all alone."

"Yes, well . . . I'm not. P.J. has an emergency," McKenna announced.

"At 1:00 a.m.?"

"DeWalla, this is Paul Watson. Do you have a computer there?"

"Of course."

"Is it on-line?"

"24/7."

"I've got to know about infants that were abandoned in Montana." He turned to Dana. "When did he take your baby? I think she's alive."

Dana gasped. "February."

"Paul, I can't give you that information. You know that."

"DeWalla, after I'm through up here in Montana, I'm comin' to Denver," McKenna offered.

"Sweetie, this girl can't live on promises alone. When will you be done up there?"

"I want to get myself a kitten first," McKenna announced.

"A kitten?"

"Yeah, do you know anyone who runs an

animal shelter up around Great Falls?"

"I might," she replied. "What are you looking for?"

"A female, of course."

DeWalla giggled. "Naturally. How old?"

Watson held up two fingers.

"Two," Toby called out.

"What color kitten are you looking for?"

Dana clutched Paul Watson's arm. "Black hair, brown eyes," she murmured.

"Did you get that, darlin'?" Toby added. "Black hair, brown eyes."

"Around Great Falls?" DeWalla asked.

"Yes, even a stray that wandered in last February will be fine," Watson added.

"You want one with any distinguishing markings?" DeWalla asked.

Paul stroked Dana's dark hair away from her tear-filled eyes. "Did she have any birthmarks or any identifying marks?"

"A tiny field of freckles about the size of my thumbnail," Dana reported.

"I want one with a few spots, DeWalla."

"Where?" she asked.

"On the lower left hip," Dana said.

Watson stared at McKenna.

"Lower left hip area would be cute," McKenna repeated.

"Bingo!" DeWalla exclaimed. "I found

you a kitten in Great Falls."

Dana began to sob.

"Is she healthy?" Paul Watson asked.

"Must be. There are three others interested in taking her home, but legally they cannot do that until next February."

"DeWalla, you are a jewel," Toby called out. "If you were here, I'd hug you, darlin'."

"And if you were here, you'd have to do a whole lot more than hug," she sighed. "Is that all?"

"What time does the shelter open tomorrow?" Watson asked.

"Eight a.m. 987 24th Street."

"We'll be there," Toby called out. "I'll call you later in the week when my Corvette is repaired. Then you and me will go dancin'."

"I'll believe that when I see it. But, my oh my, Tobias Patrick McKenna, you do help a girl to dream good."

"Night, darlin'," Toby called out.

"Night, sweetie. Good luck with the kitten."

Dana sobbed on Paul Watson's shoulder. "I've got to go to Great Falls tonight so I can be there when the shelter opens," she wailed.

"Yes, you do."

"I'll go with her," Toby offered. "I mean, unless you have other plans for me."

"Toby, it's about time I quit controlling your life. How about you just going and being the person God wants you to be."

"Do you mean that?" Toby said. "I'm fictional."

"So is the good Samaritan. Go with Dana. Besides, I'm not writing for a few days. Go on," Watson insisted.

Dana pulled away. "I'll get Diana and Duke. I'm going to name the baby Paula June."

"P.J.?" Toby said. "Yes. That's what the world needs at last, a cute P.J.!"

Dana scurried into the house.

Toby pointed to the hood of the Impala. "I see you found the laptop."

"How did you get the computer?" Watson asked.

"The Korean kid needed some persuasion." Toby pointed to his knuckles. "Seems Boudary had called and offered $10,000 cash if you came in with the disk or the laptop."

"How did he know I would go there?"

"How many public places does Montana have to send an attached file?"

"I don't know."

"DeWalla would," Toby mused. "Do I have time to drive down to Denver?"

"Are you going to treat her nice?" Watson challenged.

"I will treat her better than she thinks she deserves to be treated," Toby grinned. "You see, I did learn somethin'. Are you really gonna turn me loose?"

"I'm going to release you to the Lord."

Dana scurried out, leading Duke and Diana. "The kids made a mess in your kitchen."

"No problem. Go on. Toby's going with you."

"Is he gonna drive?" Duke asked.

"It might be better if your mama drove," Watson cautioned.

Dana hugged him again. "Paul, what can I say? They all say they love us, but no one treats us real."

"You are real to me, Dana. Now go on. Go hug on little P.J."

"I won't ever forget you, Paul James Watson."

"Well, sometime when you are parked there in the Library of Congress, tell stories about me. In some way I'll live on with you."

She finally pulled away, and within seconds the green Impala sped through the Montana night.

Watson toted in a suitcase, two boxes of books, computer bag, garment bag, and a dirty clothes sack, then wandered into the silent kitchen. Everything in the huge white kitchen was perfectly in place. He opened the refrigerator, pulled out the orange juice, and poured himself a glass. A small lavender note lay on the white tile.

"Daddy, Pete called, and Jared and Marcia wanted the four of us to play bridge. So, Pete and I will spend the night at their house, and we'll have a long session. Sorry to leave you alone. I'll be home early to clean up for work. I love you. Rudi."

He leaned his backside against the counter and sipped on the orange juice. *I'm gone for two weeks and come home to an empty house. Not that I'm complaining, Lord. It's a nice house. Well, maybe I'm whining a little.*

He didn't notice the blinking red light until he turned off the kitchen light. In the half-lit room he reached over and punched the answering machine.

"Honey, I'm on my way home. I got everything done at the foundry tonight, and Marty was insistent that I leave. She said you sounded lonelier than a lost pup. She's right. I don't know what I was thinking. I need to be with my sweet author. I'll be in about 1:30 or 2:00. Go on to bed. I'll wake you."

Watson turned the kitchen light back on and looked at the clock.

"1:20?" he sighed.

He heard the electric garage door open. He stepped to the doorway to the garage. A lady with short blonde hair and an ear-to-ear smile popped out of the Jeep Cherokee and scooted over to him.

"Hi, Paulie," she called out. "I missed you."

"Hi, babe. Did I ever mention to you that you are totally cute?"

"I think you said that once, but I figured it was another fiction line."

He shook his head. "Does this feel like fiction?" He took her hand and pulled her into the house.

Once, when they had dated only three times, he had taken Sheila to Balboa Island, and they watched the sunset. It was their first hug. It seemed to last all evening. The intensity of the hug he now felt far surpassed that one.

"I think my author missed me."

"It's been a long two weeks," he murmured. "And a long day."

"I hope you had a leisurely one. Did you stop and enjoy yourself along the way home? Did you shop any in Billings?" she asked.

"No shopping, but I did stop a time or two. I did work on a new story idea."

"How do you do that? How do you always have another story ready to go? Where do you find them?"

"Sometimes," he whispered, "the stories just seem to find me."

"Well, they aren't going to find you tonight." She tugged him toward the bedroom.

He raised his eyebrows. "Did you know Pete and Rudi are staying at Jared and Marcia's?"

She kissed his cheek and grinned.

"You told them to do that, didn't you?"

"I think it was a good idea, don't you?"

He brushed a kiss across her ear. "A very good idea."

She patted his shoulder. "How did your shirt get all wet, honey?"

He glanced down at the damp spot. "It's a very long story."

"Then it will have to wait until morning. You are two weeks behind on your kissing."

"You don't expect me to make it all up in one night, do you?" he asked.

"Yes, I do, Paul James Watson," she winked. "And I'm not talking fiction."

epilogue

the next day

A tiny dab of teal blue dotted Sheila's chin as she padded out on the deck behind the big log house. She carried two steaming cups of coffee and handed one to the man wearing University of Montana sweatpants and a plain charcoal gray sweatshirt.

His grin widened as he took the cup. "Mornin', darlin'."

She sat down on the bench beside him and scooted over until their hips touched. Cradling the coffee in her lap, she leaned over and kissed his unshaven cheek. "Morning, honey. Did you sleep well?"

"I slept wonderfully well."

"Have you been working on that new plot?" she asked.

He kissed her forehead. "Yeah, I suppose I have." With his thumb he rubbed the speck of paint from her cheek. "I see you've been painting."

"I woke up with a perfect vision of what

color that building should be in *San Juan at Dusk*."

He glanced at his thumb. "I like the color."

She kissed his lips. "It looks better on canvas."

"I doubt that," he smiled. "I saw you were busy, so I didn't want to bother you."

"And I saw you come out on the deck. I knew you were lost in a story, so I waited as long as I could."

Paul slipped his left arm around her waist and took a sip from his coffee. "Kind of crazy, babe. We give each other so much space, we sometimes forget to touch."

She rubbed her hand up and down his thigh. "Yeah, I know. Why do you think I drove back from Kalispell last night?"

"Because your sister made you?"

"Well, that too," she giggled.

"Do you think we need to do things in a different way?" he asked.

"Do you?"

"I've been pondering it."

"And?" she pressed.

"No. We can't be different. You're an artist. I'm a paperback writer. It's part of what we love about each other. We must always have the freedom to be those things, and somehow we'll stumble along through all the rest."

"I know," she murmured. "Paul James Watson, I cannot imagine a more supportive husband than you've been. My artist friends are all jealous, of course."

"And my writer friends cannot for the life of them figure out what you see in me."

"That's ridiculous."

"That's what they say. Of course, they think you're twenty years younger than me."

"Paul James Watson, you are one smooth-talking novelist. You are beginning to sound like Toby McKenna."

"Wait until you see Toby's maturity in the next book," he said.

"What are you going to call it?"

"Toby wanted to call it *Montana Underground*."

"What does Mr. Paul James Watson want to call it?"

"Right now I was thinking *Paperback Writer*."

She took his hand and squeezed his fingers. "I love it!"

"Probably doesn't matter. L. George Gossman and the gang at Atlantic-Hampton will want to change it to something boring."

"Will you let them?"

"Not this time."

"When do we leave for the lodge at East Glacier?" she asked.

"Sunday after lunch. I promised Lanny he could come over after church."

"Are you going to take your laptop?" she asked.

"Are you bringing your sketchbook?" he replied.

Their eyes locked.

She grinned. "We are, aren't we?"

"Of course, babe. We can't be anything different from what we are. The beautiful and talented artist and the . . ."

"Rustically handsome, incredibly talented paperback writer."

Shelia leaned over. Their lips pressed into each other's warmth.

"Ehhh hmmmm," Rudi cleared her throat. "Are you taking phone calls, or do you need to go to your room?"

Paul Watson sat back. "I didn't hear the phone."

In a pink fluffy bathrobe and wet blonde hair, Ruth Ann Watson padded over to her parents, cordless phone cradled in her hand. "It's for you, Daddy."

"It's not Lanny, is it?"

"No."

"Or Theo Revelage?"

"No."

"Or Dana?"

"Who?" Rudi asked.

"No, of course not. She's fictional." He took the phone. "This is Paul Watson."

"Oh, my. I can't believe it," the young woman's voice gushed. "I was calling to schedule an appointment with your secretary. I never realized I would talk to you directly. Oh, my. I'm a bit flustered."

"Can I do something for you?"

"Mr. Watson, I've read every book in the Distracted Detective Series at least three times. I just about have every word memorized in *Yellow Sea*."

"Those are encouraging words. Thank you very much."

"Mr. Watson, here's why I called. My name is Megan Fernandez. I'm a graduate student at Stanford and . . ."

"Stanford University? In Palo Alto, California?" he asked.

"Yes, I'm working on my masters in Post-World War II American Literature and, specifically, the complete works of Paul James Watson."

"What?" he gasped.

"I'm doing my thesis on your work, Mr. Watson."

"I'm flattered, to say the least."

"I, eh, sort of have a long list of questions. May I ask you some of them? If I'm taking too much of your time, I'll stop. I just can't believe I'm actually talking to you this morning. I was eight years old when I first read *Distracted in Dublin,* and I knew I had to be a writer or a detective. Mr. Watson, do you have any idea how many joyous, exciting hours you have brought into my life? My big brother died in a car wreck that year, and your books gave me sweet relief from the pain and grief. I can never thank you enough."

He slipped his fingers into Sheila's hand and clutched it tight. "You are a gracious young woman. What can I answer for you?"

"I've prioritized the questions in case I don't get to ask them all. So here's the most important one first." She cleared her throat. "Mr. Paul James Watson, where do you get the incredible ideas for your next book?"

DW